Seduction

A Club Destiny Novel

Nicole Edwards

ISBN: 978-0985059163

Cover Image by: © Anette Romanenko | Dreamstime.com

Chapter One
*** ~ *** ~ *** ~ ***

No one would ever accuse Ashleigh Thomas of being spontaneous. At least not anyone who knew her well.

If there was something that needed to be done, she planned. Usually weeks in advance and in frustratingly thorough detail. Follow that up with final preparations and then finally, once there was enough forethought and design, she just might make a decision.

Overkill?

Good God yes.

Which could only mean this was one of those times when Ashleigh was setting herself up for potential disaster.

Her house was packed up, her things already loaded into the moving truck, a handful of capable men having spent the morning doing backbreaking work as they filled the enormous metal container with everything that was near and dear to her heart. This was it. One final goodbye to her beloved two bedroom house before she was on her way.

Back to her roots.

Back to the place she had called home for most of her life.

Granted, she had taken her own sweet time getting to this point, but nonetheless, she could no longer procrastinate. Getting back to the hustle and bustle of Dallas was the next step. Leaving behind the slow, easy going life she had built on the bank of Lake Whitney, just outside of Hillsboro, was not going to be easy yet it was inevitable.

Relocating her life wasn't the difficult part. As a writer, she could easily pick up her office – also known as her laptop – and go just about anywhere. That was one of the many perks of her job.

Since she had grown quite fond of her current office space – her back porch which overlooked the rippling waters of Lake Whitney – she had worked hard to convince herself this move was for the best. Being able to wander out of her house in her pajamas, watching the random vacationer as they attempted some sort of water sport, had become one of the highlights of her day.

Somewhere in between all of the fresh air, sun and people watching, Ashleigh actually managed to write. Thirteen books in total between her two personas and she wasn't doing all that bad actually. The children's books were enough to pay the bills, as well as a convenient story to sell her grandfather. Not that he completely believed she was making a living at it.

Since he was partly right, Ashleigh never bothered to argue with him.

Her bills might be covered from her various tales of farm animals, fairy princesses and the like, but her savings was being built from the other genre she moonlighted in.

Smiling to herself, Ashleigh turned from the back windows that overlooked the serene view of the lake and went to get the last of her things.

The movers had already headed out, on their way to Dallas, so she wasn't going to put any more thought into whether her stuff would make the journey in one piece. The only thing left was to get her laptop and her purse and say one last goodbye to life as she knew it.

"Goodbye, little house. I'm sure going to miss you." Ashleigh said to the empty room, nothing but bare walls and carpet, as she put the key in the door for the last time. In a week, the new owners would be moving in, taking over and filling the small house with their own memories.

With her personal effects in tow, Ashleigh ventured down the front steps and across the small walkway to her Chevy Tahoe sitting in the driveway. Feeling a little melancholy, she looked up at the sun, letting the bright Texas sun warm her.

The late January morning wasn't as cool as the weatherman predicted – Texas weather didn't usually go with the norm – but the wind off the lake was a little brisk. Thankfully she'd remembered her jacket just in case.

Those were the sort of things she planned for.

Not the sort of abrupt change which resulted in her going back home to Dallas.

Shrugging her shoulders, figuring she had already set out on the path, might as well be in it for the long haul, Ashleigh climbed into her SUV. With a flick of her wrist, the Tahoe roared to life, the interior of the truck filled with a country song.

How appropriate.

Turning the radio up, she tried to drown out her thoughts.

Within minutes, she was on the two lane highway heading for the main interstate where she would be on her way.

Though leaving the comfortable life she had gotten used to made her nervous, there were some positives that she would be looking forward to.

Being close to her family one of them. Although only a forty five minute drive on a good day, her family was still far enough that she didn't get to visit as often as she'd like. Having lived a solitary life for so long, she was actually looking forward to being close to those she loved.

She had talked to her brother Dylan just that morning. He was essentially doing the same thing she was, packing up and getting ready to head out. With her niece, Stacey, having been accepted at the University of Texas at Dallas, Dylan had reluctantly let her move at the beginning of the semester. According to him, he was worried about her – though Ashleigh figured that was a convenient excuse – and now, he was moving back to the big city to be closer to his daughter.

Even though Stacey would have been in capable hands living with her great grandfather, Ashleigh found she couldn't argue with Dylan even if she wanted to. Since Dylan's wife passed away, her older brother had never been the same. Figuring a change might do them both some good, Ashleigh had encouraged him as much as he had encouraged her.

When a familiar tune blasted through the car, Ashleigh gave herself up to the music, singing slightly off key - ok, who was she kidding, there was no *slight* about it, it was severe. There was a reason Ashleigh didn't make a living as a singer. The thought made her laugh and sing even louder.

A second later the song was interrupted by the ringing of her cell phone, the sound coming through the speakers thanks to the Bluetooth connection in the car. Hitting the button on the steering wheel, she allowed the call to connect.

"Hey, Pops." Ashleigh greeted her grandfather cheerfully, his name coming up on the small touch screen in the dash.

"I hope you aren't driving while you talk to me." Xavier Thomas' laid back drawl drifted through the car, and Ashleigh smiled.

"You're the one who said I needed to be home before dark." She chided him as she flipped on the turn signal. "I'm just leaving, so it'll take me close to an hour to get there."

"Well, you be careful and call me if you need anything. What time did the moving truck head out?" Xavier asked.

"Not too long ago. I figure they might beat me by half an hour. They're going straight to the house to unload." Once Ashleigh had gotten a contract on her lake house, she wasted no time finding a house close to her grandfather's. It was either that, or take the chance of Pops giving her a hard time about moving back to his house.

Since Stacey and her brother, Nate, would be living in the eight thousand square foot mansion, Ashleigh figured her grandfather would have plenty of company. Dylan had insisted on moving into the guest house, rather than into the main house, so Ashleigh had opted for something just a little farther out.

Not that she minded so much living with her grandfather and her niece and nephew, but living on her own for so long, Ashleigh had gotten used to the solitude. She thrived on it. And since her schedule was usually so out of whack, sometimes her days and nights entirely flip flopped, she wanted to have her own space.

"Nate and I will meet them over there. You just take your time and be careful." Xavier drawled.

"Thanks, Pops. I'll call you when I get closer. Maybe I can pick up something for dinner though we won't have a place to eat at my house."

"We'll figure it out. See you in a little while, baby girl." With that, the line disconnected.

Baby girl.

At twenty seven years old, Ashleigh figured she was too old for the nickname her grandfather had been calling her since she was just that. Not that she wanted him to stop, because secretly she had always reveled in being his baby girl. Since he had single handedly raised her and her brother after their parents' tragic death, Ashleigh figured he could call her whatever he wanted.

Another reason she wasn't too upset about moving back to Dallas. She needed her family. Since she and Dylan had been living in the past for far too long, Ashleigh knew he was right. It was time they move forward.

Insisting on going home in a better mood, she turned up the familiar song, once again singing loud and off key. There would be plenty of time later for her thoughts to intrude. For now, she just needed to relax.

Chapter Two
*** ~~ *** ~~ *** ~~ ***

Alex McDermott was pacing the floor for the hundredth time, and based on the glare he was getting from Veronica, Xavier's assistant was running out of patience. Alex could relate. He'd run out of patience first thing that morning when he woke up to the shrill ringing of his cell phone. Damn that Logan McCoy. For some reason, that man lived to irritate him.

Just because he had found a woman didn't mean Alex deserved the other man's constant harassment.

Ever since the night of the XTX Christmas party, Logan had been ribbing him every chance he got. Apparently Logan didn't get the memo. The one that said *back the fuck off.*

Obviously Xavier Thomas didn't get the memo either because he had summoned Alex about an hour ago. And now he was making him wait.

"He'll see you now." The irritation in Veronica's sultry voice was evident, and Alex shot her a glare.

Pushing open the massive wooden door, Alex stepped inside, his eyes landing on Xavier sitting behind his lavish desk, a mischievous grin tipping the corners of his mouth.

"Thanks for stopping by on such short notice." Xavier said, his severe Texas drawl coming out aloof and disinterested.

Alex knew better. Xavier Thomas was anything but.

"Not a problem. Is something wrong?" Alex didn't know whether to stand or sit, so he opted to stand.

"As a matter of fact, things couldn't be better." Xavier stood from his chair and walked around the desk.

At seventy, Xavier was an impressively fit man, dressed impeccably in slacks and a crisp white shirt, accented by one of his many favored ties. Today's was a shiny red.

"I just got off the phone with Ashleigh. She's on the road as we speak and the movers should be here within the hour."

Alex did his best not to give away his thoughts, especially to Xavier.

Ashleigh Thomas was the bane of his existence, and from what he could tell, everyone he knew was well aware of his infatuation with the woman. Seemed that no matter what he did or said, those closest to him knew exactly what she did to him.

"Dylan mentioned it to me." Alex admitted, knowing he couldn't get anything past Xavier.

Alex was well aware that Ashleigh was permanently moving back to Dallas, although he had thought she would've done so months before when the rumors started flying. No matter how long it took her to get back, he was quite fond of the idea, but he also knew she didn't want anything to do with him. Apparently Xavier hadn't gotten that memo either.

"I need a favor." Xavier leaned against the front of his desk, crossing his arms over his chest and staring at Alex. For the first time in as long as he could remember, Alex felt the scrutiny in the other man's gaze.

Over the years, he and Xavier had developed a strong working relationship, as well as a personal one. However, he had no illusions about how quickly that relationship could turn sour if Alex were to touch one hair on Ashleigh's beautiful head. It was a given that if Xavier knew the thoughts that plagued Alex where the other man's granddaughter was concerned, he just might not see him the same way.

Not that he would ever let on, but the way Xavier's eyes were focused on him, Alex wondered if the man weren't just reading his mind.

Patience undoubtedly wasn't his virtue, but then again, Xavier knew that. "And that is?"

"I need a security system installed at Ashleigh's new house." Xavier paused without breaking eye contact. "Today."

Easy enough, Alex thought to himself. He didn't actually install the systems, so he could possibly stop by the house before she ever showed up, write up the estimate, and have one of his tech's back within the hour to complete the job. Or better yet, he could just have Dylan, Ashleigh's brother and Alex's new partner, stop by and do the prep work.

Not that he would do either, but those were options.

"That's easy enough to arrange. Have you talked to Dylan? I'm sure he wouldn't mind stopping by to check it out."

Xavier shook his head, before saying, "Dylan's in the process of helping Stacey move in. And, honestly, I'd prefer that you handle this one. I'm confident in his ability, but I prefer to have your experienced eye on this. You understand."

No, actually, he didn't.

Bracing his feet apart, feeling a tad defensive, Alex had to work overtime not to give himself away. After the last incident with Ashleigh, Alex had a feeling she wouldn't agree with Xavier.

Of course, her preference would likely be for Alex to fall off the face of the earth. Since that wasn't going to happen, and Alex was inadvertently turned on by her need to avoid him…

What the hell. Might as well go for broke.

"Alright. I have a meeting with Sam in fifteen minutes, but after that, I'll head over. Have Veronica send me the address."

"Thanks, Alex." Xavier stated, going behind his desk once again, sounding even cockier than he had moments before. "I'll have Nate meet you over there with the key."

Alex glanced at Xavier suspiciously. Why did he get the feeling Xavier was up to something?

Forty five minutes later, Alex was walking out of the main doors of XTX, toward the parking garage. He'd just spent half an hour with Samantha Kielty going over her update for the XTX project secretly labeled WTF by some of her project managers. She was well aware of what they said, and she'd started calling it the same thing, which made Alex laugh. Thankfully she didn't need much of his time, and just like last week, she advised that she was on target from both a cost and a time perspective.

Not surprising.

Alex had taken a gamble last year hiring Sam on full time as his executive vice president in order to alleviate some of the tension provoked by a hot and heavy relationship that Sam and Logan found themselves in. Since that time, she'd married Logan, and the rumors had stopped, however, her innate ability to drive projects to completion hadn't. Alex would be the first to admit, Sam was a force to be reckoned with, and though skeptical at first, both he and Dylan were excited about the skills she brought to CISS.

Her reputation preceded her, making a couple of their other clients interested in bringing her on to address some of their project issues, but Alex had been stalling. For the time being, she would remain at XTX, thanks to the contract Logan had insisted on, but there was no telling what the future held.

Climbing behind the wheel of his two year old Chevy Avalanche, Alex let the truck's navigation provide him the directions to Ashleigh's new house. If he was lucky, which he planned to be, he would still be there when she arrived. She might not appreciate that fact, but Alex was past the point of caring. If she wanted to play hard to get, he could play along with her.

For now.

Alex wasn't sure when it was that he had decided to go after the woman who had made his blood boil for far too long. For years, he'd managed to stay away from her, despite the centrifugal forces that always seemed to draw them together. Ever since the rumors started flying that she was coming back, he'd been hopeful.

Ten years was a long time to lust after one woman, but Alex had done it. Despite the twelve year age difference, which he felt made her entirely too young for him, Alex had recently found it too easy to overlook that one minor detail. Not that her age, or his, really mattered because Ashleigh had never so much as hinted at any sort of reciprocated feelings on her side. Not that he'd pushed her. Much.

If it weren't for the fact that she'd gone out of her way to avoid him for so long, he likely wouldn't have thought anything of it.

The final straw had been that damn Christmas party.

For some reason, Ashleigh had gotten him all worked up, although he wasn't sure she realized it. He'd asked her to dance, and she had graciously accepted, but when the one song was over, she had excused herself and then smiled so sweetly, he'd felt the jolt straight to his cock. Whether or not she intentionally teased him that night, he didn't know. Either way, Alex wasn't about to let her get away with it.

No, Alex had something else in store for little Miss Sweet and Innocent, which hopefully, would end with her in his bed.

That's where his current plan went into play. Not that it was much of a plan. Seduction was the name of the game and as far as he was concerned, the gloves had just come off.

It had recently come to his attention – thanks to a little investigative work on his part – that sweet little Ashleigh wasn't all she pretended to be. He'd stumbled across a very interesting fact when he was checking out her highly regarded children's book series. To be honest, he hadn't been all that interested in her books... initially.

Some creative searches resulted in a much more entertaining book series that their sweet Ashleigh was responsible for. The kind that carried a certain disclaimer on them – for mature audiences only.

As it turned out, Ashleigh Thomas was moonlighting as Ashton Leigh, writing some downright provocative stories that Alex admitted to getting caught up in. It hadn't taken him long to recognize the side of Ashleigh that wrote about deep, dark fantasies and sexual exploits so outrageous, he wondered where the hell she had learned about them. Had he not experienced a few himself, he might've been blushing by the end.

Gripping the steering wheel with both hands, Alex tried to rein in the hunger that ignited in his soul whenever he thought about her and those damn books. At the moment, the last thing he needed to be thinking about was Ashleigh and sex when he should be paying attention to the hordes of cars and trucks around him.

Navigating Dallas' traffic required skill and total concentration on a good day. Friday afternoons generally didn't qualify as good as far as congestion standards went.

As he sat on the highway, at a complete standstill, Alex reviewed the directions. Based on his knowledge of the city, the drive to Ashleigh's should only take about fifteen minutes. However, he'd actually have to be driving first.

It had been a long time since Alex had looked forward to doing much of anything, but anticipating the reaction on Ashleigh's face when she saw him was quickly becoming the highlight of his day.

It'd been ten long years since he'd seen any hint of interest on her face, but she'd been a high school senior when Logan McCoy had introduced Alex to Xavier Thomas. At seventeen years old, she'd captured his eye with her beauty, but not much else. Over the years, Alex had become close to the Thomas family, building a friendship with Dylan and a strong working relationship with the family's patriarch, Xavier.

Alex had barely gotten his business off the ground when Logan had introduced him to Xavier, and it wasn't long after that Alex landed the largest client CISS had ever known. So, over the years, Dylan had become a regular fixture at the Thomas home, and as he'd watched Ashleigh grow up, he'd found himself more and more captivated as the years went by.

In order to ensure his admiration didn't turn into infatuation, he'd kept as far away from her as possible, only it appeared that seemed to be a colossal waste of time. Since she'd continued to ignore him, avoiding him whenever possible, Alex found himself only wanting her more.

Then the years of denying the lust he harbored for the woman he couldn't have all came to a screeching halt the night of the Christmas party when Alex held Ashleigh in his arms. That night, his need to have her escalated. For a brief moment, he swore he'd seen interest in her eyes, but she had quickly masked it, followed by that sweet, dismissive smile of hers.

Now she was coming back for good, and the timing couldn't have been better. Alex knew that Ashleigh would be a challenge, but hell, besides having more business than he could keep up with, what else did he have to do?

Chapter Three
*** ~~ *** ~~ *** ~~ ***

Ashleigh pulled into the driveway of her new house in record time, traffic on a Friday afternoon unusually light coming into Dallas. She was never one to enjoy driving, and she couldn't say she was anxious to have to do that trip again, but at least she'd had some time to think and... sing. Although she was fairly certain what she was doing wasn't in any way associated to singing. At least not in a good way.

She smiled.

Who cared.

Parking her Tahoe beside a big, black fancy truck that Ashleigh couldn't place, she wondered who was there. The movers were, she could see them traipsing back and forth across her lawn hard at work. Her brother was there, his all too familiar ranch truck was parked near the street.

Curious, she grabbed her purse, opting to leave the rest of her things until she was certain she had a place for them. If she was right, her house would probably look like that moving truck had thrown up in the middle of her living room because there was no way they would know where to put anything.

She wasn't halfway up the front walkway when Nathaniel – everyone called him Nate – came bounding out of the front door, a mischievous smile on his handsome face. The boy looked so much like his father, it was uncanny.

"Aunt Ash!" Her nephew exclaimed, coming right at her with his arms open wide like he was seven, not seventeen.

"Nate." Bracing for the impact, Ashleigh laughed out loud when he stopped suddenly, standing right in front of her and waiting for her reaction.

Ashleigh walked right up to him, letting the much bigger boy embrace her.

"Ummm... Nate?" She smiled, taking a step back. "Did you know you aren't a little boy anymore?"

Nate's whiskey brown eyes danced with amusement. "Yep. No more boy. All man." He said in a Tarzan-like imitation.

"Last time I saw you, I could've sworn you were shorter than me."

"Doubtful." Nate remarked, looking thoughtful. "I'm having a hard time coming up with anyone who is as short as you are."

Slapping his arm lightly, Ashleigh laughed. At five feet eight, she was by no means on the short side. It wasn't her fault that the men in her family seemed to steal all the inches, every one of them, including Nate as it turned out, stood over six feet tall.

"So, what do you think of my new digs?" She asked him, turning to look at her little house.

"Impressive. I'm gonna have to grab my fishing pole and come hang out sometime."

Grinning, Ashleigh looked up at him. She wasn't sure the little stock tank behind the house even had fish, but if anyone would find out, it would be Nate.

"Where's your dad?" Hefting her purse up on her arm, she turned toward the house.

"Inside. He's talking to Alex."

His words had her stopping in her tracks, before glancing back at the black truck in her driveway. She should've known. Pretending she didn't care, she forced a smile. "Have you been to your new school yet?"

"No." Nate didn't look at her, keeping his eyes on the expanse of water they could see from where they stood. "Dad's taking me up there in a few minutes."

"You excited?" She knew he wasn't, if his expression was anything to go by.

"Anything will be better than where we came from." He admitted, turning back to the house, but not moving.

Ashleigh knew from talking to her brother Dylan that Nate was having a hard time at school, and it had nothing to do with academics and everything to do with the cruelty of the kids.

Just last year, the Thomas family had been shocked by Nate's revelation that he was gay. Although not a single one of them had any issues with it, including Xavier, her grandfather, which had surprised the hell out of damn near everyone, not everyone seemed to be as accepting as Nate's family. Ashleigh wasn't sure whether it was the small town, or just ignorance that had the kids being so cruel, but either way, Nate seemed to be dealing with it.

"At least the year is almost over, right?"

"I wouldn't quite say that. We've still got the rest of this semester."

"Oooh. A semester. That's like what? Eighteen more weeks?" Ashleigh laughed.

"Fifteen, thank you. Don't make it longer than it has to be." Nate teased.

"Sorry. I'll work on getting my facts straight next time." God she missed her nephew. He'd always been the fun loving, exuberant child who had kept them all on their toes. Despite the difficulties and the challenges he seemed to be facing, it was good to see he hadn't changed much.

"Well, I've put it off as long as I could." She told him, turning back to the house. "Time to check out the chaos."

Steeling herself for the *chaos*, better known as Alex McDermott – but she wouldn't tell Nate that – Ashleigh followed her nephew up the steps to the house. The front door stood wide open, the screen door propped open with a small box – great, the box read "panties and bras".

Lovely.

Every light in the house was on and the low sound of people talking filled the space. As soon as she was inside, Ashleigh remembered everything she had loved about the house the first time she saw it. Her realtor hadn't seemed too excited about showing her the place, apparently it had been on the market for quite some time, and she hadn't figured it would be what Ashleigh was looking for.

It had taken one trek through the house, and less than five minutes for Ashleigh to turn to the woman, telling her to draw up the papers. After seeing at least twenty other properties, Ashleigh had been sold almost the minute she stepped inside.

Open, airy, it was just what Ashleigh was looking for.

The back wall was nearly all glass which offered a serene view of the small pond and a handful of trees. The inside was warm and comforting, something that struck Ashleigh immediately. Dark wood floors and cream colored walls, along with stone accents on the fireplace, and the bar that separated the kitchen from the rest of the house, had caught her eye immediately. The rest was a bonus.

Speaking of bar. From where she stood, just inside the front door, Ashleigh could see her brother who was animatedly talking to the man she'd dedicated way too many thoughts to for the last decade. Alex's back was to her, and she fought the urge to stand there and stare at him while he was unaware.

Right. As if anything ever got past him.

Alex McDermott and all of his sexy as hell goodness was a weak spot Ashleigh had never been comfortable with. The man was hot as sin, but Ashleigh had sworn off his type at a young age. Or maybe it was just him that she'd sworn off.

Not that he didn't visit her in some of her hottest dreams. But during waking hours, she did her best to avoid him. Living so far away had made that easy, but apparently being this close, and the fact that he worked with her grandfather, Ashleigh would have to put forth some effort to keep him away.

Time to change the locks.

"What's he doing here?" Ashleigh asked Nate, tilting her head in the direction of the kitchen, keeping her voice low, and trying to sound interested, but not *interested*.

The look Nate shot her way said he wasn't buying it.

"He's quoting the alarm system Pops is having put in."

And why couldn't her brother have done that? She didn't ask the question out loud because she knew Nate wouldn't be able to answer, and she was pretty certain her discomfort was obvious, no reason to sound defensive on top of it.

Apparently she was going to have to have a conversation with her grandfather. She was forever grateful for him, and his need to make sure she was taken care of, but when it came to Alex, Ashleigh would rather go without.

Dylan's voice got louder, and then a deep, booming laugh echoed through the house, making Ashleigh turn to look at her brother. He was laughing. It was a rusty sound, but only because she knew he hadn't been doing much of it over the years. It was the sweetest thing she'd heard in a long time.

Sitting her purse on the counter, she cleared her throat, getting Dylan's attention. He smiled, his eyes locking on her, but the man whose back was still to her didn't do more than tilt his head to the side, a mischievous grin tilting his beautiful mouth.

Damn that man.

She suddenly wished she had checked her face in the mirror before she came in. Not that it would matter much. Wearing yoga pants, an oversized sweatshirt, and her hair in a messy ponytail, she'd dressed for comfort, not to come face to face with the hottest man she'd ever laid eyes on. But she didn't care what Alex thought. Or so she tried to convince herself.

Her appearance was the least of her worries anyway. Right now, she'd have to make every effort just to breathe.

"Hey, how was the drive?" Dylan asked, his dark eyes holding a hint of amusement. The mischievous grin on his face didn't help either.

"Uneventful." She said, stepping around the bar and into the kitchen, keeping her eyes trained on her brother and not the other man standing so easily against her counter, who appeared not to be giving her the time of day, although she knew better.

"You remember Alex, don't you?" Dylan asked by way of introduction.

Did she ever.

"I do. Nice to see you again." Ashleigh gave him a brief glance, then turned back to her brother. "What's going on?"

"Pops asked Alex to stop by to install a security system." Dylan restated what Ashleigh already knew. "Now that you're here, I need to run Nate by his new school. We've got to pick up a schedule or something."

Maybe she should offer to take Nate. The dead last thing she needed was to be left alone with Alex. Not if she was expected to keep her sanity.

She'd grown accustomed to her body's unruly reaction to the man over the years, but that one night at the Christmas party just a few weeks before had nearly sent her hormones on strike.

"Why don't you stay? I can run out and pick up dinner." One last ditch effort to keep her brother close was worth a shot.

"Can't. Maybe tomorrow." Dylan replied as he nodded back to Alex, then turned toward the front door. "Oh, and Pops said he got held up, but he'd stop by tomorrow to see how things are going."

Right. Held up her ass.

The old meddling man was interfering, that's what he was doing. For the life of her, Ashleigh couldn't fathom how Pops would think this was a good idea. Her and Alex?

"I'll walk you out." Alex offered, and Ashleigh shot him a glare. He graced her with that sexy, seductive smile that she had thought about way too many times.

Damn that man.

She fought the urge to watch him walk out the front door. Then she fought the urge to lock it and keep him on the other side where he belonged. One of the movers caught her attention as he headed toward the back of the house.

Great. They were setting up her bed.

That was clearly what she needed - more temptation. Couldn't they have waited to get her bedroom set back up until after the cocky, arrogant alarm guy left?

Of course not.

Karma was a pushy bitch, trying to test every one of Ashleigh's limits. And Alex McDermott was so far beyond off limits Ashleigh couldn't even see the warning signs from where she stood.

Her body wasn't heeding the warning signs anyway. And that was after only two minutes in his presence.

When he was around, her skin was too tight, her entire body felt flushed, and she would never have to worry about cold weather again because he heated her from the inside out.

Sex. That's the first thing that came to mind when Alex was anywhere in the near vicinity. Hot, sweaty, rip-your-clothes-off-and-throw-them-around-the-room sex. And Ashleigh would be the first to admit she constantly had sex on the brain, but that was only because she was an erotic romance author. The *only* reason.

Well, that and because she'd been introduced to Alex McDermott all those years ago.

With a sigh of disgust, she dropped her head. She had to get over this freakish infatuation with the man.

She needed some air.

Ashleigh made her way to the back deck, her eyes eating up the spectacular view it afforded her. This was the reason she bought the house. The water looked like glass, reflecting the warm glow of the sun, the crystal blue sky, and the brilliant green tree line that reminded her entirely too much of Alex's eyes.

Shit.

Mind. Gutter. *Damn it.*

Squeezing her eyes closed for a second, she fought off the image before once again opening them. Taking in the calm, smooth water, she remembered the real reason she bought the house. Inspiration.

Giving up the view from her Lake Whitney shoreline had been the hardest part about moving. When she'd glimpsed the pond through the plate glass windows, Ashleigh had been inspired. Being a writer, she took it where she could get it. Although the small pond wasn't as elaborate as the lake, Ashleigh still felt at peace here.

A quick gust of wind blew across her skin, somewhat cooling her overheated libido, and once again reminding her of the reason for the unseasonal heat wave in her girl parts. Why in the world would Pops set her up with Alex McDermott? Didn't he know how flustered the man made her?

Wait.

On second thought, she hoped not. She did not want either man knowing the affect Alex had on her. Ever.

For as long as she could remember, Ashleigh had been fighting her body's reaction to the man and doing her best not to let on that she felt any sort of attraction to him. Except for that one night when she'd lost her mind, but she was almost certain Alex didn't remember anything about that night. Copious amounts of alcohol tended to do that to a person.

She'd tried to drown the images out of her brain once or twice – obviously it didn't work *after* the fact.

"Nice view."

Ashleigh stilled. Alex's deep voice resonated through every single one of her nerve endings, sending a shiver down her spine that had nothing to do with the crisp afternoon air.

"That was part of the appeal." Ashleigh said, once again focusing on the water, not bothering to turn around.

"I can't disagree there." Alex's voice grew closer as he made his way to the edge of the deck.

Against her better judgment, Ashleigh did look at him then. The gleam in those emerald green eyes told her that he wasn't talking about the pond. "What are you doing here, Alex?"

"Putting in a security system." He said flatly, pretending he was interested in the view.

"It's a good thing you don't get paid by the hour." Ashleigh retorted. "You waste a lot of time."

"I wouldn't classify this as time wasted." The growl in Alex's rich, deep voice washed over Ashleigh's senses, sending a warm shiver across her skin.

"I better go check on the movers." Being close to him was too much.

To her dismay, Alex turned and followed her, reaching the back door and opening it before she had a chance. Ashleigh dared to look up into those glimmering green eyes and saw something sparkle there. With Alex, it was difficult to read him, but his smile was pure seduction and Ashleigh knew it was time to put some distance between them.

"When will you be finished installing the alarm and how much is it going to cost me?" Letting him hear the frustration in her voice wasn't difficult. Too bad she was more frustrated with herself than him.

"I've got two guys working on it now, so it shouldn't be much longer. And Xavier already paid." Alex stated, closing the door behind them and then turning that mischievous gleam on her once again.

Maybe she should try that whole drinking herself stupid thing again. It had been years since the last time. At least then if she was going to do something stupid – like say, go all gaga for this guy – she wouldn't remember it.

Two of the movers walked into the kitchen carrying her breakfast table, and thankfully interrupting the intimate situation that she suddenly found herself in. Being alone with Alex was not smart. No matter how much her body seemed to like the idea.

"How about dinner?" Alex asked, but Ashleigh pretended not to hear him. She'd perfected the art of pretending anytime he was around.

"What?" She turned to face him as though she needed him to clarify his statement. That was a mistake.

The man was so damn hot, Ashleigh's internal thermostat notched up a degree or two just from looking at him.

Not only was he a massive chunk of eye candy, a man Ashleigh had compared nearly every man she'd ever met to, he was also tall. At five feet eight, she was on the tall side herself, and his size was one of the things she'd always been drawn to.

At least a head taller than her, Ashleigh liked that he made her feel small in comparison. In order to make eye contact, especially when he insisted on crowding her like he was now, she had to look up. Most of the time, although she was mesmerized by his eyes, they were the last thing she was looking at though.

No, she found herself eyeing his broad chest, or his thick, ropey arms, or... well, the rest of him was off limits where her eyes were concerned.

When Alex cleared his throat, Ashleigh realized she'd been doing just that. Ogling him. Again.

"I'll be glad to go and pick something up for us if you'd prefer."

Assuming he was again talking about dinner, Ashleigh contemplated the repercussions of having dinner with this man. Knowing her, and the fact that her body had already begun to ache for him, dinner could likely lead to something more. Much more. And quite frankly, her limited experience didn't fare well for her when it came to taking on Alex McDermott.

No, dinner wasn't a good idea. But then neither was him being in her house at all.

Not wanting to be rude, her grandfather had raised her better than that, Ashleigh came up with a compromise.

"Why don't I order pizza? I'm sure your installers are hungry, as well as the movers." At least if she ordered pizza, she wouldn't risk being left alone with him.

"Pizza works." Alex smirked, then turned and walked out of the kitchen.

Thankfully he didn't look back, or he would have caught her sneaking a peek at another one of his exceptionally impressive features.

Chapter Four
*** ～ *** ～ *** ～ ***

One week later, settled and having spent more than a few hours a day writing, Ashleigh opted to take a break, which had come by way of an invitation from Samantha McCoy, Logan's new wife.

Instead of coming up with a multitude of excuses, which was her MO, Ashleigh easily accepted, hoping that the outing would help to get her mind off of the two things she'd been overwhelmed with throughout the week – being stalled on the book she was writing and thinking erotic thoughts about Alex McDermott.

It was a no win situation. If she could stop thinking about Alex, the first would likely work itself out. However, if she kept thinking about Alex, the first would likely work itself out.

Since her brain hurt from trying to do either, Ashleigh had sworn off thoughts of Alex for the night. Which was why she was standing in the living room of Logan and Sam's immaculate home, trying to feel like she belonged.

After an hour of engaging in conversations with a slew of people, Ashleigh was still feeling a little awkward.

Between Logan and Sam trying to introduce her to everyone, including Sierra Sellers, an interior designer from Nashville, Ashleigh's mind was racing, trying to put names with faces. She'd even had a brief conversation with Luke, Logan's sexy as hell twin brother, but he didn't seem to be in much of a good mood, so she'd given him some space.

At times, it was awkward trying to talk to adults about children's books, especially those who weren't parents themselves. As much as they wanted to feign interest, Ashleigh knew better.

When living a life of isolation, it was easy to find ways to entertain yourself and Ashleigh had come up with a few tricks of her own. Watching people was one of those things that both amused her and provided good material for future work.

The McCoy house was offering her a plethora of information that could be spun into some really intriguing books. Suffice it to say, these people were unquestionably entertaining. Of course, there was the most fascinating of them all, and though she had sworn him off for the night, avoiding him required some creativity on her part. The man was relentless.

Up to this point, she'd succeeded in avoiding conversation with him, but his interest was apparent, and a little flattering if she were completely honest. Although it was a day late and a dollar short as far as she was concerned. Had he remembered what happened so long ago, Ashleigh was pretty sure he wouldn't be looking at her like he was undressing her with his eyes. Instead, she hoped he'd be blushing bright red with embarrassment.

Doubtful, but she had a vivid imagination.

A commotion sounded from the front hall causing Ashleigh to turn, just in time to see Sierra nearly running out the door, Logan's twin and a sexy blond man following after her. No one seemed concerned with the drama, and Ashleigh wasn't about to get in the middle of it.

When Sam's voice drifted from the foyer, Ashleigh made out the words: *Luke, frustrating,* and *gone and done it again.*

"Hey." The familiar voice interrupted her eavesdropping. Swallowing hard, Ashleigh summoned up the nerve to turn around.

"Hi." One syllable. That's all she had to come up with. So how was it possible for it to come out choppy and a little unsure?

It was odd the effect Alex had on her. Here she was in a room filled with extremely good looking men, all successful, confident, but Alex was the only one who could make her heart pound. From his sexy, unkempt hair, to those dark, dark, emerald green eyes, to that powerful body, Alex stole her breath.

Even in comparison to Luke and Logan McCoy, identical twins who were by far the biggest men Ashleigh had ever come into contact with, Alex was just as intimidating.

Maybe even more so.

Admittedly, Ashleigh wasn't a shrinking violet. Easily above average in height, she was thin, but not terribly so. She hadn't been blessed with the luscious curves that Sam or Sierra possessed, but she could fill out a bikini quite nicely, thank you very much. Her arms were long, her legs even longer and to top it all off, she had big feet. They were nice feet, but big nonetheless.

"Walk with me."

Alex broke through her thoughts, and Ashleigh managed to fight off the embarrassment. She had spent the better part of her teenage years being shy and easily embarrassed – something she worked exceptionally hard to overcome. In turn, she had become incredibly outspoken, often too much so. So when Alex took her hand, linking his powerful fingers with hers, she took that moment to prove it. "What are you doing?"

Wow. Way to ruin a moment.

"I'm holding your hand. It's this little gesture that affords me the opportunity to touch you when otherwise you would run for the hills."

Well, ok then.

The feel of his fingers beneath hers was making her dizzy, so she let him lead her through the back door, onto the patio overlooking a stunning pool. The water glowed with alternating colors while a sound system played something jazzy from overhead. The weather couldn't have been better for so early in the year, the air cool, yet not cold. All combined, it was nice.

With Alex holding her hand, Ashleigh feared he would realize her palms were starting to sweat because his hand was hot enough to melt her insides and not because she was nervous. Ok, maybe a little nervous.

When they stopped at the edge of the pool, Alex sat on the stone ledge surrounding the hot tub, easily pulling Ashleigh down beside him.

"How's the book coming?"

Instinct had her tensing, immediately wondering which book he was referring to. There was no possible way he knew she was Ashton Leigh...

Going on that assumption, she answered, "I'm up to my eyeballs in fairy dust."

Alex's chuckle reverberated through her, rebounding off each and every molecule and making her insides dance with pleasure. Even his laugh turned her on.

"Fairy dust, huh? Does this one end with the princess taming the prince?"

"Well, of course not." Ashleigh said, trying to sound stern. "Don't you know there's no way to tame a prince? Unless of course you turn him into a frog, which I haven't done. So, no, my prince is actually a horse, who, as it turns out, is best friends with a barn owl."

Alex's shocked stare made Ashleigh laugh. "What? Do you have a fear of farm animals?"

"Not that I know of." Alex recovered easily. "That stuff really excites you?"

Ashleigh wasn't going to tell him that she managed to publish the children's books because her agent was a hard ass, and since the books were popular, she was hard pressed not to keep going. But the others she wrote... well, those were what she spent most of her time on.

"I enjoy what I do." She said honestly. "I work for myself ... mostly. And I get to meet so many incredible people along the way."

Alex seemed to contemplate her statement for a moment. "So, what do you do in your spare time? Or do you have any?"

Grateful for the change of subject, Ashleigh glanced out over the pool, watching the glowing water ripple gently in the crisp evening breeze. Sitting here with Alex was nice. She couldn't say relaxing because she was too overheated to relax, but his presence did afford her a sliver of comfort.

"I have spare time. On occasion." Whenever she took a break which wasn't all that often, she thought. "I like to run on those days when I can get away for a bit. Or, I check off one of the items on my *I haven't done this yet* list."

Alex cleared his throat, causing Ashleigh to look at him. The heat in those emerald eyes was palpable.

"What types of things?" Alex's voice sounded strained, and the way his eyes darted down to her lips had Ashleigh's stomach tightening.

"Horseback riding is one of them. I've never done it, so I figure it's something I should at least try. Skiing. Possibly riding a four wheeler. Those types of things." She wouldn't mention the other items on her list that were for her eyes only, like skinny dipping, or having sex in a public place. Or having sex period.

Ashleigh fought the urge to fidget. She often wondered whether her secret list would have more interesting things on it if she had, in fact, ever had sex. Hell, she came up with some astronomical scenes, some she hardly believed would ever happen. At times, she could almost picture herself in those scenes. Not that she would share that with Alex.

Nor would she tell him that she was Ashton Leigh. No reason to give him the wrong impression. Those were fantasies she came up with, and not necessarily her own. But if he knew, would he think they were?

That was the same question she asked herself about anyone who knew her. If she was outed, would her friends and family be disappointed in her? Would they be concerned about her warped mind? Not that she thought it was warped, nor did her readers apparently.

"You've never been skiing?"

Grateful he was keeping the conversation on simpler topics, Ashleigh responded, "Nope."

Her list was long. So many exciting things she wanted to do. Along with the exhilaration of trying something for the first time, Ashleigh sometimes needed to get out of her own head for a little while. Having new things to conquer gave her that brief reprieve. Since she didn't have enough time to do them all at once, she would just write them down for the future. "What about you? Are you a skier?"

"Not much, no. I've been a couple of times, but can't say I'm good at it."

"See, that's the part that doesn't matter. As long as you've tried it once, you can say you've done it. Then you know whether you liked it or not, regardless of how good you are."

Ashleigh took a chance and looked at Alex. He looked lost in thought, and, not for the first time, she wanted to get inside his brain and rummage around. She was pretty sure she'd find some fascinating things there.

Chapter Five
*** ~~ *** ~~ *** ~~ ***

Alex was having a hard time concentrating on the words Ashleigh was stringing together. Between the intoxicatingly sweet scent of her hair, and those luscious pink lips, his brain wasn't functioning because it was suffering from blood loss.

Although his dick wasn't having any issues paying attention.

That was the problem with being around Ashleigh. Or thinking about her. Or dreaming about her. He was rendered completely useless because his body was on overload. From the sweet scent of her glossy, brown hair, to the gleam in her whiskey brown eyes, to those more than perfect lips, Alex couldn't get enough of her. He wanted to run his tongue over the seam of her lips just to find out if she tasted as sweet as she smelled.

He might just get punched for that one.

"I've never been horseback riding either." He offered, hoping they were still on the same topic. "Never has been my thing, I guess."

"Not a cowboy, Alex?" She teased.

He liked when she teased him. A lot.

Since she usually had her guard up when he was around, being with Ashleigh when she was relaxed and talkative was a first for him.

He'd come upon her in the living room, not expecting her to be there, and he'd been like a moth drawn to a flame.

At the moment in time when he saw her standing there, looking ridiculously hot in a pair of tight, faded jeans and cowboy boots – or were they cowgirl boots? Hell, it didn't' matter. She was fucking hot – he hadn't been able to turn away from her.

When he had taken her hand, her long, slender fingers linking with his, he'd made a point to walk outside, rather than to find the first available room so he could feel those soft hands on other parts of his body.

Not that she would have gone for any of that. Not Ashleigh. She wasn't the playful type. Or at least not when he was around.

He was suddenly interested in changing all of that.

"What are you doing tomorrow?" He asked, standing suddenly from the restless hunger that surged through him.

"Tomorrow?" She asked, sounding surprised.

"Yes. Saturday. What are you doing on Saturday?" He repeated, taking her hand and pulling her to her feet.

"N-nothing." She stammered. "Well, that's not entirely true. I sort of need to unpack a few things, and I had planned to go running in the morning."

"What about tomorrow afternoon?" Since Ashleigh wasn't deflecting his question, or flat out pretending she didn't hear him which was usual for her, Alex was going to keep pushing.

"Other than trying to get in some writing, I don't have any plans."

"Go out with me." Alex didn't phrase it as a question because he wasn't going to offer her an out.

"Where?"

Alex chuckled – mainly because he was overjoyed that she didn't flat out tell him no. "It'll be a surprise."

Ashleigh kept her eyes locked with his as she seemed to contemplate his invitation. He silently willed her to say yes while praying she wouldn't say no. This was the most conversation they'd shared in all of the time he had known her, and quite frankly, Alex didn't want it to end, but he had somewhere he needed to be. He didn't want to leave her without at least making plans to see her again.

A few seconds turned into an interminably long minute before she finally smiled, and the sweetest word he had ever heard emerged from her lips. "Ok."

If he wasn't damn near forty years old and scared he'd freak her out, Alex would've fist pumped the air in celebration. Instead, he let his eyes graze her lips. The temptation to kiss her was overwhelming. So much so that Alex couldn't resist.

With a small measure of hesitance, he leaned down toward her, waiting to see if she would back up or worse, push him away. When she didn't, he leaned a little closer. "Kiss me, Ashleigh." He whispered the words and waited patiently to see what her next move would be.

When Ashleigh leaned in, meeting him halfway and pressing her warm, soft lips against his, the world erupted in fireworks and song – although he was pretty sure that was all in his head. He pulled her closer, pressing his body against hers as their lips met briefly. Since he'd already acknowledged patience wasn't his strong suit, Alex took it one step further.

Using one hand to hold her close, he used the other to cup her chin, tilting her head slightly so he could better the angle and slip his tongue into her mouth. She didn't immediately react, but once Alex dipped his tongue just a little farther, her lips parted and he took advantage, kissing her with everything he was.

In turn, Ashleigh blew his mind as she kissed him back, her hands going around him, pulling him even closer as she pressed against his erection, making him moan. *Fucking hell.*

For all the time Alex had fantasized about this moment, he'd never dreamed it would be like this. The woman was sweeter than nectar and so damn soft. With her body crushed up against his, their hips aligned damn near perfectly, as though they had been made to fit together.

Time needed to stand still so Alex could get his fill of this woman in his arms, but, unfortunately, the sound of the door opening behind them had Ashleigh pulling away abruptly, although she used him as a shield to block her from the view of whoever had come out.

Leaning down, knowing he had only seconds before she retreated entirely, Alex whispered in her ear, "We'll pick up where we left off tomorrow, Ash. We have a date, and I'm holding you to it."

Ashleigh nodded her head but didn't look at him.

Alex knew he had made ground that night, so he let it be for now. Tomorrow would be another day. And after the chemistry they'd just shared, he would need time to prepare himself for the explosion that would likely rock his world because it was inevitable.

"See you tomorrow." He kept his voice low, then leaned in and dropped a kiss on her lips before turning to go.

Chapter Six
*** ~~ *** ~~ *** ~~ ***

Alex woke up the next morning with a hard on to rival all. Morning wood paled in comparison to the steely length of his cock after having dreamt about Ashleigh and the kiss they'd shared.

He contemplated getting in the shower to take care of business, but after looking at the clock, he cursed. Jumping out of bed, rearranging himself so he didn't cause any harm, he rushed to the closet to change. Within seconds, he was in the kitchen, grabbing a bottle of orange juice from the refrigerator and his car keys and wallet from the counter.

He only hoped he wasn't too late. With a lead foot, he floored it out of his driveway, doing his best to keep to the speed limit until he hit the open road.

This is what he got for not setting his alarm. Had it not been for the dreams, Alex would've been up before dawn as was normal for him. Instead, he'd overslept because he'd been thinking about Ashleigh when he finally crawled into bed the night before. Apparently he drifted off somewhere in between remembering the kiss they shared and fantasizing about all of the things he intended to do to that woman.

Damn.

If he kept thinking about her, he'd never find any relief from the ache between his legs. Adding some speed, he entered the highway ramp and headed south. Ten minutes tops. That's all he needed.

Since the sun was just coming up, he figured he had a few minutes to spare, but he wasn't willing to risk it. Turning up the volume on the radio, he tried to distract himself with the morning news. It didn't help much.

Thankfully the cops hadn't been out, or they had turned a blind eye because Alex was pretty sure he wouldn't have been able to drive away with just one ticket after that. He pulled into the driveway of Ashleigh's house at the same time she was walking out onto her front porch.

He made it.

Figuring she was confused enough at it was, Alex remained in the truck, lowering the window and waiting for her to come closer. The look on her face was one of shock and awe. The same way he must have looked last night when she had kissed him back.

"Hey," he smiled when she approached. "Hop in."

"Umm." Ashleigh hesitated, glancing up and down her street as though she were expecting someone. "I was about to go for a run."

"I know. You still are. Get in." Alex didn't stop smiling as Ashleigh finally moved in the direction of the passenger door. He leaned over, flipped open the door and pushed. He didn't get it fully opened, but he was able to at least get it started.

"Where are we going?" She asked, taking in his appearance as she climbed in.

Yes, he was in his running gear. Little did Ashleigh know, but Alex ran as well. Maybe not as much as her, he didn't know her routine, but he did manage to get in two runs a week, at least.

"White Rock Lake." He told her as he put the truck in Reverse and backed out of her driveway.

When he got home the night before, he'd researched some of the trails close to her house, and then he picked one he was familiar with. He didn't frequent this particular trail, but he knew it was an easy one, and being a pleasant morning, they'd get the opportunity to enjoy the view. Not that he would find a view nicer than the one sitting beside him.

"I've read about that one." Ashleigh contributed, buckling her seatbelt and seeming to relax somewhat.

"It's usually busy, a lot of runners. This early we'll have some space to ourselves though. Have you found another that you like yet?"

"Not yet. I've run the neighborhood a couple of times and one trail close by, but I haven't had much time to go exploring."

Alex didn't know how this would work out, but after last night, he'd thought of nothing but her and seeing her first thing in the morning was worth the physical exertion. If he was lucky, she might just want a running companion on a more frequent basis. He could get accustomed to having more motivation when it came to his weekly exercise regimen.

"I didn't know you were a runner." Ashleigh broke the silence a few minutes later as Alex steered the truck onto the highway.

There are a lot of things you don't know about me, Alex thought to himself, but he said, "I try to get out a couple of times a week. Sometimes I'm not as successful as I'd like."

"I religiously go five times a week, but that's because I don't go to a gym." Ashleigh admitted, still looking out the window, rather than at him.

"How far do you run?" Sneaking glances at her as he drove, Alex let his eyes skim over all of that sleek, smooth skin revealed by her running shorts.

"I'm up to nine. My goal is to get to ten. Since I don't care about the amount of time it takes, I often don't push myself as hard as I should."

Nine miles? Alex suddenly wondered if he'd be able to keep up with her.

He wouldn't let her know that he only ran five miles at the most, but he did it in under an hour, so he was pretty impressed with his accomplishments. He wasn't looking to be the fastest, and quite frankly, he was generally impressed that he ran at all. With so many things going on in his life, he found working out one of those things he had to focus on just to keep it at the top of his priority list.

"Well, I'm impressed," Alex admitted. "I'll do my best to keep up."

Ashleigh laughed.

Alex liked the husky sound she made and the smile that tipped her lips was an added bonus. He was well aware that beauty was in the eye of the beholder, but when God created Ashleigh, it was obvious He had a bigger audience in mind.

The woman was classically beautiful, with her high cheekbones, strong jaw, pert little nose and perfect lips, all coming together on a flawless face. Her long dark hair, with its sun kissed highlights, normally hung down past her shoulders but was now pulled up in a ponytail. She was long and lean, with golden skin that tempted him to touch her.

Over the years, Alex had watched her grow from a stunning teenager into a gorgeous woman, and he'd battled his own hormones for every one of those years. When he first met her, she was far too young for him. He'd been twenty nine, she only seventeen and although she'd physically caught his eye, he knew better.

Then she turned eighteen and without the law and his own moral compass interfering, Alex had given it more thought. He'd played it out in his head and realized that at thirty years old, he had nothing in common with an eighteen year old. If he'd only wanted sex from her, that would've been one thing.

It wasn't until about the time that she turned twenty five that Alex seriously considered his infatuation with the woman. She'd grown up significantly, and surprisingly, so had he. That's about the time that his friends started giving him a hard time about it. Now, all these years later, he was glad he had waited, but feared they'd built a friendship that wouldn't translate into much more.

But they had come too far for him to turn back now. Considering their history, and her uncanny ability to keep him at a distance, Alex considered this progress.

Twenty minutes later they were pulling into one of the gravel parking lots. At the crack of dawn, only the very determined were out, so they weren't going to have to worry about finding a place to park. Selecting a spot closer to the trails entrance, Alex pulled in and shut off the engine.

If he didn't know better, Alex would've thought the truck was on fire based on the way Ashleigh bolted. After she took a swig of her water, she set the bottle in the console between them, grabbed her iPod and was out the door.

He followed suit, joining her at the front of the truck where she proceeded to stretch her legs, continuing not to look at him.

He'd never been the type to be self-conscious, and considering he had on a shirt, shorts and shoes, he felt he was presentable. But the way she was avoiding him, he was beginning to wonder if there was something wrong with him.

Insecure much?

Instead of wondering what was bothering her, Alex did as he normally did. He asked.

Taking her slender arm in his hand, he turned her so she was forced to look at him. When the tips of her breasts brushed against his chest, he sucked in a breath, realizing how close they were and the image of their kiss from the night before replayed in his mind. Instead of giving her space, he crowded even closer, inhaling her clean, fresh scent. Tipping her head toward him, Alex forced her eyes to meet his.

"What's wrong?" He asked.

"Nothing."

He might've believed her if she hadn't been so quick to answer.

Gently cupping the side of her neck with his hand, he enjoyed the soft feel of her skin against his fingertips. The gentle pulse in her neck was faster than he expected, giving him a momentary rush. Despite her attempt to disguise her reaction, Alex knew he affected her.

"Then why won't you look at me?" Keeping his fingers on her chin, his other hand cupping the back of her neck, Alex fought the urge to kiss her right there in front of God and everyone.

~~*~~

Ashleigh stared back into the greenest eyes she'd ever seen.

Her reaction to him was ridiculous on a grand scale. As though it hadn't been hard enough to make it through the night without dreaming about his hands on her, or the firm, gentle stroke of his tongue in her mouth, he'd had to go and show up at her house.

During the drive, she'd had to accept that she was pleasantly surprised to see him, and that had pissed her off. She didn't want to look forward to seeing him, yet here they were and once again, he was touching her.

After the explosive chemistry that ignited between them the night before, she didn't have any illusions about what would happen between the two of them if she would just give in. The way he stood in front of her now, his body so close, his hands so gentle where they scraped against her skin, she knew that given half a chance, she would probably do just that.

Her first mistake of the day had been agreeing to go with him. Her second... climbing into the small cab of his truck and breathing in the intoxicating scent of the man. With his sinful voice washing over her as they drove, her body had come alive, and for the first time in her adult life, she found herself wanting something she knew she shouldn't want.

But the whopper of them all was standing here, her body pressed against his, their eyes locked on one another and his presence consuming her.

"I'm just preoccupied." She lied. She wasn't looking at him because she wasn't sure she could control herself if she did.

Clad in a tight black t-shirt and gray running shorts, Ashleigh was gifted with a view of the man she hadn't had before. Seeing so much of him should be off limits. Between those powerful thighs and his thick, sinewy arms, Ashleigh had wondered briefly if she would even be able to run. Every muscle in her body had turned to gooey noodles, offering her very little support.

She dared to look him in the eye, and the moment she locked onto those glowing emeralds, she knew why. Along with the heat she saw reflected there, she also saw genuine concern and to know that she had caused it didn't make her feel any better.

"I'm fine. Really." She said unconvincingly. "It's just..."

Just what? What was she going to tell him? *It's just that I can't stop thinking about that kiss? I can't help but want to touch you. Everywhere.*

Ummm... no.

She couldn't tell him that because Alex would likely play to her weakness and she would find herself in his bed – or hers – only to end up wanting something she could never have. Considering she could never say no to the man, she could in no way give him the impression that she wanted him.

"I'm just excited about the trail." Wow, even she didn't buy that one. "You ready?" She pulled away from him.

Breaking the contact was like unplugging from an electrical socket.

"Ready as I'll ever be," he answered, looking somewhat disappointed.

Forcing her ear buds into her ears, Ashleigh set out at a relaxed pace, needing to get warmed up. Although thanks to Alex's wicked touch, she was already pretty damn warm.

Later that afternoon, Ashleigh was sitting on her back patio, her laptop in front of her, and her mind drifting to places it shouldn't be. The morning run had left her invigorated, a restless energy pulsing through her. Alex had allowed her to keep up with him, and although he tried to tell her that it had been the exact opposite, she knew better.

They'd managed the full nine miles in just under two hours, and Ashleigh was so wired, she could have gone another nine. Instead, they had walked for a solid ten minutes before returning to his truck.

When he dropped her off at the house, they still hadn't done a lot of talking. The energy had been throbbing inside the small confines of the truck, and Ashleigh had been forced to ignore it. And him.

Thankfully, when they reached her house, Alex simply pulled into the driveway, shot her a beaming smile that had her insides quivering, before telling her that he'd see her later. And if she had been at all disappointed, she ignored that too.

Now as she sat in front of her computer screen, desperately trying to keep her focus, her mind kept wandering. The most pressing item on her mind – how Alex had forgotten they had a date.

Although, for all she knew, he could have figured the early morning run counted, but as far as she was concerned, that wasn't normally how dates went. Ok, so she didn't have much experience in the dating arena, but she was pretty sure that wasn't how they normally went. Having gone on her fair share, Ashleigh had had more first dates than follow ups, so she certainly wasn't an expert.

And it wasn't as though she were sitting there pining away for the man because she wasn't. She wasn't! What did she care if this morning had been their date? It was nice. Fun. Not what she expected, but it was what it was.

Alex was a complex man, she knew that from experience. He was also busy with his company and remarkably few people came before his precious CISS. Not that she blamed him because he'd worked hard to build the company and if it meant to him what her writing meant to her, she guarded it with her life.

So maybe he hadn't forgotten, maybe he was just busy. She should've been too, so what was she sitting around complaining for? Could it be that she was anxious to see him again? That would've been the complete opposite from how she felt just a week ago.

Toggling back to her Word document, she tried to focus on the words, tried to get her mind on the story. It took only a few minutes before she was immersed in a new chapter, fingers furiously flying over the keyboard.

So when her cell phone chimed, signifying an incoming text, Ashleigh damn near came out of her chair. Excitement fizzed through her veins as she anticipated who it might be.

Grabbing her phone like it would run away, she used the touch screen buttons to get to the text. Her chest bubbled up with anticipation when she saw the unfamiliar number. Normally it would register the caller based on her address book.

She touched the envelope to open the text.

We still on for our date tonight?

Ok, so maybe he hadn't forgotten.

I thought this morning counted as our date

Yes, she was playing hard to get. Sue her. She waited impatiently for his response.

Not hardly

Unsure how to respond to that, Ashleigh waited for him to continue.

Dinner sound good?

Yes and no, she thought. Yes, she was hungry. No, she didn't think she could eat if she were anywhere near Alex. He caused her body to flare up, and her insides to churn which wasn't conducive to digestion.

Since she couldn't very well tell him that, she simply answered *yes*.

Good answer.

His reply made her smile and her insides to riot.

You have two choices.

Not what she expected. Ashleigh didn't want choices. If he gave her an out, she was likely going to take it because in all honesty, Alex scared the bejesus out of her.

Dinner at my house.

Ashleigh waited patiently for the *or*. That option certainly wasn't her first choice.

You get to choose whether you drive over here or I pick you up

Well, hell. What did she say to that? She'd already agreed to dinner, she couldn't very well say something had come up. Going to his house was definitely not a good idea. Too many temptations.

The only option would be for her to drive herself. At least that way, she would have the opportunity to run out if things got too hot. Which she undoubtedly knew they would.

I'll drive.

Committing to what she knew would be the biggest mistake of her entire life, Ashleigh waited for him to provide her with his address. She didn't have to wait long before he gave her the information that would get her there, as well as the time she was expected. An hour.

Damn the man was optimistic.

Although she had showered earlier that day, she had yet to do anything with her hair or makeup. If she was smart, she would throw on a pair of sweats and head over there as is. That would teach him.

But no, she wasn't smart when it came to Alex, so she snatched up her cell phone and laptop and high tailed it inside. She didn't have much time.

Chapter Seven
*** ~~ *** ~~ *** ~~ ***

Alex refused to pace. Yet he was pacing.

Damn it.

Returning to the kitchen, he checked the bread warming in the oven before heading out to the back patio to check on the steaks. He expected Ashleigh to arrive any minute, and he wanted everything to be perfect.

Using his best dishes – he could thank his mother for those; one of the few things she'd ever given him – he had set the table and retrieved a bottle of wine.

Now if Ashleigh would show up, he'd have it made. Instead, he was awaiting her arrival like some love struck teenager who had yet to go on a real date. That was so far from the truth, Alex almost laughed. For a man who'd had his share of women over the years, he should be used to this by now.

But this was Ashleigh Thomas. The woman he had resisted for as long as he could remember on principal alone. His friends liked to hound him about it, giving him shit almost every day about the way he lusted after her, but had yet to *go* after her. Well, he was proving them wrong now, wasn't he?

The doorbell rang, and Alex steeled himself. Where the hell was the confidence he normally exuded?

When he opened the door, his breath hitched in his chest. Replaced was the woman from this morning – filling out a pair of running shorts like no one could – with the stunningly beautiful woman before him. The woman must have a penchant for tight jeans that hugged her curvy hips, and those damn tight t-shirts that lovingly clung to her magnificent breasts.

He'd never envied a t-shirt until now.

"Hey." She greeted him and Alex realized he'd been staring at her like an idiot.

"Come in. You're just in time." Stepping back so she could enter, Alex inhaled as she passed by, once again, damn near getting high from her intoxicating scent.

"I didn't know what to bring, and I didn't know what you were making, so… here." Ashleigh thrust a bottle of wine at him.

Alex reached for the bottle, their fingers touching as he took it from her. Once again there was an electrical current of awareness that passed between them. There was no way she didn't feel it, but from the look on her face, it hadn't fazed her the way it had him.

"Thanks." Alex turned the bottle so he could read the label.

"My brother said you like wine, and I'm not an expert, but I've heard that's a good one."

"One of the best." Alex said, still shocked that she had gone to this much trouble. The wine she brought was hard to find, and since he hadn't given her much notice, she obviously had it on hand.

Tipping the bottle in the direction of the kitchen, Alex pointed the way. "Dinner's almost ready. As a matter of fact, I better check the steaks."

Alex left Ashleigh in the kitchen where she was sitting her purse down on the bar and openly eyeing his space. He hoped she liked what she saw because Alex had worked hard for his home. Mainly physical work because he had designed the house himself, hired the subcontractors, and after many hours of blood, sweat, and tears – his own – he'd finally accomplished what he was going for.

The result was a three bedroom house that he could guarantee was unlike any other in his small neighborhood. Sitting on three acres, he had the privacy he desired, along with a view to rival them all.

Similar to Ashleigh's house, Alex's had an open floor plan and a large manmade pond behind it. Since he hadn't wanted to block his view, he had forgone a fence, leaving remarkably little privacy should one of his neighbors behind him choose to break out the binoculars.

A pool had been a must, due to the hot Texas summers, and he had creatively managed to block the view of prying neighbors by strategically placing various plants and trees. Not that he had needed any privacy thus far, but if Ashleigh was going to be a regular guest, Alex knew all bets were off.

Flipping open the lid on the grill, Alex checked the steaks before removing them from the grate and sliding them onto a nearby plate.

When he reached the kitchen, Ashleigh had donned an oven mitt and was pulling the bread from the oven. His eyes raked over the woman performing a mundane domestic chore, and another surge of lust zipped through his veins. What was it about her that made him go up in flames?

Setting the plate on the table, Alex returned to the stove to get the roasted vegetables he'd cooked earlier, before following Ashleigh into the dining room once again.

Waiting until she sat, Alex poured the wine then took the seat across from her. He realized he'd never invited a woman back to his house for dinner, and having Ashleigh there was making him nervous. There were so many things to think about – were the steaks cooked right? Did he forget anything? Did she like wine or did she just bring it?

Disgusted with himself for being obnoxious, Alex took a deep breath before filling his plate. He wasn't allowed to be nervous. He wasn't a damn teenager.

"This is great," Ashleigh commented, breaking some of the tension.

"Thanks."

"I didn't realize you cooked."

Alex glanced up from cutting his steak and noticed the mischievous gleam in Ashleigh's eyes. Was she teasing him?

"I bet you didn't know that I went to culinary school either, did you?" Alex taunted her.

"Actually, no." Ashleigh's eyes widened like his statement was the most absurd thing she had ever heard.

"Well, that's not surprising since I didn't actually go to culinary school."

Her smile lit up the room, and that seductive laughed warmed him from the inside out. How he had managed to stay away from her for so long was beyond him. Other than the random company party that Ashleigh would attend, or an impromptu invite to Xavier's house, Alex had managed to keep Ashleigh off his mind. But the moment he saw her again, no matter how much time had passed, he'd spend days trying to get her out of his head.

That had all been up until he had kissed her. Since then, there was no erasing her from his mind. She was a permanent fixture at this point.

"Dylan tells me CISS is branching out."

Alex took the opportunity for what it was.

"That's the plan. XTX is still our biggest client, but we've seen an abundance of interest lately. Cole Ackerley attended a vendor's conference in Vegas earlier in the month which seemed to have drummed up some business."

"How's Dylan doing with all of this?"

It was no secret that Ashleigh and her brother were close. Alex also knew she was concerned about Dylan and the way he'd been coping with his wife's death eight years prior. He wasn't normally one to share personal information about the people he knew, but he knew Ashleigh only wanted to know because she was loved Dylan.

"He's coming around." Alex told her as he placed his fork on his plate and reached for his wine glass. "I think now that he's close to Stacey, and Nate is doing better, it'll get easier for him."

"He's had a hard time since Meghan died." Ashleigh admitted, a sudden sadness etched into her beautiful features.

"It's been a long time." Eight years to be exact. And though they had all given him a wide berth, it hadn't been easy. Being his friend, Alex had considered interfering on more than one occasion, but thought better of it. Dylan had been devastated after losing his wife and Alex figured it wasn't his place to determine when he should put the past behind him and move on.

"He's been cooped up for years, running that ranch and essentially living in total seclusion. I don't see how he could get out from under the memories even if he wanted to."

Ashleigh watched him, her brown eyes full of emotion. "When he tried to talk me into moving back," she began, "I told him that the only way I would come back was if he did. That resulted in a couple of long discussions, but I think in the end, it all worked out."

"How does it feel to be back?"

Ashleigh picked at the food on her plate before turning her attention to him. "I didn't think I would ever want to, but I'll be the first to say it's been good for me."

"How so?" Or better yet, why hadn't she wanted to come back? That wasn't a question he was willing to ask her yet.

"Dylan isn't the only one who's been isolated. And just like my brother, I brought it on myself." She told him, sipping her wine. "Last night's party? That's the first time I've been out for anything other than book signings or one of my author groups."

Alex could totally relate. "Don't feel bad. Other than work, I don't venture out much. Logan's always trying to get me to hang out, but now that he's married, it isn't the same." Alex and Logan had been known to tie one on every now and then, but since the man up and got married, Alex hardly saw him.

Other than the party Ashleigh was referring to, Alex hadn't gone out much lately either. Not even on a date.

Ever since the word had gotten out that Ashleigh was thinking about moving home, Alex hadn't found much interest in dating. What that said about him, he didn't know.

"So, tell me about this book writing business." Alex said, encouraging her to open up more.

~~*~~

Ashleigh had to hand it to Alex; he was trying hard to make this as uncomfortable as possible. It wasn't working.

From the moment she pulled into his driveway, she wondered what brought her to this point. Not to dinner specifically, but to Alex in general. For years Ashleigh worked to avoid him and he'd returned the favor.

If only she had forgotten about that one night the same way he had, she might just be able to sit at the dinner table, carry on mundane conversation and not feel as though she were not supposed to be there.

She could go on and on about writing, or any other topic he seemed to be interested in, but in the end, where would it leave them?

"What are we doing?" Ashleigh finally asked, sitting her fork down and pushing her plate away.

"Last I checked, this was called dinner." Alex commented slyly, but the concerned look in his eye told Ashleigh that he was thinking the same thing she was.

"Why are we doing this, Alex?" She really wanted to know.

The kiss they shared last night was as unexpected as it was riveting. Having him show up at her house unannounced, spend two hours running with her, had been overwhelming, to say the least. And now, here they were attempting to converse over dinner when it was clear the only thing going on between them was a little chemistry.

Ok, a lot of chemistry.

Instead of answering, Alex surprised her by pushing back his chair and taking his plate to the kitchen. Feeling like she had brought the black cloud over their attempt at a date, she followed behind him, scooping up her dishes as well.

Depositing them alongside his on the counter, Ashleigh stopped to look at him. Watching as he pulled a long neck bottle from the refrigerator, she waited.

And waited.

Instead of talking to her, he apparently decided to ignore her altogether. Proven when he opened the beer then continued out onto the back porch leaving her staring after him.

Figuring he needed a little space, and she wasn't opposed to the idea either, not to mention she wasn't sure what to do next, Ashleigh busied herself with cleaning the dishes and putting them in the dishwasher.

That didn't take as long as she hoped and she found herself fidgeting as she looked from the back door then back to the wall. What the hell was she supposed to do now?

If she was smart, she would grab her purse and walk out the door, leaving Alex to his temper tantrum. She should pretend this never happened and do her level best to forget what it felt like to kiss Alex McDermott. Forget how sexy the man looked in running shorts and a tight t-shirt. And forget that, for most of her adult life, she had lusted after this man.

Since that wasn't likely to happen, she did what her heart warned her not to do. She turned on her heel and stormed out onto the back porch.

Chapter Eight
*** ~~ *** ~~ *** ~~ ***

"Thank you for dinner." Ashleigh stated as the door clicked shut behind her.

She fully intended to tell him goodbye and then be on her merry way, but a sliver of hope surged up from somewhere deep inside when Alex turned and shot a glance her way. He didn't look happy, and that tiny spark was doused the moment he turned his back on her again.

"Alrighty then." She muttered before inserting some steel into her spine and standing up straight. "I guess I'll be seeing ya." With that Ashleigh turned to go.

"Wait." Alex's voice broke the silence and had Ashleigh stopping in her tracks.

She had one hand on the door knob, ready to haul ass and pretend this night never happened – pretend the entire day had never happened. Instead, she stood there, anticipating what he would say next. To her dismay, he didn't continue, and with a suddenly heavy heart, she knew there was nothing left to say.

They had given it a shot, Alex even more so. After years and years of the chase, apparently the next step wasn't all that he thought it would be. She turned the knob and took one step inside before she was abruptly pulled backward, Alex's solid body colliding with her back, his arms wrapping around her.

In that one instance, all thought was erased from her mind as she allowed Alex to turn her in his arms, pulling her against him and all of the pent up frustration burst free when his mouth collided with hers.

Lips, firm and soft, melded with hers, and she let herself get lost in his kiss. Wrapping her arms around him, everything she had ever held back came barreling forth in a rush, leaving her breathless and aching for this man.

Sliding her hands into the hair at his nape, she let the silky, cool strands caress her fingertips. When he backed her against the rough stone of the house, his erection pressing intimately against her lower belly, Ashleigh thought of nothing more than having him the way she almost had him so many years ago.

When he cupped her face in a gentle, tender gesture, Ashleigh fought to maintain control. The heat she could handle. The inferno erupting between them was familiar, expected, but the way he touched her, held her close, was more than she expected. More than she wanted. When he broke the kiss and pressed his forehead to hers, Ashleigh tried to breathe normally.

"I'm sorry," he mumbled, his breath warm against her cheek.

"For what?" She didn't want apologies, she wanted to go home and forget this night ever happened.

"For making this awkward."

"Well, I think it's safe to say it's not your fault."

"In a way, it was." Alex pulled away, taking her hand in his and walking toward the steps that led down into the yard. When he stopped and sat, she had no choice but to follow suit.

"I've waited a long time for this, Ash."

Ashleigh sat motionless; her hand enveloped in his much larger, much warmer one. The deep rumble of his voice was like warm honey sliding over her skin and the remnants of his kiss had her lips tingling.

"Me too." She admitted when he didn't continue. "But that doesn't mean it'll work out." There were no guarantees, she knew, and just because they had spent years dodging one another, the thrill of the chase leaving them both wanting more, didn't mean anything.

"I think we should start over."

Staring out at the water shimmering in the moonlight, Ashleigh contemplated how they could do that. Starting over usually meant that everything in the past was to be forgotten. Her problem? She couldn't forget the past. Even if he couldn't remember it.

But sitting here beside him, Ashleigh was content for the first time in as long as she could remember.

"What if it's not that easy?" Ashleigh asked him, the question weighing heavily on her mind.

"Why couldn't we? We deserve to give this a chance."

Give *what* a chance? The chemistry? Where would that leave her when it was all over? Ashleigh didn't like the idea of giving in to this man for however long he was willing to have her only to be left wanting something she knew he would never give her.

Then there was the experience issue. Alex was so far out of her league when it came to experience with the type of sexual chemistry that pulsated around them when they touched. At twenty eight years old, it was difficult to admit it, but she was a virgin. The closest she had ever come to having intercourse had been with the very man sitting beside her, and they had never even gotten out of their clothes.

How would he handle knowing that? It wasn't like she was going to tell him. Or maybe she should, just to gauge his reaction.

She couldn't answer his question because she was confused. Confused and scared of her answer. Instead, she glanced over at him, "I really should be going."

Alex nodded his head, acknowledging that, for now, the subject was closed. Before she could stand, Alex made his way to his feet, gently pulling her up by her hand until she stood nearly at his height on the steps.

"Just so we're clear, I can be relentless in my pursuit of what I want." Alex said calmly, quietly. "And I want you, Ashleigh. I've always wanted you."

Ashleigh swallowed down her rebuttal, wanting desperately to remind him that he had been the one to push her away all those years ago. He had been the one to turn and run when she would have so easily given in to him.

"You don't know anything about me, Alex." She warned him, knowing that if he knew who she was, this would be all the more difficult.

"I know more than you think I do."

But not the pertinent parts, she thought to herself.

"Let me walk you out." Alex offered, taking her hand.

Surprising her yet again, Alex didn't plant another soul scorching kiss on her before she left. Instead, he told her to expect the unexpected.

The good thing was… that was her motto.

~~*~~*~~

Alex did as he promised, he gave Ashleigh space. How he managed, he still wondered.

For the last two weeks, he'd only seen her twice. Once they had gone to Club Destiny for drinks, which he'd practically had to beg her to do, and the other time, he had convinced her to go horseback riding.

If he never got on the back of a horse again, it would be too soon. Although there weren't any mishaps, thank goodness, Alex much preferred to keep his feet planted firmly on the ground. Not have his ass perched on top of an animal that could crush him if his mood changed.

She had laughed at his obvious distaste, which as it turns out, only made him want her more. And hadn't that been a swift kick in the ass. The staying away from her part was what got him the most.

Thankfully he'd been a little preoccupied with other things. First of all, work. CISS was eating up all of his time which had led him to finally reach out to Cole Ackerley. Admittedly, he needed help and Ackerley was one of the best in the PR department. Having him come onboard would reduce some of the stress on Alex.

Since Dylan wasn't quite pulling his own weight, Alex was trying to cover that as well, which was beginning to pull him under. It wasn't that Dylan didn't have the necessary skills to succeed, but the man seemed to be lacking the motivation. And that was the reason Alex was taking the time to meet with Dylan for lunch.

"Table for two, please." Alex told the hostess when he entered the restaurant.

Due to their conflicting schedules, Alex had opted to meet for a late lunch so they could be on neutral ground for the conversation that was inevitable. Since the restaurant was more or less empty, Alex didn't need to request a table that would offer a little privacy.

The hostess seated him promptly, and he advised that he was expecting someone. When the waiter stopped by, he ordered two beers and then began checking his email on his phone while he waited.

Prompt as always, Dylan joined him a few minutes later.

"Hey." Alex greeted his friend and business partner as Dylan took the empty seat across from him.

"Is it just the two of us?"

Nodding his head, Alex grabbed a menu from the holder on the table. "I ordered you a beer." Then he found himself stalling.

Earlier that day, the idea of this meeting had been a good one. The conversation had played out seamlessly in his mind while he drove to the restaurant, but now that Dylan was sitting across from him, he was beginning to have second thoughts.

The two men perused the menu, drank their beers, chit chatted about nothing significant and otherwise avoided the issues at hand. When the waiter came back around they ordered then waited for him to step away again.

"Spill it." Dylan stated in his laid back Texas drawl so much like his grandfathers. "I know you have more appealing choices in lunch companions, so why don't you just cut to the chase."

"Alright." Alex said, downing the rest of his beer before signaling the waiter to bring another. Dylan was right, Alex just needed to come out and say it. "I don't know any other way to say this, but when I asked you to come onboard, I wasn't looking for a receptionist."

Dylan's reaction wasn't one of surprise, or even anger, which was what Alex originally expected. Instead, he glanced down at the table briefly before meeting Alex's eyes once more.

With a resigned sigh, Alex elaborated. "When I asked you to be a partner in CISS, I didn't mean a silent partner. I didn't need money, and I don't need someone to answer the phones." Alex told him, all of the pent up frustration coming to the surface. "You sit around the office answering the damn phones like it's what you were born to do."

"Someone has to answer the phones." Dylan remarked without heat.

"But not you. Fucking hire someone. Or just have them forwarded to my phone like they've always been." Alex told him, sitting back in his chair. "Look. We've been friends for a long time. I know what you went through, and I'm still so very sorry, but, Dylan, she's been gone for eight years."

"I know." The sadness in Dylan's eyes shone bright, making Alex feel like a jackass.

"Meghan wouldn't want you to stop living. Now that the kids are older, you've got the rest of your life ahead of you, man."

"Preaching to the choir, brother." Dylan said, taking a long swallow of beer. "I've heard it all before, and I'll tell you the same thing I tell everyone else. You don't know what it's like. You don't know what it's like to go from one day having the love of your life and your best friend right there beside you, only to have her taken completely away the next. She's gone, and I feel like I died right along with her. The only thing that has kept me going was taking care of my kids. Now that they're old enough to take care of themselves, I don't have anything else."

"Bullshit, man." Alex bellowed, sitting forward in his chair, resting his elbows on the table. "You know that's a load of shit, Dylan. You've got Stacey and Nate, Xavier, Ashleigh. Every one of them depends on you. *Needs* you."

"I get it."

Alex knew he wasn't telling Dylan anything he didn't know already, but when it came to CISS, he needed to take it to the next level. Bringing on Samantha and now Cole meant they were equipped to branch out. Something Alex had dreamed of. And he wanted Dylan to be part of that.

"Cole accepted my offer," Alex said, changing to a less sensitive subject. "He's officially onboard starting next week."

"That's great news." Dylan stated, picking at the label on his beer bottle. "I think he's just what we need to help divert some of the strain off of you. And yes, I know I need to do more."

Alex wanted to hear how Dylan planned to do that.

The waiter interrupted, bringing their food and offering them a brief reprieve. Alex took the opportunity and let Dylan breathe for a minute.

When Alex finished, in record time no doubt thanks to not eating that morning, he pushed his plate away and downed more of his second beer. "What's your plan?" He prompted.

Dylan pushed his plate away, then leaned back in his chair, propping his elbow on the empty chair beside him. "Since the residential security services are growing astronomically, I think I'm going to focus on that. I've got some ideas, and I want to bring on a couple of people – sales people."

Alex noted the renewed interest in his partner's eyes. Dylan needed something to focus on and bringing him onboard had been one of the best decisions he'd made. Once Dylan took off, there would be no stopping him, Alex knew.

Dylan continued before Alex could contribute. "We've got all the installers we need, and I want to hire someone to manage them, but I need some folks driving sales. What do you think?"

"I think this is the reason I wanted you to go in business with me, man. You've got great ideas and the direction you're going is one I wish I had time for before now. Do you have any candidates for the sales positions?"

"I've got one. Guy named Jake. I went to school with his aunt. If you know of anyone, send them my way. I'd like to get them hired by the end of next week if possible." Dylan's voice had gained a significant amount of confidence.

"I've got a couple, actually." Alex added.

This was the Dylan Thomas he had known before his wife had succumbed to cancer eight long years ago. The man who stopped at nothing to accomplish his goals. The man who was like the Energizer bunny... kept on going because each idea was bigger and better than the one before.

"Alex, I want to thank you." Dylan interrupted Alex's thoughts, surprising him.

"For what?" Alex asked. "I should be apologizing –"

"Don't." Dylan stated adamantly, his tone containing none of the laid back country boy that Alex was used to. "I needed this. I need to get on with my life. Moving was the first step, which I can thank my sister for. Speaking of..."

Oh shit. Alex hadn't expected the sudden topic change, and he wasn't quite ready to talk to Dylan about his little sister.

"I've heard you and Ashleigh are seeing each other." The laid back, country drawl was present once again. Alex wasn't deceived by his friend any more than he was by Xavier when he pulled the same stunt.

"We're seeing each other." Confirming Dylan's statement, Alex wasn't willing to go further. "Trust me, man. You don't have to warn me off of her. I've been doing it for years. I can only promise you that I won't intentionally hurt her. As for anything else, I don't know, but I'm going to see where it goes."

Dylan laughed, making Alex's back straighten.

"Man, I was just gonna ask whether you were taking her to Luke's reception."

Fuck. Way to speak out of turn, McDermott.

"But now that you mention it," Dylan began, "I trust you have her best interest in mind. She's my little sister, and I'm protective of her, but you already knew that. I don't want her hurt, but she's also a big girl who can take care of herself. You won't see me trying to interfere." Another laugh. "But I can't say the same for Pops. You know he's going to be all over this as soon as he gets word."

Oh, Alex was more than aware of what Xavier would have to say as soon as the news got out. Even if Xavier did have a hand in pulling the two of them together, he'd still have something to say.

Alex didn't look forward to that day.

Chapter Nine
*** ⁓ *** ⁓ *** ⁓ ***

Ashleigh no longer had to worry whether her cell phone was working or not. The call from her agent proved that it was. Even though her original excitement over who might be on the other end had been doused when Madeleine's sweet voice echoed through the speaker, it had been renewed after five minutes on the phone.

Her agent was clearly satisfied with her last submission, the book about the horse and the barn owl that Ashleigh had pondered over for far too long. At least now it was out of the way, and she could move on to her current project.

This one was keeping her up at night, but not with worry. Her bout of writer's block had long since moved on, and she was writing furiously, the pages all but writing themselves.

She had one man to thank for her renewed burst of creativity. At least where the sex was concerned. As it appeared, her hormones were roaring like wildfire, and she was able to conjure up some juicy, erotic scenes, which worked out well for her hero and heroine.

At least someone was getting laid these days because it certainly wasn't her. But then again, she and Alex had come full circle in the dating game.

She had committed herself to making just as much of an effort as Alex, although, at times, she wondered if maybe she should resume life as she knew it before moving back to Dallas.

For the last few weeks, she'd been busy. Her social life had taken off like a jet airplane, which meant the time she wasn't spending with her grandfather and niece and nephew, she was spending with Sam and Sierra. As for Alex, well, she hadn't seen nearly enough of him in the last two weeks for her wellbeing, but more than enough for her sanity.

Apparently he had gotten a look at her list of things she wanted to do, and he was bound and determined to check off each and every one. There were a few items she hadn't written on her list, and sometimes she wondered whether they just might get around to them as well.

To top it off, he was being a perfect gentleman.

Too perfect in fact.

So much so that they hadn't shared another kiss since the night he'd invited her over for dinner. Ashleigh had no idea what was going on with him, but something was. He was cordial, friendly, but nothing more.

On top of that, something or someone was taking him away frequently. She didn't think he was going far when he left, but he was obviously going somewhere. One afternoon when he had taken her fishing, something she had on her list, she'd thought about asking him, but instead chickened out.

That had been an interesting day, but not one she cared to relive. Apparently fishing was not her forte. Too much down time in her opinion. But hey, to each his own and all that.

Delving back into her work, Ashleigh was trying to work out a scene that she was having trouble with. A sex scene. Imagine that.

Lunch with Sam and Sierra earlier in the week had provided her a little insight, but not nearly as much as she hoped for. She'd gone with the intention of getting some hopefully discreet details of what it was like living the ménage lifestyle. Since she didn't have any idea about the subject matter, she was hoping for details from the experts so she'd gone out on a limb and asked for their help.

So how she ended up sharing way more information with the two of them than they had shared with her, she had no idea. Although she got a brief glimpse into what it was like to be the focal point of two men, Ashleigh had found they were way more interested in understanding how she was still a virgin.

And no, maybe a twenty eight year old virgin wasn't the norm these days, but it wasn't unheard of. By the look on Sam's face, Ashleigh would've thought she was the oldest living person yet to have ever had sex. It was comical actually. Kind of.

Much to their dismay and her own, Ashleigh couldn't answer the question as to why she'd never had sex. There had been a couple of men in her life who had sparked her interest, but they'd never made it that far. Could've been cold feet on her part, or it might've been the hope that had been burning bright and obnoxious in her chest for ten long years.

Either way, Ashleigh would admit to having harbored some crazy, mixed up feelings for Alex through the years. Anger, admiration, hurt, love. Pick one.

If she thought about it – which she did... a lot – she could almost put a name to those feelings. Infatuation. The man encompassed everything she hoped to find in a lover – he was gorgeous, intelligent, and dominating. Yes, the last one unquestionably had caught her interest when she was old enough to know what it actually meant. Or what it could mean.

Ashleigh remembered the day she met him. It was at her grandfather's house and she'd just gotten home from school. She'd been a high school senior, she remembered that much. And in her teenage mind, he'd been much older than her, although she didn't know by how much. At the time, it hadn't mattered one single bit. She had fallen head over heels in love the moment she laid eyes on him.

It didn't take long for Alex to become a regular fixture at the Thomas household and in her teenage dreams. He quickly began working as the head of security for XTX on a contractual basis. Then he'd established a friendship with Dylan, which had Alex coming around when her brother was home. He and Logan were friends – college roommates if she remembered correctly – which meant Alex was invited anytime Logan was present.

Needless to say, she saw as much of Alex as she did her grandfather there for a while. At first, she'd been smitten.

It wasn't until he started treating her like she had a contagious disease and if he came anywhere near her, he'd be stricken with it. That didn't stop him from sneaking glances of her from time to time. She was aware of each and every one, but over time, she grew irritated with his aloofness and she moved on.

Looking back on it now, Ashleigh had been far too immature for him, especially considering the age difference. At twenty eight, twelve years didn't mean a thing. But at eighteen or even twenty, it meant everything. They had absolutely nothing in common. Other than a little physical attraction.

Then there was the small detail of his marriage. By the time she met him, he'd been divorced for years, but knowing he had been married, Ashleigh had accepted the fact that he wasn't likely going to be a one woman man, though she had no idea why they had split up. She still didn't know.

Not knowing the story, she didn't care to be enlightened back then, although now she was more than a little curious. Just the fact that he had been married put him in an entirely different category than any boy or man she'd ever met. Suffice it to say, she kept her distance. And so did he.

Until that one night.

The week before graduation, Ashleigh had convinced Pops to let her stay in the guest house for a few weeks while she got ready to go off to college.

Since Dylan didn't live at home at the time – he'd already gotten married to Meghan, and they had even had both Stacey and Nate by then – Ashleigh had wanted to see what it was like to live on her own as well. Reluctantly, Pops had given in to her request.

To celebrate her graduation from high school, Pops had thrown a party the likes of which Ashleigh had never known before. There had to have been one hundred or more people in attendance, yet out of all those people, she'd never seen Alex. Not until he stopped by the guest house a couple of hours after she went home.

Being eighteen and finally out of school, Ashleigh had a misconception of what it meant to be an adult. And adults had visitors, so she'd invited him in.

That was her first mistake.

He was more than a little intoxicated, barely able to stand on his own, but she was all grown up, she could handle anything he could dish out. Or so she thought.

They had talked for a little while, neither of them having much to say because it was blatantly obvious, they had absolutely nothing in common. Likely the dwindling conversation had led to what happened next.

They had been sitting on the couch, not much space between them, when Alex leaned over and kissed her lightly on the lips. Her *first* kiss.

Ashleigh remembered it like it was yesterday.

"What was that for?" Ashleigh asked, shocked by the intensity of her body's reaction to the feel of Alex's lips against hers.

"It was just a kiss."

Just a kiss? There was nothing "just" about that kiss. She knew she shouldn't push the issue because it was evident Alex was intoxicated, but Ashleigh couldn't seem to stop herself. "Why'd you kiss me?"

"Don't know." He said, leaning in a little more.

Ashleigh knew it was going to happen again and despite the intense feelings that one kiss had ignited she knew she shouldn't want him. But the intelligent side of her brain was being suffocated by her hormones and she found herself hoping he would.

Instead of waiting for him, Ashleigh leaned in closer, her eyes locked with his before catching a brief glimpse of his perfect lips. Before she knew what happened, she was on her back on the couch with Alex's impressive body on top of her, pressing against her in the most delicious way, infusing her with heat and longing.

"I shouldn't want you, Ashleigh."

For the life of her, she didn't know why not. They were both consenting adults, and there was something obviously between them. So when Alex pressed his lips to hers yet again, Ashleigh gave into him, pulling him closer and giving back as good as she was getting.

Shaking off the memory, Ashleigh tried to push it away. She would not go there. Not right now. Thinking about that night never did anything more than put her in a bad mood.

~~*~~

Alex tossed his cell phone into the center console, throwing the truck in Drive. Pissed off and in desperate need of a bright spot in his week, he pulled out of the XTX parking garage and aimed the truck toward Ashleigh's house.

After that phone call, he wanted to simply turn off the ringer, hang out with the one woman who would be able to make him smile at this point. That had been his plan all day anyway, and though the phone call from Jessie had been somewhat expected, he was going to pretend it never happened.

His ex-wife had made it her life's work to suck him into the mess she called a life, but today he didn't have the patience, nor the desire to try and rescue her from herself. He'd been spending way too much time with her as it was trying to talk to her, calm her down, or chase off that good for nothing boyfriend of hers.

Not today.

Ten minutes later he was pulling into Ashleigh's driveway, trying to get his bearings. He was frustrated, and he knew he needed to take a minute to clear his head. The last person he wanted to see his temper was Ashleigh. Having not seen much of her in the last two weeks, showing up at her house unannounced was going to be bad enough.

He needed to see her. Need being the key word.

Ever since their afternoon of horseback riding, Alex had purposely backed off a little bit. She was getting to him in ways he hadn't expected. The desire was there, but it always had been. It was the other feelings stirring around inside of him that had made him take some time to process exactly what was happening between them.

He wanted her in ways he feared she couldn't handle. And until today, he'd been able to reason with himself. Today his need for her had intensified, and he wasn't strong enough to resist it. So instead of doing the right thing, he'd given in to temptation, despite the perfect excuse to stay away for at least one more day.

After a few minutes, his blood pressure had finally reverted to the more normal range, and he exhaled a sigh of relief. It took a lot to get Alex riled up, but today everything seemed to be stacking up against him. Even the thought of seeing Ashleigh was getting him worked up but for an entirely different reason.

Alex exited the truck, glancing at Ashleigh's Tahoe parked in the driveway. At least she was home. It would have been the perfect end to a shitty day for him to have driven all the way there to find out she wasn't.

When he made it to the front door, he rapped his knuckles on the wood, pacing back and forth in front of the door while he waited. A good minute later, he figured she wasn't going to answer. Thrusting his hands in his pockets, he stood on the porch for a minute, wondering where the hell she might've gone.

Glancing around toward the side of the house as he walked back to his truck, he stopped. It was worth a shot.

Alex turned the corner and saw Ashleigh sitting at a table on her back deck, her fingers flying furiously over the keys on her laptop. For a brief moment, he just watched her.

She was breathtaking. Her hair was piled on top of her head in a clip, and from where he stood, it didn't look like she was wearing makeup, which made sense because she was still in her pajamas. He couldn't ever remember a time when he was still in his pajamas at three o'clock in the afternoon.

"Hey," he called out, not wanting her to see him standing there staring at her.

Ok, so maybe he startled her. There was a little squeak, a little jump, and now she was staring back at him with her hand clutched over her heart.

"What the hell are you doing?" She asked, obviously not shocked for long.

He grinned. "I could ask you the very same question."

Alex made his way up the steps, his eyes glued to the woman standing before him, dressed as though she had just crawled out of bed. He'd like to drag her back there.

"What are you doing here?" She rephrased her question, her hands now on her hips.

"Bored." He lied, but smiled as he said it.

"I find that hard to believe. Dylan said you guys are busy, so I know that's not it."

"Ok, I just wanted to see you. That better?"

The smoldering look in her eyes told him that she definitely liked the answer, but he was willing to bet she wasn't going to verbally agree.

"What are you writing?" He asked, glancing down at the computer that sat on the table between them.

Ashleigh glanced down, her eyes wide before she slammed the lid closed. Obviously she didn't want him to see what she was writing. If he had to guess, she wasn't writing about horses and owls like she'd told him before. He grinned again.

No, he grinned *still*. Since the moment he laid eyes on her, he'd had a permanent smile on his face.

"Nothing." She covered quickly, looking slightly embarrassed.

"Nothing, huh?" He was tempted to grab the computer, just to see what she'd do. He knew about her pen name, he knew exactly what she was writing about, even if she wouldn't admit it.

But, he wasn't in the mood to get slapped at the moment. Ashleigh wouldn't take too kindly to him intruding on her personal space, so he kept his hands in his pockets.

"Well, since you aren't working," he made a point to look back down at the laptop, then back up at her, "I was thinking we could do something."

"Something?" The skeptical look in her eye had him biting back another grin.

"Sure." He said, closing the distance between them. "What else you got on that list?"

Ashleigh surprised him when she didn't take a step back, allowing him to stand close enough to inhale her fragrant scent. She smelled like vanilla and sunshine. It should've been outlawed in all fifty states. It was that damn good.

"I'm thinking... swimming." Because he wanted to see her in a damn bathing suit. Or nude would be fine with him. Either way.

"*Swimming?*"

Was it him or was she tongue tied? She wasn't smiling, but nor was she frowning. She looked confused.

"Yes, you know, water... pool. It's heated and it's nice out." *And you would be in a damn bathing suit which would be hot as hell in itself.*

"Ok."

He cocked his eyebrow, staring down at her suspiciously. Sure, he definitely liked the idea of getting Ashleigh wet – in more ways than one – but he got the distinct impression she was up to something. His Ashleigh would've come up with an excuse to make him leave. Instead of questioning her, because he wasn't an idiot, he slid the back of his finger down her smooth cheek. "Ok, then. Go get your stuff and I'll wait right here."

~~*~~

What the hell was wrong with her? Swimming? *Seriously?* It was only sixty degrees outside at best. What in the world was she thinking?

Ashleigh grabbed her laptop from the table, turned and darted inside the house as fast as she could. Depositing it on her bed, she turned to her dresser to find a swimsuit.

Ha! Served her right. Staring down into the near empty drawer, Ashleigh took stock of the one and only bathing suit she'd unpacked as of yet. It was a two piece – two very small pieces – and it was bright, neon pink. Admittedly, it didn't look all that bad on her when it was the middle of the summer and she'd had a chance to get a little sun. Right now, in February, she wasn't sure which would be brighter, the bathing suit or her pale skin.

And now she was shaking. Actually, she'd been trembling since Alex had scared the daylights out of her a few minutes ago. Apparently those tremors were causing her to lose brain cells.

She hadn't expected Alex to show up, so when he walked across her back lawn, her brain had lost some of its functionality. Apparent by her agreeing to go swimming. At his place. Those two things combined were a recipe for disaster. Especially considering her libido was in overdrive after the last couple of chapters she'd written.

Her body didn't seem to be caught up with her brain's reluctance because five minutes later, Ashleigh was traipsing across the living room, a small bag containing the neon pink bikini in hand.

"Ready?" Alex asked from his perch on the arm of the sofa.

No, not really. "Yep." She blurted.

Alex stood, once again towering over her, and she wondered what he was waiting for. Standing there like an idiot, she watched him until a sexy as hell smile tipped his lips.

"After you." He said, holding his hand up in the direction of the door.

Good grief. Her brain was overloaded, and now she wished she'd reconsidered this astronomically stupid idea.

By the time she was safely inside Alex's truck, buckled up and staring out the side window, her stomach was a jumble of nerves.

"Do you swim a lot?" She asked, because, at this point, only stupid things were coming out of her mouth.

"No, not really." Alex glanced at her, then back to the road, "In the summer, I get out a few times a month, but since I'm not home much, I don't."

"When I was a kid, Dylan and I would get in the swimming pool at Pop's house all the time. Even in the winter and sometimes when he didn't remember to heat it."

"That's commitment." Alex laughed.

"I was on the swim team in high school. For one year anyway. Turns out I didn't want to be a fish like I once thought." Actually, it turned out she was way too shy and far too awkward to go out in public and compete in anything. She froze the few times her coach had tried to get her in the pool.

"No?"

"No. I found my writing niche while I was in high school though." At least writing gave her exactly what she was looking for. Solitude. "Turned out to be a great way to escape. I could become someone else for a little while. Like a fantasy coming to life."

"What did you write about back then? I couldn't imagine a teenage girl had much interest in writing children's books."

Ashleigh laughed. "There wasn't much rhyme or reason back then. I'd write short stories and most of them didn't fall into any specific category."

Her parents had died before she was old enough to even remember them, and Ashleigh found herself fantasizing about the mother and father she never had, putting their stories down on paper. It helped with the grief.

"And now?"

"And now *what?*" She asked. Ashleigh didn't know where he was going with this, but she was half tempted to push him.

She knew, thanks to Sam's admission, that Alex was well aware of her pen name. Oddly, she thought he'd be more determined to get her into bed because of that fact.

Originally she wondered if Sam had been mistaken, but Ashleigh didn't think so. There was a gleam in his eyes when he talked about her writing. He knew, he just wasn't going to bring it up.

"Do the children's books hold your interest?"

"For the most part, yes." That was partially true.

"Have you thought about writing something else?"

"Like what?" A knot formed in her stomach. This conversation was going in the wrong direction.

"Oh, I don't know. Mysteries? Romance, maybe?"

Or erotica? She wanted to say the words out loud, knowing that's what he was hinting at, but she didn't.

Before she could answer his question, he was pulling his truck into his garage, shutting off the engine and closing the door behind them. The confines of the truck were intimate enough, but with the outside world shut completely out, the intimacy was almost disturbing.

She sighed, unable to keep up the facade any longer.

"When were you going to bring it up?" She asked bluntly, needing to get this out in the open. As much as she valued her anonymity, it was too hard to try to hide something that was out in the open anyway.

"Bring what up?" Alex's dark eyebrow rose.

For the last week, Ashleigh had fantasized about how this conversation would go. Never once had she dreamed that Alex would feign ignorance. Turning her back on him, frustrated and still a little shaky, she pushed open the passenger door and stepped out of the truck.

She needed a moment to breathe and although she wasn't claustrophobic, being closed up in his truck with him was just too much. When she was close to him, his unique scent alone made it hard to think, and that was something she couldn't afford when Alex was around.

Alex walked around the truck and stood beside her. "Talk to me."

"I know that you know." She told him, wishing he would take a step back because he was much too close. It was hard enough to breathe, hard enough to think when he was near, but this close, she didn't stand a chance.

From where she stood, looking up at him, she could see the darker flecks of green in his already dark eyes. His lashes were long and thick, and there was a day's worth of stubble decorating his strong chin. The man was beautiful if that was an apt description for someone who exuded so much masculine power.

"What do I know, Ashleigh?" He asked, taking a step closer, if that was even possible, and successfully blocking her between him and the unmoving vehicle at her back.

"You know that I'm Ashton Leigh." She spouted before she could think better of it.

"So?"

"What do you mean 'so'?" Putting her hands on his chest, she tried to push him away, but he didn't budge. "If you're thinking that I'm anything like her –"

"Shhh." He whispered, brushing his finger over her lips. "I don't *think* anything."

Didn't he? Didn't he think she was wild, spontaneous and openly adventurous when it came to sex? It's what she wrote about, so it would make sense, wouldn't it?

"I've wanted you since the first day I met you, Ash. Long before you began writing. I don't have any preconceived notions about who you are or what you want."

He wanted her?

His admission sent a shockwave of lust rippling through her insides. Without thinking, she glanced down at his lips, then back up to his eyes.

"Stop looking at me like that." His voice was firm, but he didn't move away from her.

"Like what?" She almost choked on the words.

"Like you want me, too."

"I do want you." There was no reason to deny it.

They might be playing a game, but he knew good and damn well that she wouldn't have gone to his house to go swimming if she didn't have a hidden agenda. Friends they might be, but not close friends. And never would she have put herself in this position if she hadn't hoped for something more to happen between them either.

"Ashleigh." The way he said her name was a warning, and her body didn't heed it worth a damn.

In a move totally unlike her, Ashleigh instigated what happened next. With her hands still pressed against his chest, she was no longer trying to push him away; instead, she slid them up, feeling the solid muscle and his strong heartbeat beneath her fingertips. Cupping his jaw, she pulled him closer. She wasn't sure if it was the weather, or what was sparking between them, but something was making it hotter than hell in that damn garage.

Chapter Ten
*** ~~ *** ~~ *** ~~ ***

Alex didn't move a muscle. Well, unless his dick counted. He stood as motionless as possible while Ashleigh tortured him with the soft tips of her fingers against his jaw. Since the moment she'd put her hands on him, he'd been frozen in place, waiting for her next move.

That was no small feat for Alex. When it came to any sort of intimacy, he generally shied away from it. Unless of course it was sex. That was an entirely different story. When it came down to it, Alex ensured he was in control and his partners were always aware of it too.

But right here, right now, with Ashleigh... this was different.

He wanted to crush his mouth down to hers, to press his body to hers, to grind his throbbing erection between the juncture of her thighs and find some sort of relief from the overwhelming lust that bubbled inside of him.

"Kiss me, Alex."

Alex didn't kiss her; he just stared down at her like she'd lost her mind. Did the woman even know what she did to him? Did she know how hot she made him burn?

"Kiss me like you want to kiss me." She insisted again, not moving her hands from his face.

God she was going to kill him.

"Are you sure?" He needed to know whether she understood what she was signing up for. Alex was not a gentle lover.

"I'm positive." There wasn't even a hint of uncertainty in her tone.

"Baby, I can't promise I can stop once this starts." Standing in the middle of his garage, Alex knew he'd at least get her into his house, but the second he let loose on her, there might be no turning back.

"Just a kiss, Alex. For now." Ashleigh grinned, and that little spark she lit with her bold words turned into a full blown inferno. She was going to be a challenge, he knew.

Easing closer, her fingers sliding up the side of his face until they laced into his hair, he closed the gap between their mouths. When she closed her eyes, he slid his tongue over her bottom lip. When she moaned, he damn near lost it.

"So sweet." He whispered, not meaning to talk at all, but he was doing his damnedest to hold onto an ounce of his control.

Her little pink tongue darted out, meeting his on the edge of her lip and Alex pressed his body against hers. When she pulled his head down closer, he knew he was no longer in control of what was happening. She was.

Then she kissed him and just like the last time, everything came down to this one single woman, and the way she gave herself over to him. He plundered her mouth with his tongue, taking everything she offered, delving deeper, gripping her head and holding her close as though she might try to move away.

Not Ashleigh. Instead, she tried to get closer. Much closer. Until he had no choice except to hoist her up, letting her wrap her legs around his waist, his steel hard cock pressed into that sweet spot between her legs.

Her sensual moans were the music that went along with the light show going off behind his closed eyelids. This was more than he'd imagined, and yes, he'd given plenty of thought to what it would feel like to take this woman. To bury himself deep inside her and make her cry out his name as she came around his cock.

Breaking the kiss, he moved down the side of her neck, inhaling her fresh, sweet smell. He used one hand to pull the neckline of her t-shirt back so he could reach the gentle ridge of her collarbone, licking and kissing as she squirmed in his arms. Latching onto the skin, he suckled, knowing he was going to leave a mark on her perfect skin, but not caring. He felt like a teenager, touching a woman for the very first time and wanting nothing to stand between him and what would be the most pleasure he'd ever experienced.

Writhing in his arms, Alex traced his lips back up over her neck, higher until he met her mouth again, scared to death of what he might do if he let this get out of control. She'd turned on the heat, his body set on broil, and the flames were likely to make him lose every possible good intention he'd ever had.

He didn't know how much time passed as they made out in his garage, but he finally managed to pull his lips from hers. Staring back at him, Ashleigh's whiskey colored eyes were now darker, swirling with the passion he could physically feel just beneath the surface of her flawless skin.

He held her against him, pressing his forehead to hers as he tried to catch his breath. She didn't sound like she was faring any better than he was. Her fingers were still laced in his hair, her nails grazing his scalp and sending tingles down his spine.

"What am I going to do with you?" He said the words out loud, but he didn't expect an answer.

"Anything you want."

Oh, Lord have mercy. He was not going to survive this.

~~*~~

Ashleigh had no idea what had come over her.

Alex made her want things she'd only ever read or written about. She wanted to experience every single thing her brain had ever come up with at the hands of this man. And after that kiss, she knew she was going to be in for the ride of her life.

As strange as it was, she meant what she said. Maybe her alternate personality was more a part of her than she thought. When he touched her, Ashleigh didn't feel any of the trepidations she thought she would. The way he kissed her, as though he needed it as much as she did just to sustain life, made her legs weak.

When he set her back on her feet, taking a step away, Ashleigh realized where they were. In the moments when they had been pressed against one another, his tongue in her mouth, where they were hadn't mattered. Hell, nothing had mattered but the sensual taste of him, the urgency in his touch. He had somehow tapped into that other part of her that had absolutely no inhibitions.

Leaning around her, he opened the truck door, snatching her bag from the seat before taking her hand in his and leading her into the house. He didn't say a word and she was afraid to ask what they were doing because she had an idea.

Would he take her straight to his bedroom?

"Hungry?" He asked when he opened the refrigerator door.

Was that a rhetorical question, she wondered. She was hungry alright, but it wasn't food she wanted.

"I'm good." She answered, only a few feet separating them in his open kitchen.

This was the part she had trouble with. She couldn't wrap her mind around how she was supposed to act. If they were, in fact, going to have sex, would he just take her to the bedroom and get it over with? That's not how it happened in the books she read, or the ones she wrote, but hell, those weren't real. Were they?

"You can change in the bathroom." Alex said, pulling her brain back to present.

Change? What was she going to change into?

Oh, good grief. Her mind was in the gutter. They had come to his house to go swimming and apparently that was still his intention. Letting her gaze rake over him, she noticed the hard outline behind the zipper of his jeans. He obviously still wanted her, so why was he thinking about swimming?

"I'll meet you out back." Alex said, a small smile teasing his lips before he turned away.

Ashleigh grabbed her bag from the counter and went in search of the bathroom. The last time she'd been at his house, she hadn't seen much of it, other than the dining room and the kitchen. Now, with the chance to explore for a moment, she was curious as to how Alex lived.

As it turned out, the guest bathroom was off the living room, down the same hall that led to what appeared to be the master bedroom. Feeling a little bold, Ashleigh glanced into his room, taking in the warmth that greeted her.

Just like the rest of the house, the bedroom was rich with dark colors and wood accents. The bed was made, which wasn't surprising for a man who always needed to be in control, and there was no clutter. The heavy wooden furniture fit nicely in the oversized room, and all of it tied together to fit the man perfectly.

For a brief moment, she could imagine herself sprawled out on his bed, his gloriously naked body above her, as he drove his cock relentlessly into her, over and over until she couldn't contain the orgasm that would skyrocket her into another world.

Jerking from her reverie, Ashleigh glanced around nervously, praying Alex wasn't standing beside her, watching as she fantasized about what it would be like to... well, what it would be like.

Sneaking back the way she came, Ashleigh slipped into the bathroom to change. She was a little nervous about donning a bathing suit in front of Alex, especially after what had happened a few minutes before. Nervous, yet excited.

Stripping off her clothes in record time, she pulled on the hot pink bikini and looked at her reflection in the full length mirror on the door. Well, the good news was that her skin wasn't as bright as the bathing suit. The bad news was that her skin was flush, and she was pretty sure she was glowing.

She felt like a different woman than the one who woke up that morning. Her body was alive with all sorts of feelings, sexual tension coursing through her veins. Could this be it? Could today be the day when she finally succumbed to the overwhelming urges that had been building in her for years? If her body had anything to say about it, she would.

Glancing in the mirror, Ashleigh smoothed her hair down and smiled. "Stop smiling, you goof." She told the reflection staring back at her.

Despite what had happened in the garage and the emboldened way she felt, something seemed off about Alex. She knew he couldn't be nervous. The man had probably been with a thousand women... and didn't that thought make her sick to her stomach.

With the smile successfully wiped away, Ashleigh pulled her clothes back on over her swimsuit before wandering through the house and into the backyard. From her spot on the patio, she had a perfect view of the perfect man. And she only thought seeing him in gym shorts and a t-shirt had been riveting. That's only because she hadn't seen him without a shirt.

Alex was standing by the pool, wearing a pair of swim shorts that were longer than the running shorts he had worn, but the absence of a shirt made her mouth water. With his back to her, Ashleigh outlined every hard angle and toned muscle with her eyes. Across his back, from shoulder blade to shoulder blade, from his neck down to just above his waist was a tattoo of what looked like a tiger's face, the eyes a brilliant teal blue.

As if the guy could get any sexier. Holy crap!

His shoulders and arms were corded with well used muscles while his back was brawny and ripped. A narrow waist and trim hips caught her eye right before she stopped and ogled his extremely fantastic behind. The man was masculinity in its finest form.

"You going to stare all day, or are you going to join me?" He called out as he stepped into the pool, never looking back at her.

Oh good grief. She'd been busted, and now her face was hot with embarrassment. Sucking in a huge gulp of oxygen, Ashleigh steeled her spine and committed herself to whatever happened next.

Chapter Eleven
*** ~~ *** ~~ *** ~~ ***

From the moment the door clicked, signaling Ashleigh had joined him, Alex had felt her eyes on him. After what transpired between them in the garage and the heat the woman inspired in him, Alex knew he was going to go up in flames. Which was another good reason for getting in the pool. At least there he'd be able to cool off, even if the water was warm.

The sound of Ashleigh's bare feet on the concrete sounded behind him, coming closer, and he had to force himself not to turn and look at her. Seeing the woman in a bathing suit was probably going to blow his mind.

"Um, Alex..." Ashleigh called out to him, and he knew he had no choice but to turn around.

Looking up at her, all but gloriously naked in that tiny hot pink bikini, he had to close his mouth or risk drooling down his chin. Not a good look for him, that's for sure.

"Are you sure about this?" She asked when he finally made eye contact.

Was he sure? Hell no, he wasn't sure, but it was inevitable. At this point at least. Going back up two steps, he held out his hand for her until she moved closer. Lacing his fingers with hers, he hoped he could withdraw some of her strength because he was suddenly feeling a bit woozy.

Once in the water, he released her hand, but remained close, crouching low, leaning his back against one of the side walls with his hands holding the edge above his head.

"So, when did you start writing erotic romance?" He asked.

Ashleigh leaned down into the water, letting it come up to her neck before she turned back toward him. "It's been about five years now, I guess."

Alex wondered if something specific had made her want to venture into that genre, or if it was something she just wanted to do all along. Asking her those questions was awkward though. Since his secret was out, or rather hers was, Alex didn't quite know how to broach the subject.

"Have you read my books?" She asked, her gaze fixed on his face.

Well, that was one way to do it.

"Yes." He admitted truthfully. Some of them he'd read more than once, and that was saying something because he wasn't much for reading.

"All of them?" She wasn't closing the gap between them, but she wasn't going farther away either, so Alex considered that a good sign.

As long as he remained holding on to the edge of the pool, keeping his ass as far away from her as possible, she'd be safe. At least that's what he told himself.

"Except for the last one that came out. I haven't had a chance to go out and get it yet." But he planned to.

"So what'd you think?"

Wow, now that was a difficult question if he'd ever head one. What did he think? Did he tell her that he couldn't get the image of her in some of those kinky positions out of his head? Or maybe he told her how he wanted to see her tied to his bed while he had his wicked way with her. Or possibly how he wanted to see her in the playroom at the club, naked, and on her knees in front of him while others watched.

The last one might not really be true, but some of her vivid descriptions had had him imagining exactly that scenario. Hot or not, Alex had never been into voyeurism.

Regardless, he couldn't tell her any of those things, no matter how true they were because although she wrote about stuff like that, he was pretty sure she only considered them fantasies.

"They're interesting." He admitted, his body warming by several degrees as she made her way over to him.

"Are you nervous, Alex?" Ashleigh asked. "Because I'm thinking if anyone should be nervous, it should be me."

He laughed. That should be the case, yes. And no, he wasn't nervous, he was just hell bent on keeping his hands off of her so he didn't scare the daylights out of her. "Why should you be nervous?"

"I don't know." She said, her demeanor changing immediately to the Ashleigh he knew well. She turned away from him, moving farther into the pool and farther away from him.

He knew how it looked from the outside, but the last thing he was trying to do was push her away. In fact, he wanted her closer. Much closer. Like close enough for him to bury his cock inside of her while she rode him right there in the water. Instead, she must've thought he was trying to keep his distance for other reasons.

He had more control than this, but for the life of him, he couldn't conjure up an ounce.

"Come here." His mouth said before his brain caught up to it.

Ashleigh didn't turn though. Instead, she kept walking until she was wading into the deeper end of the pool and over to one of the stone ledges that acted as a seat. Ok, so he would obviously have to go to her.

Releasing his death grip on the pool's edge, he stood to his full height, the water coming up to his hips before he closed the distance between them. Since the pool wasn't very deep, Alex walked right up to where she was sitting. Easing her legs open, he maneuvered between them, placing his hands on her silky thighs.

"Look at me, Ashleigh." He told her when she was doing her best to avoid him. Lifting her chin, he forced her to look him in the eye.

"I've read your books, but not until I knew you had written them. They're fucking hot if you want to know the truth." He paused. "Too fucking hot."

"That's kinda the point." She smiled, but it didn't quite reach her eyes.

"Honey, I won't lie to you. I enjoyed them immensely. Is that what you want to hear?"

"Maybe." There was a glimmer in her eye. He got the impression this was turning her on.

With the hand that was still on her thigh, he reached for her hand, pulling it closer to him until he placed it directly on the hard proof. "See what you do to me? You make me hard, Ashleigh. When I read your books, it only made me want to do those wicked things to you." And then some, but he wasn't going to tell her that just yet. "But it isn't what you write that makes me so fucking hard. You do that. Not Ashton Leigh. You. Ashleigh."

When her palm pressed against his erection, Alex groaned. "Baby." It was the only warning he could get out.

"Show me, Alex." The seductive temptress said, her little pink tongue darting out to lick her bottom lip before she caught it between her teeth.

"Show you what?" He was riding a mighty fine edge right now, and what she said next would likely send him over.

"Show me what happens when you lose control."

Oh, fuck! There was absolutely no holding back, it wouldn't have mattered if he was a fucking superhero, he could not keep his hands off of her. Alex pulled her into his arms, close enough she had to wrap her legs around his waist. And that's when he lost every remaining ounce of control he possessed.

~~*~~

Yes!

This was the man she wanted.

The man who hungered for her, not the one who sat back on the sidelines trying to restrain himself.

Ashleigh had always been attracted to Alex. Always. For as long as she could remember. But it was his fierce determination and his dominating personality that drew her to him. The man kissing her senseless, his large hand pressed against her back, holding her to him, was the one she ached for in the dark of night.

Her body was on fire, and no amount of water was going to douse the flame that he had lit inside of her. Ashleigh could feel his erection, solid and firm between her legs, and she wanted to feel him inside of her. She wanted the hard length of him filling her, wanted him to be lost in the same tumultuous feelings she was.

The need was so fierce, so hot, she didn't know if her body could contain it all before she broke apart.

"I need to taste you." Alex said when he broke the kiss.

She was game.

"I'm afraid I can't be gentle." His words sounded as though they were torn from somewhere deep inside him.

"I don't want gentle. I won't break." She told him, once again pulling his mouth down on hers.

As he used his tongue to expertly rob her of all common sense, Ashleigh reached behind her and released the string that tied her bikini top behind her neck. The small pink fabric easily dropped, freeing her breasts to the cool air and Alex's penetrating gaze.

"Lean back." He instructed, pulling his mouth from hers.

Ashleigh did as she was told, leaning back with nothing behind her except water, gripping his hips with her thighs and his forearms with her hands to keep her from going under. She was floating, literally, but emotionally she was soaring.

This conflagration that had ignited in her blood was foreign, yet addictive, and she couldn't seem to get enough. She wanted Alex to touch her, to ground her in the moment, but he seemed content to just look at her and that penetrating gaze of his was unsettling.

The air caressed her breasts, sending cool chills over her skin. But when Alex latched onto a nipple, heating it with his mouth, her body began to tremble from the inside out.

"I've waited ten fucking years for this, Ashleigh." Alex's gruff tone sent shards of pleasure ripping through her as he plumped her breasts with his hands as he licked the pebbled tips.

"Alex. Please. It's not enough." And it wasn't nearly enough. She'd never been this worked up; her body had never throbbed in various places at the same time.

"What do you want me to do to you, Ashleigh?"

Was that a trick question? She wanted him to do *everything* to her. Over and over again until she didn't know her own name.

But she wanted to touch him too. She wanted to taste him. That's something she didn't have any experience with. She almost did, but Alex had turned her away that night.

Forcing the depressing thoughts away before they took hold, Ashleigh pulled herself up into his arms once again. Lifting her right breast, she held it closer to his mouth.

"Lick me." She ordered him, feeling oddly empowered and more sexually aggressive than she ever imagined. She wanted him to lose control, and in order to do that, she had to push her own limits.

When his tongue snaked out and swirled around her puckered nipple, Ashleigh watched in awe. There was something to be said about watching because it definitely stimulated certain areas of the brain. The same areas that controlled her orgasm if she had to guess since she felt the tingling start to intensify.

"Suck me." And boy did he. "Alex!" She screamed his name; the pain ricocheted from her nipple to her clit and back again, setting off mini detonations along the way.

She wasn't ready to come yet. Not until she got to play with him some more. And not until he was inside her.

Gripping his head in her hands, she held him to her breast before pulling him away easily. "I want to taste you. I want to feel you in my mouth."

"God, woman." Alex was breathing hard, his chest heaving. "You're going to be the death of me."

Yeah, well... if that was the case, they were going to go together because her circuits were overloaded and she wasn't so sure her body knew what to do with the intense pleasure.

Reaching down between them, Ashleigh found what she was looking for. Gently stroking him through his shorts, she wanted to know what he felt like against her bare palm. Feeling bolder than she expected, she slipped her hand into the waistband of his shorts, finding the satiny hard length of him and stroking slowly.

"Let me taste you." She said as their eyes met. "Please."

Alex groaned as she stroked, but he carried her to the steps that would lead out of the pool. The brisk air tickled her skin, goose bumps breaking out up and down her arms. Thankfully he carried her into the much warmer house before heading to his bedroom – no make that bathroom – where he deposited her into the standup shower.

"Take off your bathing suit." Alex told her as he turned on the water, his eyes focused on every inch of her exposed skin.

Feeling modest for the first time since she got there, Ashleigh fumbled with the tie on her back before finally managing to release it. Her breasts were already uncovered, so that was the easy part. Lowering her wet bikini bottoms down her legs took more effort than it should have.

Once they were around her ankles, she kicked them free and stood before him, completely exposed in more ways than one.

Chapter Twelve
*** ~~ *** ~~ *** ~~ ***

Alex could only stare at her.

Standing in his shower, naked as water streamed down her sinful curves, Ashleigh was the most beautiful woman he'd ever seen. Her long, dark hair was slicked back from her face, her lashes were beaded with water, and those rosy pink nipples were puckered and begging him to taste her again.

When she said she wanted to taste him, he almost lost it. The most he had ever done was imagine what it would feel like to have Ashleigh's lips wrapped around his cock, but to hear her beg to do just that was more than he could take at the time.

Where he had gotten the idea that she might be timid and not open to the same things he was when it came to sex was beyond him. But even though she could voice her desires, Alex got the impression she was new to this. How new, he had no idea and he damn sure didn't want to think about her being with another man.

"I think I'm a little overdressed." He told her when the water warmed, and he turned the spray toward her.

"I think so, too."

Ashleigh didn't try to cover herself from his wandering gaze, but he got the impression she wanted to.

"Take off my shorts." He might be pushing the limits with her at the moment, but she was testing his control. On purpose.

If she wanted to let loose the beast within him, Alex was going to make sure she knew what she was getting herself into. He could do gentle and tender when he wanted to but, not with this sort of hunger raging just beneath the surface.

Her eyes darted from his, down to the erection tenting his shorts and back up before she moved closer. Once their bodies were almost touching, Ashleigh put her hands on his hips and began to push his shorts down, his erection straining to be free.

Without hesitation, which alone was the most erotic thing he'd ever witnessed, Ashleigh lowered his shorts down until they fell to the floor. Once they were a puddle on the tile, Ashleigh used her pink tipped toes to pull the fabric closer to her before going to her knees.

"Fuck." Alex groaned as he watched. Honestly, he hadn't expected anything like this from Ashleigh. Not the sweet, polite girl he'd had a hard on for for the better part of ten years now.

Backing to the wall so he could brace his legs, Alex watched as she touched him. It was like she was doing this for the very first time and the thought both thrilled and scared him.

Surely she wasn't...

No way. She was almost thirty years old.

When she circled her fingers around his shaft, slowly gliding her petal soft hand up and down, he found himself captivated by the scene. It was like he was standing outside of his body watching, but that couldn't be because it felt way too fucking good.

"Suck me." He repeated the words she'd said to him earlier.

Alex slid his hand into her hair, pulling her closer as steam rose up around them, filling the bathroom with warmth. She swiped her tongue over her lips before using it to caress the head of his swollen cock, making him jerk in her hand.

She glanced up at him and smiled before pulling him deep into her mouth.

"Fuck." The single word escaped when he sucked in his breath, his hands instinctively gripping her hair tighter.

She proceeded to lap at him, sucking lightly, scraping him gently with her teeth, and essentially attempting to blow his mind. And in that moment, he knew she'd never done that before, or if she had, the bastard hadn't shown her how much he enjoyed it because she seemed almost... scared. And if not scared, she was most definitely uncertain.

"Suck me, Ashleigh. Take my cock in your mouth and suck. Use your tongue, baby." He encouraged her, holding her head to him with one hand while gripping the base of his cock with the other and feeding it into her mouth.

"That's it, baby. Stroke me."

Taking her hand beneath his, he showed her how much pressure to apply as she stroked his shaft while bathing the head with her tongue. It was so fucking good, but he damn sure wasn't going to come yet. As tempting as it was to let go and watch her swallow every last drop, Alex wasn't done exploring her yet.

Pulling his cock free of her mouth and her hand, he helped her to her feet before pressing his lips down on hers. He probed her mouth with his tongue, devouring every inch he could taste. When he broke the kiss, he let the water pour over them for a second while he stared down at her.

"Did I do it wrong?" She asked, and her self-doubt had him gritting his teeth, disbelief and anger filling his mind.

He felt as though she had stabbed him in the heart. The insecurity he saw in her eyes nearly leveled him. "Baby, you've got the sweetest mouth. I'm just not ready to come yet."

A small smile tilted her lips before he kissed her lightly.

"Now it's my turn," he said as he turned her so she was positioned where he had been, her back to the wall. He lifted her leg and placed her foot on the ledge before lowering himself to his knees.

The dark curls that shielded her sex were trim and neat, and he took a moment to glide his fingers through them before separating the soft pink folds beneath. He had to focus on breathing because the only thing he wanted to do was to get lost in this woman.

~~*~~

Ashleigh needed something to hold on to because she was pretty sure her legs were not going to hold her up once he... "Alex!"

The sensation was overwhelming, shards of electricity bolted through her, exploding as it touched exposed nerve endings and leaving her light headed. His tongue slid through the sensitive tissue, barely touching her, but it was too much. Her orgasm ignited, a fierce eruption blasting through her and making her knees buckle.

There had been no time to prepare, no way to know that the raspy warmth of his tongue would send her plummeting over the edge upon impact.

"I've got you, baby." Alex said, holding her hips as he continued to kneel between her legs. Her muscles wouldn't work, her bones had turned to mush, and she was flooded with a devastating sensation of fulfillment. Something she'd never felt before.

When he had actually stood back up, she didn't know, but he was once again holding her against him, his fingers trailing down her spine as she fought for breath. He must think she was an idiot.

And then he was kissing her, pressing her against the cool tiles of the wall, his warm body flattened against hers, all of those sinfully sleek muscles rippling with tension beneath her fingertips. His kiss was gentle, sweet, yet she could taste the restrained hunger. When he reached behind her and shut off the water, she could only lean against the wall, hoping he didn't expect her to walk because she wasn't certain she'd be able to.

For a brief moment, he disappeared out of the shower, allowing her a second to suck in a breath, leaning her head against the wall and trying to pull herself together.

So that's what it meant to have a mind blowing orgasm. She almost laughed at the thought. Here she'd been writing about it for years, and the self-induced ones weren't even in the same galaxy as what Alex had just done to her.

He returned a moment later with a bath towel that he used to dry her completely. When he lingered a moment longer than was necessary between her legs, Ashleigh whimpered. There was still an ache in that general vicinity, and there was only one man capable of making it go away.

Thankfully Alex lifted her and carried her back to his bedroom because she wasn't going to be able to walk on her own for at least a little while. That one orgasm had drained her of all remaining energy. More so than any ten mile run she could have ever gone on.

"I need to taste you again, Ashleigh." Alex whispered in her ear as he came down on top of her.

She couldn't say a word because she couldn't muster up the strength, but she was pretty sure she wouldn't survive another orgasm of that magnitude. So when he started trailing liquid fire kisses down her chest, her belly, then between her legs, she let go and let herself feel.

Her skin was hypersensitive, making every touch, no matter how small, nearly unbearable. The way his rough palm caressed her hip, her thigh, before the tips of his fingers opened her to his hungry gaze. The air cooled her overheated skin, but he was quickly ratcheting up her body temperature by the heated look in his eyes.

She tilted her head on the pillow so she could see what he was doing and when his tongue delved into her slit, she almost came off the bed. He was being gentle, but other than her own hands, which felt entirely different than this, she'd never been touched there. Not like she could tell him that though.

The ache intensified, her clit beginning to throb with need once again, so she put her hands on his head and pushed him between her legs, lost to the power of the climax building inside of her.

~~*~~

Alex was having a hard time controlling himself. Feeling Ashleigh's body trembling beneath his touch was intense. He'd been with plenty of women in his lifetime, but he'd never noticed the sensual way their body responded to him. Until Ashleigh.

Alex didn't think he'd ever get enough of her.

After what just happened in the shower, which still had his mind reeling, Alex couldn't help but wonder again whether she'd ever been with a man or not. The way she reacted, he'd be inclined to say she had not, but he couldn't wrap his mind around it. That just didn't happen this day in age.

Easing between her legs, he used his thumbs to open her swollen lips so he could lap at the moisture he found there. She tasted like dark storms and deep promises, and he wanted to feast on her for hours, hell maybe even days. Giving in to what she wanted, he let her pull his head into her as he thrust his tongue inside her warm, wet heat before teasing her clit with his thumb.

Her moans were echoing in the room, a throaty, sexy sound that made his dick throb and his balls ache. He wanted to bury himself inside of her, to feel her grip him, hold him in her fiery depths until she shattered beneath him. Instead, he settled for flicking his tongue over her clit while inserting one finger into her warm, wet pussy.

"Alex."

The way she moaned his name set off something dark and possessive inside his soul. If he had anything to say about it, his name would be the only one to ever come out of her mouth again like that.

He wanted to dominate her. He wanted to pleasure her until her every thought was filled with him. He wanted to own her – heart and soul.

"Alex, please." Ashleigh begged. "I need to feel you."

That was all he needed before he removed his finger from her silky hot depths and came over her again. Staring down into her eyes, he brushed his thumb across her bottom lip. "I want you to taste yourself on my lips."

When their tongues met, he tasted her hunger, inhaled her passion and knew in that moment that what they did next was going to alter the course of his life forever. He had dreamed about this day, harbored a burning desire to take her in the most elemental of ways and now that the time had come, he prayed when it was over he'd be able to control himself.

Reaching into the nightstand, Alex pulled out a condom and ripped open the foil packet. With as much finesse as he could muster, he slid the latex over his throbbing cock before easing himself between her legs once more.

Using his knees, he pushed her legs wider before guiding the tip into her moist heat. When her fingernails dug into his back, he leaned in closer, holding his upper body off of her with his arms.

"Are you sure about this?" He needed her to be with him in this because if he was right, once he was inside of her, there would be no turning back.

"Yes." She whispered. "Alex, please. I need to feel you."

Alex pushed in deeper, her muscles gripping him painfully, so much so that he wondered whether her body would be able to take him.

"Relax, baby." Putting his mouth on hers, he lightly kissed the edge of her mouth, running his tongue over the seam of her lips before slowly gliding his tongue inside, at the same time he pushed deeper into her body.

"You're pussy is so fucking tight." He groaned the words as the pain gripped him. She was tight. Tighter than he thought possible and she wasn't relaxing as he'd told her. "Look at me, Ashleigh."

Those amber eyes locked with his and he saw so much raw emotion there that his heart skipped a beat.

"Let me love you." He hadn't expected to say the words, but they came out anyway. "Relax."

When she wrapped her arms around his neck and pulled him in for another earth shattering kiss, he thrust inside of her, and when she whimpered, he stilled instantly. Pulling back, he stared down at her and his heart damn near came right out of his chest.

Holy fucking hell...

Ashleigh must have seen the recognition in his eyes because she crushed her mouth to his and began thrusting her hips while trying to pull her in deeper. He was buried to the hilt inside of her, and if he wasn't careful, he was going to come just from the realization alone. She was a virgin. He was the only man who had ever been inside of her.

The thought shocked him. So much so that the beast he harbored tore free, yanking the last thread of control from his grasp and he lifted her hip, changing the angle and began thrusting hard and fast into her. Over and over, delirious with the pleasure of being inside of her, knowing he was the only man who had ever felt the exquisite bliss of her body.

"Come for me, Ashleigh." Alex told her when she dug her fingernails into his back, pulling him closer. "Come for me, baby."

Drenched in sweat, he continued to pound inside of her, knowing he wasn't going to last much longer because being sheathed in her body was like heaven on earth and the only thing that could have been better being if they'd been skin to skin. Since he couldn't change that, he just focused on where their bodies were joined as one.

"That's it, baby." He encouraged her when her pussy gripped him tighter, her muscles clamping down on him until he was gritting his teeth so that he didn't come too soon. "Come for me." He growled the words, insisting that she let go and give in to him.

Apparently that was all she needed because she screamed his name, her fingernails scoring his skin as her body shook beneath his and an animalistic growl escaped as his own release ripped through him.

Chapter Thirteen
*** ~ *** ~ *** ~ ***

It was hard to believe that a full week had gone by since the night she and Alex had done the deed. Well, that's what she referred to it as. He seemed to be thinking it was more than that. Oh, she did too, but she definitely wasn't going to let him know that.

Not after what had transpired between them.

There was no way Ashleigh could tell him how he had rocked her world, so much so that she was pretty sure it had tilted on its axis, and she was now walking upside down through each and every day. Since that night, Ashleigh had stayed at Alex's house once and him at hers once.

But that wasn't the part of this whole mind boggling ordeal that was throwing her for a loop. That was caused by Alex's insistence on being sweet and gentle with her. If he wasn't careful, she was going to hurt him. In a bad way.

To have made it to twenty eight without ever having been with a man, to experience the mind shattering orgasms that Alex had given her was hard enough to grasp on its own. But for him to want to constantly go back to bed – yes, the man insisted on having sex in the bed – she knew she wasn't going to be able to take much more.

He said he had read her books, so he knew the thoughts that went through her mind. Did he think she just came up with those ideas because someone else might find them sexy and hot? Hell no. They were the fantasies that she dislodged from that dark side of her brain. The side that wanted passion and ecstasy – outside of the bedroom would be nice.

More than once, she'd figured this was all her fault. First of all, she hadn't told him that she was a virgin, and when she'd seen the recognition on his face, she'd nearly cried. He didn't cringe, he didn't panic... no, something very possessive had flashed in his bright green eyes, and it had shot an arrow straight through her heart.

On top of that, Ashleigh had been hiding who she was as an author, worried it would make people think of her differently. She was beginning to think that was the case with Alex, only he was thinking that she didn't want any of those things she wrote about. He couldn't have been more wrong.

She should've known better. After that one night at the guest house, Ashleigh should have seen the signs then. He was treating her like she would break if he handled her too roughly. She might break some other things if he didn't get that out of his head.

A decade ago, Ashleigh had seen the prelude to what they shared the other night in his bed, but Alex had apparently been scared that long ago night. She remembered the argument he'd had with her, the way he had cut her to the bone with his words. Words she was pretty sure he didn't remember.

"Ashleigh, wait." Alex's deep voice reverberated through the room as he pulled away from her.

He was on top of her on the couch, her shirt was unbuttoned, her bra unhooked, and he had been doing wondrous things to her nipples with his skilled tongue. And she had innocently weaved her hand between them, wanting to touch him, wanting to make him crazy with need, the same way she was. And since he was on top of her, she wasn't so sure why he was telling her to wait. He had all the power.

"What's wrong?" She asked, staring up into the glowing emeralds in his eyes.

"How can you ask me that? Fuck." He pushed himself up, a little unsteady, but he finally made it to his feet.

"Did I do something wrong?" She asked, fumbling to get her bra hooked and holding her shirt together, trying to cover herself.

"No. And that's the problem. You're doing everything right, but we can't do this. We, Ashleigh. You and me."

"Why not?" For the life of her, she didn't understand, but she knew from the glare he was pinning her with that he was about to tell her.

"Because you're too damn young for me. Too sweet. Too innocent. You can't handle a man like me, Ash." With that, he stormed across the room.

"And what makes you think that?" Fury ripped through her gut. What the hell made him think she couldn't handle him? From the looks of it, she was doing a damn good job so far.

"I know you, Ash. You need someone to love you. Someone to make love to you. I'm not that man."

"And what do you need?" She asked, figuring since he thought he'd pegged her it was only fair she understand where he was going with this.

He surprised her when he walked back toward her, roughly pulling her against him. The force of his movements had her stumbling into him.

"Baby, I need a woman who will go to her knees and let me bury my dick down her throat without needing meaningless words."

A sharp bolt of lust burst from her core, radiating downward. Something about the graphic image he put in her head made her want to do just that. But apparently, according to Alex, she wasn't that type of girl.

Not that she even knew what type of girl she was when it came to sex. She'd never been with a man before. Not like this.

"You're not ready for that. And I'm not ready for you, Ash. No matter how bad I want to fuck you, it'd never be enough."

Ashleigh pulled away from him then, shocked and hurt by his statement. She prayed it was the booze talking, but something told her that the truth was coming out. She wanted him to go, but he was too drunk to drive, so she did the only thing she knew to do.

"I'm taking you home. My brother can bring your truck to you tomorrow."

"No." He insisted, but stumbled as he tried to make it to the door.

Ashleigh grabbed her keys from the table; pocketing his while she was at it so he couldn't get to them, before following behind him. It took a little manipulation, but she finally got him into the passenger seat of her car and gratefully he closed his eyes and passed out.

The memory still pissed her off and made her want to hit him. Apparently ten years didn't change his mind because Alex was still treating her like fragile porcelain.

She needed to come up with a plan to change his perspective, to educate him a little more. She didn't want to be the dominate one in the relationship, she wanted to be dominated. She wanted to relinquish control to this man.

The stories she wrote, and the stories that Sam and Sierra had told her were what she wanted. She only wondered how hard she would have to work to penetrate his thick skull.

~~*~~

"Alex?" The timid voice on the other end of the phone had Alex stopping abruptly. He had just walked out of Xavier's office and was heading to his car, hoping he could stop by Ashleigh's for a little while when his phone rang.

Stopping midstride, he asked, "Jessie? What's the matter?" Alex wasn't sure he wanted to know the answer to that question.

"Can you come over? I think he's –" The words were cut off and a gruff voice erupted in the background seconds before the call ended.

Alex took off at a run, dialing the number back and praying Jessie would answer the phone. When she didn't, he focused on getting into his truck and getting out of the damn parking garage.

By the time he was on the highway, at least another fifteen minutes before he could make it to her house, Alex had a pretty good idea what the hell was going on. He tried dialing her phone again. This time someone answered, but it wasn't Jessie.

"What the fuck do you want?" The angry words were slurred, but Alex heard them loud and clear.

"Where's Jessie?" He asked, putting his foot to the floor.

"What the fuck do you care, McDermott?"

Fuck. The irrational voice was all too familiar, and Alex still couldn't understand what the hell was wrong with Jessie that she would let the bastard keep coming back. "Jeff," Alex tried for calm, "where is Jessie?"

"Hell if I know. The crazy bitch took off."

Alex gunned the engine, gritting his teeth to keep from swearing. It would only piss Jeff off more and not being able to come between him and Jessie at the moment, Alex was at a loss.

"Did she leave?"

"Fuck if I know. Why don't you come over and try to save the day like you always do, McDermott? You know that bitch just eats it up, you always coming to her rescue and all." Jeff rambled.

Alex wanted to hang up, but at least with Jeff on the phone, he knew where the man was at. "Is she hurt?" He had to ask the question, although it would likely set Jeff off.

"What the fuck do you care?" Jeff repeated himself, obviously good and drunk which was when he usually went on the rampage and found himself over at Jessie's despite the restraining order.

"Did you hurt her, Jeff?" Alex annunciated slowly, hoping the man would answer. Taking a hard left, Alex pulled into Jessie's neighborhood.

Jeff still wasn't answering him, but now that he could see Jessie's house from his truck, he didn't have to keep him on the line. Without saying a word, he disconnected the call before pulling into the driveway and throwing the truck in Park.

Jessie's car was there, but he didn't see her outside, so he went to the door, knowing he'd better gear up for a fight because if the past was any indication, it wasn't going to be pretty.

"Jessie!" Alex called out to her when he walked in the open front door. He glanced over at Jeff but didn't speak to the man. He was sitting on the couch, acting like he owned the place.

That definitely wasn't the case because Alex knew who owned the fucking house. He did.

"Where is she?" Alex stopped short, staring at the skinny bastard lounging on the couch. What the hell Jessie ever saw in the man, Alex would never know.

"Fuck, dude. Are you stupid? I told you on the phone I don't know where she's at."

Alex wandered through the small two bedroom house, glancing in both bedrooms, the bathroom, but Jessie wasn't there. He didn't figure she was, but he had to try. Going through the kitchen, he walked out onto the back steps, glancing at the separate garage.

"Jessie." He called out to the only other place for her to have possibly gone.

When he opened the door, he found her lying on the floor, curled into a ball, crying.

"Damn it, Jessie." Alex said without heat as he went to her and cradled her in his arms. "What the hell did he do to you?"

She was bruised pretty badly, but some of them were already fading, so Alex knew they weren't all from today. But her lip was split and bleeding, and there was a gash above her right eye. A red haze clouded his vision, long since forgotten memories rising up from the ashes, and for a fraction of a second, he considered going inside and kicking the living shit out of Jeff.

Instead, he inhaled slowly, the scent of gasoline and mildew filling his lungs. He could think of so many other places he'd rather be.

"Jessie, I need to get you up." He needed to check for any other wounds, see if she needed to go to the hospital.

When he reached for her hand, he found her wrist contorted at an odd angle, and she was holding it close to her body. Son of a bitch. The bastard broke her fucking arm.

Pulling out his cell phone, Alex did the only thing he knew to do. He called 911 and gave them the address. He informed them to bring the police because Jeff was violating the restraining order against him. When Jessie started to grumble something, he ignored her.

Half an hour later, the ambulance was taking Jessie to Baylor of Dallas and Alex was talking to the officer on the scene. Jeff's drunken ass had been hauled away after a little bit of a scuffle, which would hopefully keep him in protective custody for a little while.

As soon as Alex pulled off the street, heading to the hospital to take care of the paperwork for Jessie, he dialed Dylan's phone number.

"Hey." Dylan greeted. "Where are you?"

"Sorry, man. I was handling a personal matter when you called earlier. What's up?"

"I wanted to see if you'd be up to meeting Jake tomorrow morning in the office."

Alex had to think about who Jake was, but then he remembered Dylan was in the process of hiring a couple of sales people for the home security side of the business. "I'll be in early, but then I have to head out around noon. Cole and I have to go talk to a guy in Austin. What time will he be there?"

"I'll have him come in around eight if that works for you." Dylan told him.

"Sounds good. See you at eight."

"Hey, Alex. Is everything alright?" Dylan asked, obviously picking up on Alex's frustration.

"It will be." He said vaguely. "Look, I gotta go. I'll see you in the morning."

With that, Alex tossed the phone in the passenger seat and focused on getting to the hospital. This was fast becoming the worst part of his week.

Chapter Fourteen
*** ~~ *** ~~ *** ~~ ***

Ashleigh was sitting in a booth, in the far back corner of the small diner, across from Sam. She had suggested a different place than their normal steakhouse lunch, hoping a change of scenery might do her some good.

"Where's Sierra?" Sam asked.

"I don't know." Ashleigh said looking up from her menu. "I thought you would know."

Confusion backlit Sam's celadon green eyes before she glanced at the door. "I talked to her this morning. She said she wasn't feeling well, but that she would try to meet us. I guess when I didn't hear from her, I thought that meant she'd be here."

"Did she say what was wrong?" Ashleigh hadn't talked to Sierra in a week or so. The woman was busy with her interior design business, and between that and juggling two men, apparently she didn't have much free time to talk. Aside from their weekly lunch dates.

"No, she didn't. But, you know, she hasn't been feeling well for a while now."

"Do you think...?" Ashleigh let the question die off. She didn't want to stir up gossip, especially where her friend was concerned.

"Do I think what? Spill it, Ash."

Leaning over so only Sam could hear, Ashleigh glanced at the door and then back at Sam. "Do you think she's pregnant?"

"Oh my God!" Sam exclaimed sitting upright. "I hadn't even thought about that." A mischievous smirk split Sam's pretty face and made her eyes dance with happiness. Who would've thought?

"I wondered about it the last time we met. She's been eating a lot more lately, not that the woman obviously has to worry about that, but it's not like her. And she's talked about not feeling well in the mornings."

"Holy crap. That makes perfect sense."

"I wouldn't say anything to anyone just yet though. We'll have to talk to her first."

"Of course." Sam stated, glancing down at her menu and acting like nothing had happened. How did the woman do that?

Ashleigh stared at the words on the laminated sheet of paper in front of her and tried desperately to keep her mind on the menu. Instead, she wanted to ask Sam a question while the two of them were alone. Not that she wouldn't have asked the same question if Sierra had been there, but she was sort of leery of sharing too much personal information with too many people.

When the waitress stopped by and took their order, refilling their water glasses before she left, Ashleigh conjured up the nerve.

"What's it like being with Logan?" And wow, that did *not* come out the right way.

Sam looked at her with a cocked eyebrow as if trying to understand what she was getting at.

"Good grief. Not like that." Ashleigh smiled. "If I'd been using my eloquent gene, I would've asked what it's like to be in a relationship with a dominating man."

Sam laughed. "I was beginning to wonder about you there for a minute. I mean last week you were asking about threesomes and this week about Logan."

Ashleigh blushed. Last week she *had been* asking about threesomes.

Since her friends were obviously having way more sex than she was, she was trying to get a better understanding of what goes on in their unique relationships.

Sierra was in a permanent relationship with two men, and they all three shared one another while Sam was married to Logan and they had recently invited Tag Murphy as a third in their relationship. The ménage thing must have something going for it because her friends seemed incredibly happy. All the time.

"When you say dominating, I'm assuming you're talking about in the bedroom."

"Does it have to be in the bedroom?" Ashleigh said with a sigh of disgust.

"Um..."

"Sorry. I didn't mean it like that. It's just that Alex –" Realizing what she was about to reveal, Ashleigh closed her mouth tight.

"Holy shit." Sam squealed. "You did it, didn't you?"

Ashleigh knew her face was as red as the checkered squares in the ugly tablecloth on every table in the restaurant, but she couldn't stop herself.

"Tell me." Sam insisted, taking a sip of her water.

"Yes." Ok, so there it was. She'd admitted to her friend that she'd done the deed. Now she just needed to get some perspective on how to fix it.

"And?"

"And what?" Ashleigh asked, confused.

"How was it?"

"Off the charts amazing." That was the honest to God truth. Every time was better than the last, their bodies were so in tune with one another, Ashleigh was convinced they'd each been created with the other in mind.

It wasn't that the sex was lacking, it was the spontaneity. Ashleigh would never get enough of Alex, but she wondered if they'd eventually get bored with one another.

"So why do I get the impression there's a *but* in there somewhere?"

"It's just that..." Ashleigh didn't know how to say it.

"What? Is it boring? Is Alex bad in bed?"

It was her turn to laugh. "Hell no. He's amazing. It's the bed part that I've got a problem with."

"Is there something wrong with his bed?"

"No. Not necessarily." There wasn't anything wrong with the bed per se; it was the fact that it was the only place he seemed to want to be when they had sex.

"Ok, spit it out." Sam said, sitting back in her chair and looking far too serious for the conversation they were having.

"I think he's worried he's going to break me when we have sex. At first, before the first time, he was the same Alex I've always dreamed about. Commanding, dominating, sexy as hell. And then bam! We have sex for the first time, and he's treating me like I'm blown glass and one wrong move and I'll break into a million pieces."

"So that's why you wanted to know what it's like with Logan." Sam put two and two together. "From the impressions I've always gotten from Alex, he's pretty dominating himself. Is that not the case?"

"That's what I thought too. That was part of my original attraction to him. I'm beginning to think I have some misconceptions on what it means to be controlled."

"I've read your books; you're certainly right on the money." Sam smiled but then looked serious again. "Did you tell him you were a virgin before you slept with him?"

"Um, no. But I don't think he had any problems figuring that out."

"Ash, I think it's safe to say he's just scared. He's the only man you've ever been with. And my guess, since he's a member of the club, he's got some pretty kinky fantasies. He's just worried that you won't be able to handle it."

Ashleigh was immediately taken back to ten years earlier when Alex had all but told her that exact same thing. "How do I make him realize I won't break? I mean shit, he's read my books. He knows what I think about."

Sam grinned that sly grin of hers. "I think it's time you showed him."

It did not take long for Ashleigh to come up with a plan. That was one of her specialties, remember? Well, in order to execute the plan, she had to get Alex to show up at her house. Since she was trying to make it a surprise, she left him a voicemail, as cryptic as possible but getting to the point.

He needed to be at her house. As soon as possible.

She'd been sitting on the back deck enjoying the fairly warm February evening, again working on her most recent novel when she heard his truck pull down the driveway. When the butterflies erupted in her belly, she forced herself to remain sitting where she was though that was nearly impossible, and the trembling in her legs proved it.

The front door was unlocked, so hopefully he would either come through the house, or walk around the way he did before. She wasn't sure what she would do if he didn't think she was home and decided to leave.

Too late to worry about that now.

Ashleigh pulled up the page she had worked on earlier, leaving it open on her laptop screen. Thankfully it was dark outside, but again, that was in the plans as well. The veil of night was needed for what she had in mind. After all, she was open to adventure, not public indecency.

With her nerves doing the jitterbug, she was now barely sitting on the edge of her chair. Where was he?

Ashleigh hadn't seen him for the last couple of days – he was busy, she was busy... same ol', same ol'. However, they had made a point to talk to one another several times a day. Which was why Ashleigh knew something was off with him, but he wasn't revealing his secrets and she wasn't asking.

The sound of the back door caught her attention, and she turned the computer so it was facing her perfectly and she stared at it as though lost in thought.

When he approached, she was aware of his intoxicating scent first, and she fought the urge to squirm. Not long after she was assaulted by the delicious smell of him, his big, warm hands were on her shoulders, gently kneading the muscles there.

"Mmmm..." There was no way to hold back her groans of pleasure when he touched her. It was an instinctive reaction.

"I got your message." He said, leaning down to place a kiss on her cheek and Ashleigh stilled.

He would be able to see the screen, which was the intention. Now she just prayed that he read the words.

"What're you working on?" He asked, nuzzling her neck still, and Ashleigh lifted her hand to hold his face close to hers because it felt too damn good. The slight bristle of his five o'clock shadow, the warmth of his breath, and that delicious cologne he favored were a heady combination.

"Just writing." She forced the words out, although she was now leaning her head to the side, giving him better access to her neck.

When the nuzzling stopped, Ashleigh held her breath, waiting for him to say more. But he didn't say anything, and the only give away was the way his hands tightened slightly on her shoulders. She smiled. It was the reaction she hoped for.

Score.

Alex was reading.

When he approached, she was not expecting him, but in the same instance, his presence made her body come to life. What was he doing there, she wondered. At that moment, it didn't matter why, as long as he was willing to continue touching her like that.

Slipping his hands inside her loose fitting shirt, he cupped her breasts, still standing behind her, his arms hanging over her shoulders. She couldn't see him, but for some reason that only heightened the sensation because she could feel his warmth, smell his unique scent, which overwhelmed her senses as it was.

Ashleigh didn't know how much Alex had read, but she knew he'd at least made it that far. His hands slipped just inside her shirt – and yes, it was loose, and the top buttons were open – palms down on her chest, easing beneath the lace of her bra. It was erotic and stimulating, and felt so damn good that Ashleigh couldn't help but lean back into the chair, hoping he'd take the hint.

"Unbutton your shirt," Alex ordered.

Ashleigh didn't hesitate because she feared if she did, he'd take it as an excuse to tone it down and this was exactly what she was looking for. It had all of the ingredients for a hot, steamy encounter, and though she might have had to manipulate him to get him here, it was happening, and that was all that mattered.

With a flick of her fingers, Ashleigh had the remaining few buttons on her shirt undone, the fabric hanging open. The computer monitor shining brightly allowed her to see what he was doing. The only problem – that would also allow any curious neighbors the ability to see as well. She briefly considered closing the laptop, but then figured it would give Alex another reason to take this little episode in the house and she refused to let that happen.

"Unhook your bra." Alex's dark, sultry voice washed over her, caressing her skin and making her nipples pucker. She flipped the clasp between her breasts and allowed the cups to separate, freeing her breasts to the cool night air.

"So pretty," Alex whispered, his breath closer to her ear. "What happens next, Ashleigh?"

Oh God! He should know what happens next. It was right there on the screen. Wasn't he going to read it? Her head fell back against his chest when he pinched her nipples between his thumbs and forefingers, rolling them gently.

"Read it to me." Alex continued to fondle her breasts, but that was as far as he was going and according to what she had written, there was so much more they were supposed to do to one another, right there on the deck.

His fingers tweaked her nipple a little harder, making her cry out.

"Now." He said gruffly. "Tell me what they do next, baby."

He was pushing her.

Here she had thought this would be simple, write a short erotic scene, let him read it, let their passion take over, igniting a fire in the dark, and all would be right again. Instead, Alex was going to push her, see how far she would go.

Fine. She could do this.

Glancing down at the screen, she picked up where she assumed he'd left off earlier, reading aloud.

Delving his fingers into her bra, he caressed her skin, lightly teasing her nipple... Ok, they were apparently past that part. Ashleigh skimmed down a paragraph.

As she removed her shirt, allowing the cotton to fall to the chair beneath her, the cool night air caressed her skin, but the contrasting heat from his hands made her moan.

"Take it off." He said gruffly, continuing to squeeze her breasts, a little harder than before, making her moan and fight to get her shirt and bra off.

"Read it to me, Ashleigh," Alex leaned down, brushing his jaw against hers, "but, I expect you to do everything you have written on that page." He paused, nipping her neck with his teeth, "Unless it's a part for me."

Nodding her head, she was unable to find her voice. Here she was, sitting topless on her back porch, the only light was that from her computer screen, but it lit up the area enough that Ashleigh could see everything Alex was doing. But it wouldn't have mattered if she could see or not, the feel of his hands on her skin was torturous. Her nipples were sensitive, her breasts swollen, but she needed more.

It was a good thing she wrote it so she'd get as much pleasure from it as he would. Glancing back down at the screen, she continued to read:

When he leaned over her from behind, sucking one breast into his mouth, she gripped his head, holding him to her as her body writhed with restrained ecstasy.

Alex leaned over, forcing Ashleigh to tilt to the side as his chest came over the chair and his wicked hot mouth latched onto her right breast, his tongue lashing her nipple while he sucked the sensitive mound into the hot furnace of his mouth.

"Alex!" It was too good; she didn't want him to stop. Ever.

He had to pull away so she could read the screen. It didn't matter that she had written it just that morning, her senses were overloaded, which meant her brain wasn't functioning normally.

As though sensing her need, he walked around to the front of her chair, before divesting her of her leggings, the only remaining clothing she had on.

Ashleigh's nerves rioted and for a brief moment, she worried she was having second thoughts.

Alex didn't give her time to think about it though before he was pulling the spandex leggings down her hips while she lifted her bottom slightly to make it easier. When he stopped and stared up at her, kneeling at her feet, she held her breath for a moment. She couldn't let him see that she was questioning her sanity for the first time since she'd let her desires get the best of her. It was his cocked eyebrow that spurred her on because she was absolutely not going to be the one to ruin this moment. Picking up where she left off:

Once her clothes were an obstacle he no longer had to overcome, she held her breath, waiting to see what he would do next. She wanted to tell him to taste her – Ashleigh's face flamed as she swallowed hard, but continued reading, never looking up at Alex's face – *to tease her clit with his tongue, suck the hardened bundle of nerves into his sexy mouth while he speared her pussy with his fingers.*

Still unable to look at him, Ashleigh flinched when his big palm flattened against her belly, forcing her back into the chair. She held her breath, letting the warmth of his hand infuse not only her body, but her soul as she sought the comfort of the man there with her.

Yes, this had been her idea. Yes, Ashleigh was anxious for Alex to live out her greatest fantasies with her, but it hadn't been until him that she felt safe enough to have even dreamed of putting herself in this situation.

"So pretty." Alex whispered, "I love to taste your sweet pussy, thrust my tongue into your hot, wet heat. I live for it." Alex murmured against her mound, his warm breath sending chills racing down her spine.

Spreading her legs farther apart, wanting him closer to the heart of her, Ashleigh hung her knees over the arms of the chair, opening herself to him completely. Watching, her eyes were transfixed between her thighs where he was using his index finger to trail through her juices, grazing back and forth through her slit, teasing her clit before going back down. Alex didn't thrust his finger inside of her like she wanted, he slowly pushed in, bending the digit as he seemed to be searching for something inside of her.

"Oh God!" Ashleigh bucked her hips as her entire body spasmed. "Oh! Don't stop!"

Her brain wasn't functioning, but her nerve endings were, and the spot he touched was overly sensitive, and remarkably responsive. At first she had no idea what he was doing, but then it dawned on her... G-spot.

"Oh my..." Ashleigh sucked in air, pressing her shoulders into the back of the chair as she tried to thrust her hips, wanting him to increase the pressure. When he pulled his finger from the depths of her pussy, she had to bite her cheek to keep from crying out. Why did he stop?

He resumed his exploration of her wetness, sliding his finger up and down, pushing firmly on her clit from time to time. Ashleigh moaned her pleasure, never wanting him to stop because it felt better than she'd ever imagined, more erotic than even her deepest fantasy and that was saying something.

Alex was taking his part of the story seriously, using his tongue and his finger to torture her, but when he ventured from the script, dipping his index finger deep inside of her before retreating, then easing lower, tracing her anus, Ashleigh almost came apart. No one had ever touched her there.

"Lift your hips, baby." Alex demanded, his mouth latching onto her clit once again.

She wasn't sure she could lift them anymore because she was at an awkward angle in the chair, half sitting, half leaning, her ass nearly hanging off the seat while her knees were propped on the armrests. Instead of questioning him, she pushed herself farther into the chair, and he used his hands to lift her bottom, bringing her pussy to his mouth, continuing to feast there, making her crazy with need.

Ashleigh wasn't going to last much longer. Her orgasm was building, tingling sensations spiraling in her womb, her muscles gearing up for the aftermath of the implosion.

Alex lifted her rear another inch and his tongue was no longer in her pussy. He ventured lower, and Ashleigh closed her eyes, giving herself over to the foreign feeling, the delicate nerves wrought with arousal as he reamed her anus with his tongue.

Taboo, unmentionable, forbidden... call it what you will, but Ashleigh was quickly soaring toward an orgasm unlike anything she'd known before. It was amazing, this new feeling, and she didn't want him to stop, but she didn't know what to ask for.

"So good, Alex. Don't stop. Please don't stop."

Much to her relief, he didn't stop, but he did slow his ministrations. Ashleigh kept her eyes closed, not sure she wanted to see what he was doing because it was erotically intense, not to mention it was something she wasn't certain she should enjoy quite so much.

"Relax, baby." Alex's firm command broke the silence, filled only by her choppy breaths.

Ashleigh squeezed her eyes shut, trying to relax. His tongue reamed her anus again, his finger slid into her pussy, and he continued to torment her. Then he switched, and Ashleigh's body tensed. His finger slid into her anus, the foreign feeling exquisitely painful while his tongue latched onto her clit, her body fighting to understand the warring sensations until she couldn't make out anything but the overwhelming, piercing pleasure that erupted in violent tremors in her womb.

Ashleigh instinctively gripped his head, holding onto him as though that would keep her from soaring out of her body as her orgasm ruptured, shattering her into a million pieces.

It look her a few minutes to come back to herself, especially enough to pick up where they had left off. Opening her eyes, she saw the heated emerald green glow staring back at her, and she could only smile.

"Better?" Alex asked.

"Immensely," she grinned.

"So what happens next?" Alex asked, and Ashleigh glanced up at the computer screen. After that, she didn't know if she could handle much more, but the best parts – or so she had originally thought before that exhilarating experience – were still to come.

~~*~~

Alex didn't move from where he was kneeling between Ashleigh's splayed thighs. He couldn't move, actually. He was on his knees, the hard wood biting into his knees, but he was more concerned about the pressure of his jeans on his throbbing dick. He was going to explode if he moved an inch, he feared.

After that little experiment, Alex was fighting the fierce urge to bend her over that damn table and bury his cock in her ass. It was the most sensual thing he'd ever seen, and the eager responsiveness of her body told him she had enjoyed it as much as he had.

Now he just needed to wait for her to pick up the story where she had left off. And yes, maybe he'd improvised just a little, but it was so fucking worth it.

Ashleigh's whiskey brown eyes glowed from the laptop's bright light, and he was torn between seeing the shimmering desire in her eyes and gazing down at her pussy because he was hanging by a very thin thread. If she didn't get on with it, he was going to free his cock and bury himself in her sweet, warm depths.

"Her body was sated, but her need still burned just beneath the surface. The need to touch him, to taste his masculine heat against her tongue," Ashleigh read as Alex watched her sweet lips move. "She wanted to kneel between his thighs as he forced his cock to the hilt in her mouth, using her in ways she'd only ever dreamed of."

If Alex wasn't mistaken, Ashleigh was blushing which made sense because her voice was a little shaky and she wouldn't look at him. He didn't know what came next, but he got the gist of what she wanted. Hell, he'd gotten that the moment he'd seen her screen and the words that had his blood taking an immediate U-turn, heading straight for his cock.

He stood, forcing his sore knees to straighten. "Sit up." He told her as he unhooked the button on his jeans, pulling down the metal tab on his zipper before pushing the denim over his hips.

Gripping the base of his shaft, he waited patiently while Ashleigh righted herself in the chair before he quickly gripped the back of her head, holding her hair firmly and pulling her toward him.

"Open." He insisted, and he suddenly felt woozy, overwhelmed with desire as he took control of this woman. Knowing that was what she wanted turned him on all the more and the adrenaline that flooded his veins had his body throbbing.

He forced the swollen head of his cock past her lips as soon as they parted, not giving her time to hesitate. Her eyes darted to his, and in the dim light from the computer Alex recognized the passion, the need. He also recognized that she was trying to tell him something.

He'd been treating her like a fragile doll, being gentle, easy, keeping things relatively simple; scared he might send her running if she caught a glimpse of the things he wanted to do to her. Staring down at her now, Alex knew he'd made a mistake. Instead of keeping her close, showing her how good and sweet it was when they came together, he'd been pushing her away because she was seeking something from him. Something he hadn't been fulfilling.

"Suck me." Alex bit out, barely restraining the hunger. Gripping her chin firmly, he held her as he pushed his cock into her mouth slowly, not letting her move, insisting on controlling this, controlling her. "Harder, Ashleigh. Suck my cock."

Fuck! It was too good. Both the feel of her hot mouth on his cock and her eagerness to give herself over to him, they were pulling him dangerously close to a release that he wouldn't be able to control.

Using both hands, he slid his fingers into her hair, holding her head completely still as he began fucking her mouth, forward, back, over and over, faster and deeper, praying he didn't make her gag, but needing this more than he thought possible. He'd been holding back for too long, scared to send her running, and now he was afraid he wouldn't be able to turn back.

He didn't want to turn back. This was the side of him that he was familiar with. The man who wasn't gentle, taking what he needed while giving back at the same time.

"Aaahh... Baby. Fuck." Alex growled. "Take me deeper. That's it." He wasn't going to be able to hold off. She was milking him. "Ashleigh!"

He wasn't sure what he was saying anymore. He needed her; needed her to help him because he was suddenly overwhelmed with a multitude of sensations and emotions all coming together, overloading his circuits.

When her cool, smooth fingers cupped his balls, gently massaging, Alex lost it. He roared into the silence of the night as the tingling sensation raced up his spine, shattering his mind and all of his senses while he flooded her mouth with his seed, holding her still until she sucked every last drop from his body.

It took everything in him not to crumble to the floor. Staring back at her, seeing that mischievous grin on her face, Alex knew he'd been right. She was teaching him something, and he might not be the most brilliant man, but he could assure her he wouldn't need another lesson.

Unless of course it was going to be anything like that because he was definitely willing to sign up for her classes if that's the way she taught a lesson.

Chapter Fifteen
*** ~~ *** ~~ *** ~~ ***

Slow on the uptake? Ok, he'd admit to that, but not much more.

After the night before when Ashleigh had nearly made his head explode – well, she did succeed with one, but he wasn't talking about that one – Alex had committed to doing this her way. To hell with the gentle, sweet lover he'd been trying to be for her. She wanted something more, and he was hell bent on being that man.

He had left her a message a little while ago, asking her to meet him at his office. He hadn't come up with any excuses because seriously, what was he going to tell her? Instead, he'd left her a very thorough message, offering her detailed instructions. Now he just had to wait.

Thankfully Dylan and Cole were out of town, having gone back to Austin for a follow up meeting with a ranch owner looking to venture into the hotel business. They were talking big business, and since Alex had hit it off really well with Travis Walker, he'd wanted Dylan to get a feel for the man. If all went well, they'd be looking to expand south a few hundred miles.

Forcing his restless legs to remain still, Alex remained at his desk, toggling between screens on his computer, actually doing a little work while he waited. It was the only way to keep his mind off of what he hoped would happen in less than fifteen minutes if Ashleigh was on time.

After Ashleigh's not so subtle hint the night before, Alex had given some serious thought to his actions. He wasn't sure what it was about her that brought out the possessive protector who wanted to wrap her in cotton batting and keep her locked in a room where no one could hurt her, him included.

And that was the problem... he'd always seen Ashleigh like that. Ever since she was young, he'd wanted to protect her. From men like him mostly. He'd been infatuated with her and at thirty years old, she'd only been eighteen. It was unacceptable in his mind, but he'd been enthralled. Thankfully he'd kept his distance, but somewhere in the back of his mind, he'd conjured up some pretty steamy images of the woman.

If he didn't know better, he'd bet his balls that they'd been real. Except that couldn't be true because the first time he kissed her at Sam and Logan's party, Alex had known he would've remembered.

Having stayed away from her had been the right answer then, but not anymore. Alex had taken her to his bed, and if he had anything to say about it, she'd never walk away from him. Not if he could help it. Ten years was a long time to lust after someone, and despite his reminder that they weren't exclusive, weren't in a relationship, Alex had this niggling feeling that he wanted to be. Another first for him.

A knock on his door announced Ashleigh's presence and Alex glanced up at her, his eyes drawn to all of the creamy skin she had on display.

Ashleigh didn't normally wear anything except jeans and a t-shirt, or not that he'd seen anyway, so on his message, he'd left her a little instruction on what he expected her to wear.

Standing before him in a short skirt, a flimsy little sweater, and a pair of fuck me boots, Alex wasn't sure he'd be able to move from his chair. Her hair was pulled up into a messy pile on her head, held there by a silver clip while thin, curled strands hung around her face.

His dick jumped.

"Fuck." Alex exhaled, worried if he didn't, he might just pass out from holding his breath.

Ashleigh's smile widened, and Alex's eyes were fixated on her pink glossy lips.

Well, that was until she moved.

When she took a step into his office, gently closing the door behind her, his greedy eyes were tracing every luscious curve of her body and the seductive way she moved. Her body was made for sin, and Alex was beyond tempted.

"Did you need to see me?" Ashleigh asked sweetly, moving closer to his desk.

Alex stood, aware he'd never be able to hide the erection tenting his slacks, but he didn't necessarily care to either. Stepping out from behind his desk, he retraced her steps, going to the door and locking it. There wasn't another person in the building, but Alex wasn't one to invite trouble. At least this way, they'd have privacy.

And for what he wanted to do to her, they'd need it.

Glancing at the black, leather couch in the corner, then back to his desk, Alex's body hardened even more as he envisioned Ashleigh sprawled out naked on either.

"I did," Alex answered her question, turning his gaze back to her, "but I was thinking I needed to see a little more of you."

Ashleigh's back straightened, but her smile didn't falter.

"Take off the sweater," Alex stated, perching on the edge of his desk.

If Ashleigh only knew the libidinous thoughts darting through his mind, she might not be grinning, but then again, after the stunt she pulled on him the night before, maybe she would.

"I figured since you had your fantasy at work," Alex raked his eyes over her bare breasts, "it's time for me to have mine."

Ashleigh wasn't wearing a bra, which meant she'd paid attention to his voicemail. Although he hadn't told her what to wear, he did tell her what not to wear.

"Now the skirt." Alex instructed, returning his gaze to her eyes.

Ashleigh shimmied out of the skirt, leaving the boots on and just like he'd told her, she wasn't wearing anything underneath the sweater and skirt. Absolutely nothing. But that wasn't what had Alex's eyes widening and his dick throbbing like a bad tooth. Holy shit.

Alex couldn't tear his gaze away from the smooth, taut skin over her mound. She'd waxed, and now all of those pretty curls were gone, leaving nothing but sexy, sleek skin. "Damn, baby," he groaned, "are you trying to kill me?"

"Not yet." Ashleigh smiled. "I'm not through with you yet."

Alex wasn't through with her either. Not by a long shot.

"Come here." He instructed, and she walked toward him, clad only in those black, knee high boots that made his dick harder than a steel spike. "You waxed your pussy." It wasn't a question; the proof was there in front of him.

"Yes." She admitted although her smile dimmed somewhat.

"You know what that does, don't you?"

Ashleigh looked confused now, her eyebrows shifting.

"No."

"Have a seat right here." Alex said, standing from his desk and trading places with her. "Spread your legs."

He wasn't sure he'd be able to get through the next few minutes before he was pounding his cock into her sweet body, but he'd give it the old college try.

"It means you'll be more sensitive." Kneeling before her, Alex shouldered his way between her thighs, letting her sit on the edge of his desk while her knees were propped on his shoulders and his face was buried between her thighs. "To my touch."

Blowing warm air across her bare mound, he used his fingers to separate the soft, wet folds before using his tongue to slide between them, then outlining her lips, before delving between them again.

He hadn't expected this so suddenly, but being between Ashleigh's thighs, inhaling the sexy, musky scent of her arousal and lapping her warm juices was quickly becoming Alex's favorite thing in the entire world.

It was evident his light teasing was driving her wild, but she tried not to move, her fingers gripping the edge of the desk rather than his head as he had anticipated. Stroking her clit with a few more measured licks, Alex forced himself back to his feet before taking her hand.

"I've always had this fantasy," Alex began, pulling Ashleigh into him, cupping her head with his other hand before kissing her. Alex didn't say another word until they were both breathless.

"What's your fantasy?" Ashleigh asked, her voice sounding huskier than he'd ever heard it.

"Well, first one was to have the sexiest woman alive naked in my office." He grinned down at her. "Since that one came true, I figured I'd go for broke."

Watching Ashleigh suck her bottom lip between her teeth, Alex groaned. She was the sexiest thing he'd ever seen.

"What's your second fantasy?" She asked.

Leaning in, he nipped the fleshy part of her ear, using his tongue to trace the outer shell while he cupped her pert breasts in each hand, plumping them before tweaking the turgid nipples, "I want to bend you over that couch and bury my tongue and then my fingers in your pussy."

When she moaned, Alex knew she liked the idea.

"Then I want to bury my cock in your ass, fucking you until you stop begging for more and come around my dick."

To Alex's surprise, Ashleigh didn't back away, but he caught the slight sway of her body as she processed what he was telling her.

"Do you want that, Ash? Want to feel my cock buried to the hilt in your sweet ass?" Alex wanted it, for fuck's sake. He couldn't think of anything else since he'd fucked her ass with his finger the night before.

Figuring she'd unleashed the beast, he'd show her what it was she was asking for. He wasn't tame, he wasn't easy, and he damn sure wasn't going to hold back from her a second longer.

"Tell me." He said, sliding his hand between her legs, using his fingers to part her smooth lips, dipping his finger through her slit then sliding one finger in the warm depths of her pussy. "I want to hear you say it. Tell me to fuck your ass, Ashleigh."

"Yes," Ashleigh moaned, riding his fingers as he began a slow, gentle thrust inside her warm body.

"Yes, what?" Alex wasn't about to let her off the hook.

"I want you to fuck my ass, Alex." The words were barely a whisper. "God, I want it so bad."

Alex suddenly felt way too overdressed for this little party. Taking her hand, he inserted it between her legs, replacing his as he guided her to do what he'd just been doing. "Play with yourself, Ash."

Alex took a step back, unbuttoning his shirt as he watched her. She didn't look nearly as confident as she had when she walked into his office a few minutes ago, but she was doing as he instructed. With swift movements, Alex wasted no time removing his clothes, tossing them on the chair before stalking his way back to her.

"Come here." Alex took her hand, pulling her as he backed over to the leather couch before lowering himself onto it. Once he was on his back, he smiled up at her. "Sit on my face so I can taste you again."

Alex pulled her closer, not letting her back away though he was fairly certain she wasn't going to do so. Ashleigh might not have spoken many words, but her moans and groans were sheer bliss, and if he pegged her correctly, she'd been waiting for this day for a long time now.

Lifting one leg, he held it above him before she eased it to the side of his head. In seconds, he was between her legs, looking up into the swirling golden brown of her eyes as she kept her gaze fixated on him.

"Lift," Alex instructed, "then put your hands on the arm of the couch." That way she was on all fours, her breasts hanging above his head, begging for his touch. But first, he wanted her to come in his mouth.

~~*~~

Ashleigh couldn't quite believe what she was doing. Stark naked – except for the high heeled boots – in Alex's office was definitely outside the realm of even her darkest fantasies. Maybe that's because she hadn't realized Alex had an office outside of her grandfather's company. Yet here she was.

Since the second she stepped into his office, she'd sensed the side of Alex he'd been hiding from her for the last few weeks. Instead of the sweet, gentle lover she'd grown familiar with, the dominant, salacious man she'd fantasized about over the years was front and center. The hunger in his eyes was hot enough to set off the smoke alarms.

And now she was perched on his couch, his head between her thighs as she held herself above him, the exquisite feel of his tongue exploring the oversensitive lips of her bare mound driving her wild.

Yes, Alex has been correct. Having her pussy waxed had left her hypersensitive to any and all sensations. Her panties had even set off tingles inside of her when she least expected it. What had pushed her to do it, she didn't know, but when she'd bared herself to him, and his eyes had widened, hungrier than before if that was even possible, Ashleigh knew she'd done the right thing.

Trying to hold herself off of him, Ashleigh reveled in the feel of Alex's expert tongue as he lapped at her, teasing her clit relentlessly. She wasn't at all familiar with this position, but she found that lowering a little of her weight onto his mouth allowed her to control the friction of his tongue on her clit.

It was perfect, the ability to thrust against his firm tongue had her grinding her hips onto his mouth as he used his arms to lock onto her thighs, not allowing her to move if she wanted to. But she didn't. No, she just wanted to grind onto him until her body took flight.

So when he stopped abruptly, Ashleigh wanted to scream.

"Turn around," Alex told her and she had to think about it for a second. If she were to turn around...

Ohhhh! Now Ashleigh definitely liked that idea.

Quickly and effortlessly, Ashleigh rearranged herself so she was turned the opposite way and now his glorious cock was readily available to her eager mouth.

When he latched onto her clit again, Ashleigh pressed against him, but then busied herself with stroking his cock with her tongue, exploring his taste as she used her hand to gently cup his balls, fondling him gently until he was moaning against her pussy, the vibrations intensifying her body's reaction.

They continued this exploration for long minutes and Ashleigh had gotten lost in the taste of him, the silky feel of his cock against her tongue as she lapped every long inch of him, when a sharp, biting pain ignited in her, stilling her instantly.

She fought the urge to bite down because his cock was filling her mouth, but the pain was acute, albeit brief. Alex was using his finger to fuck her ass the way he'd done the night before, and though it had been uncomfortable initially, it didn't take long for Ashleigh to begin thrusting back against his finger while once again laving his cock with her tongue.

Exquisite sensations rocketed through her, and she was unable to pinpoint exactly where they were coming from. It could've been his tongue on her clit, or his thumb in her pussy, or his fingers in her ass. She didn't know, but she didn't want him to stop.

Releasing his cock from her mouth because she could no longer focus, pushing up onto her hands, using his thighs as leverage, Ashleigh began riding his mouth and his fingers simultaneously.

She was close... so close.

And once again he stopped. This time she did release a growl of frustration, but that only caused him to chuckle. Before she could ask what he was doing, he was lifting her off of him, and then she took over, putting her feet on the plush carpet before standing.

"On your knees." Alex instructed, and Ashleigh had heard that line before.

When she went to her knees before him, she was baffled when he moved around behind her, rather than in front of her where she expected.

"Put your hands on the couch and don't move."

Ok. Placing her hands on the black leather cushion, Ashleigh waited patiently, not glancing back, instead trying to talk herself into this. It all sounded good on paper, but the pain had been real, even if it did disappear quickly, she knew this wasn't going to be pleasant.

Alex lowered himself to his knees behind her, and Ashleigh was once again infused with his warmth as his solid chest pressed against her back. His mouth trailed fiery hot kisses between her shoulder blades and her body broke out in chills, the feeling intense. She loved his mouth on her, everywhere.

His arms snaked around her waist, his hands zeroing in on her breasts, cupping them firmly then squeezing.

"I need to be inside you, baby." Alex said, and Ashleigh got the impression he was asking more than telling this time.

Despite her fear, she wanted this. To feel Alex inside of her, in every way possible, was the only thing she could think about.

"Please." It was the only word she could come up with because he was squeezing her breast with one hand while dipping his finger in between the crack of her ass. This time something cool was probing her, and it took a moment to register.

He was still using his finger, but he must have included lubrication this time which helped ease some of the discomfort. Initially...

A few gentle thrusts of his finger had her beginning to feel good, wanting him to thrust harder, faster, but instead, he slowed yet again before pushing two fingers into her. Ashleigh bit her cheek, willing the burn to cease.

"Fuck my fingers, Ashleigh." Alex crooned and his smooth, sultry voice nearly sent her into hyperspace, taking her mind off of the pain.

He continued to thrust into her while she pressed back into him, her pace increasing.

"Alex." Ashleigh was looking for a lifeline because the friction was sweeter than she expected, and her body was beginning to tremble with the first signs of her orgasm. "Please, Alex."

Her body was coated in perspiration, her arms beginning to slip on the leather as she leaned forward, Alex kneading her butt cheeks as he fucked his fingers into her slowly, shallowly, over and over.

"That's it, baby." Alex groaned.

Ashleigh could feel him moving behind her, his fingers slowing until he retreated fully, leaving her feeling empty. He'd teased her for long minutes, her body confused on what it wanted and what it needed, her orgasm having built numerous times only to be doused repeatedly.

Then his hands were on her hips, and she felt the wide crest of his penis pressing against her puckered hole, the pressure more than she expected, more than she thought she could bare.

"Play with your clit." Alex ordered as he leaned around her, using one hand to spread her bare pussy lips, the heat of his fingers a welcome sensation when otherwise there would have only been pressure and pain.

Doing as he said, Ashleigh used her fingers to touch herself, stroking her clit with rough, hurried movements, trying to make her body react to the erotic stimulation and praying her brain would shut off momentarily.

"Alex, it hurts." She admitted, ducking her head against the cushion, fear making her body tremble.

"Push against me, Ashleigh. Bear down on my dick."

Ashleigh didn't know what he wanted, but she did as she was told, pushing her hips into his, the wide girth of his cock pressing into her, pushing past the tight muscles painfully until...

"Oh, God!" The pain disappeared and she was left with only an overwhelming sensation of being full. Her hand resumed its torturous pace on her clit while Alex began increasing his pace, shallowly thrusting into her ass.

When his hand took over, his mouth hot on her back, she knew he wasn't going to last, and she prayed he'd hurry. Her body was having a hard time keeping up with itself, and this was erotic as hell.

"That's it, Ash. Ride my cock, baby." His voice was gruff, strained as he began ramming into her, his strokes going deeper, his pace quickening.

"Fuck me, Alex! Please fuck me." She begged, needing something more to push her to the edge.

When Alex's finger delved into her pussy, she squirmed against the invasion, shocked by the intensity and for a brief second, she wondered if this is what it felt like for Sam and Sierra. The mental imaged flashed through her mind as her orgasm erupted, and she bit her cheek to keep from screaming out.

"Fuck. Baby, I'm going to come. Ashleigh! It's too good."

Ashleigh held on as Alex followed her over the edge with blinding, intense fury.

In that moment, Ashleigh knew two things: One, she was quickly falling for this man and the ramifications of that scared her half out of her mind. And two, there was no way that Ashleigh would ever find another man who could sate her the way Alex could.

In the end, she knew the devastation would be abysmal, and she promised that no matter the outcome, she'd walk away with the memories of this moment right here, when she had given in to the fact that Alex McDermott owned her – mind, body, and soul.

Chapter Sixteen
*** ~~ *** ~~ *** ~~ ***

Alex had no sooner walked in his back door when Jessie came walking out of the guest bedroom. "How are you feeling?" He asked as he passed through the living room on his way to the kitchen.

He needed a beer and he needed one bad. After that long ass drive to Austin and back, Alex wanted nothing more than to sit back and relax. The only thing that would make it better was if Ashleigh was there with him. Since he'd been busy with work and she busy with a deadline, he hadn't gotten to see her in two days now – not since that smoking hot scene in his office. The mere thought made his blood pressure soar.

But, instead of sneaking off to Ashleigh's, he'd be sitting at home with his ex-wife, hoping she would get well enough to go home. He had made a point not to spend the night at Ashleigh's since Jessie had been released from the hospital, and it wasn't because he didn't want to. No, he'd much rather be with Ashleigh, but truth be told, he was worried about Jessie, but more than that, he didn't trust her.

Not a good place to be, honestly.

"A little better. My arm hurts, but the Advil is helping." Jessie said softly as she curled up on his couch.

The doctor had offered pain meds, but after a brief chat with him, they opted not to go that route. Jessie was a recovering addict, and the last thing she needed was something to entice her.

"Thanks for letting me stay here. I'm just scared to go back home." She said when he took a seat on the empty couch across from her.

"Well, Jeff's in jail for a little while, so I think it would be safe for you to go home if you wanted to." He wasn't trying to push her out the door, but a gentle nudge wasn't going to hurt.

It's not that he didn't like Jessie because he did. Hell, he'd been married to the woman. Although that little sham of a marriage was for entirely different reasons, but for some reason, Alex felt like he'd been here before.

Different man, same circumstance.

Alex met Jessie at a strip club when he was twenty-one years old. She was supposed to have been eighteen, but as it turned out, she lied about her age and provided a fake id. Being that she was a dancer at the club, that had caused quite a few problems.

But it hadn't been the club giving her the most grief. It was her father. So when Alex found out that Jessie was being abused at home, he'd come to her rescue and the only logical way to get her out of that mess had been to marry her. He didn't recommend it to anyone, but he had done it nonetheless.

They were married until she turned eighteen which was only a couple of months. Then they got the marriage annulled, and Alex had mistakenly thought that would be the end of it. He and Jessie were friends, and he wished her well and all that.

As it turned out, Jessie was a walking disaster. Her time at the strip club had led to some intense addictions – to both drugs and alcohol. Given that she had no one else to turn to, Alex again stepped in to save the day. And for damn near twenty years, he'd been coming to her rescue every time she needed him.

The problem was, he was beginning to think there was something more to these little stunts she pulled. Was she faking it? No, of course not. Her broken arm was proof of what Jeff had done to her. But the story he gave the cops was an entirely different one than the one she offered.

In Jeff's version, Jessie had called him to come over, and once he was there, she instigated the fight, telling Jeff that the only thing she needed to do was to call Alex and everything would be taken care of.

Her version varied, depending on who she told it to. What she told Alex was that she had just gotten home from work when Jeff showed up. He proceeded to beat her because she wouldn't go and get them something to eat. She'd been scared and injured, which was why she called Alex.

The scared and injured part he believed. The rest sounded like total bullshit. But what was he going to do about it? He'd spent the better part of two decades saving her from herself so to give up on her now seemed a little cruel.

"Do you mind if I stay here for a couple more days?" She asked sweetly.

Alex knew he was being played, knew she was doing the same thing she did every other time, but just like always, he conceded.

"Two days. But by this weekend, I need to get you home." He had plans for the weekend and Jessie didn't factor into them at all.

Pushing up from his chair, Alex took his beer and headed to his room. "I need to take a shower, but then I'll order pizza or something. Give me fifteen minutes." He told her without looking back.

Fifteen minutes almost on the money, Alex was back in the living room hunting for his cell phone. Jessie was in the kitchen pouring a glass of tea, so he called out to her. "Have you seen my phone?"

"It's in here on the bar." She told him.

"Thanks." He said absently as he grabbed his phone. "What do you want on your pizza?"

"It doesn't matter. I'll eat anything."

Alex hit the buttons to take him to his previously dialed calls. That was the only way he knew the pizza places number because he always forgot to add it to his contact list. As he was rummaging through the numbers, he noticed the last call that came in.

Ashleigh.

At seven twenty three.

But it wasn't a missed call.

"Did my phone ring while I was in the shower?" He asked Jessie, turning to look at her. She got that same look on her face that she normally did when she was about to lie.

"Some girl called. I told her you were in the shower and that I'd tell her you called."

Fuck! "Why the hell did you answer my phone, Jessie?"

Those damn tears welled up in her eyes, and she flinched like someone was about to hit her and it pissed Alex off. He was suddenly no longer hungry, so he grabbed another beer from the fridge and took his phone to his bedroom.

The second he had the door closed behind him, he dialed Ashleigh's number.

No answer.

Imagine that.

Son of a bitch.

No matter how he tried to explain, this was not going to work out the way he wanted it to.

~~*~~

Ashleigh couldn't believe what she'd just heard. Some woman had answered Alex's cell phone. Worse than that, the woman said he'd have to call her back because he was in the shower.

That bastard.

Although they hadn't talked about being exclusive with one another, Ashleigh had assumed as much. How could she not after all the things they'd been doing and that wasn't even including the sheet scorching sex.

Shame on her, apparently.

When her phone rang a few minutes later, she just stared at the screen as it lit up with Alex's name and number. There was no way in hell she was going to answer it. Not now. Not ever. As far as she was concerned, they didn't have anything more to say to one another.

So why did she want him to explain? Why did she want to give him the chance to tell her exactly why that woman was at his house and that it wasn't because he was a slime ball and sleeping with her while sleeping with other women.

That was her heart talking, not her brain.

Ignoring the phone, Ashleigh grabbed her laptop and went out on the back porch. It was dark outside, but the small light fixture and her computer would provide enough to do what she needed to do.

It was true, readers wanted emotions when they read the stories they loved. They wanted heat and lust and chemistry. Ashleigh could give them that at the moment because she was angry and hurt. No better time than the present to put it all down on paper.

At least this way, she might possibly be able to keep the tears at bay. She was fairly certain that once she let them go, there'd be no stemming the flow, and she just might drown.

How had she been so stupid?

Chapter Seventeen
*** ~~ *** ~~ *** ~~ ***

By the time the weekend rolled around, Ashleigh had successfully written another one hundred pages and ignored just about as many calls from Alex. They had nothing to say to one another, so she wasn't sure why he bothered to call.

She'd been tempted to answer a couple of times, but she reminded herself how smug that woman sounded on the phone and thought better of it. One time, just so she wouldn't be inclined to answer it, she tossed her phone in her underwear drawer.

Ignoring it had become second nature by now, but when it rang Friday afternoon, she glanced at it just because. Grabbing the phone, she hit the answer button.

"Hey."

"Let's go out tonight." Sam's sweet voice rang through.

"Where to?" Ashleigh definitely wasn't opposed to the idea, but going to Club Destiny wasn't going to be her first choice although she knew it would be Sam's.

"Where else?"

Anywhere? Ashleigh wouldn't voice it, but that was her first thought. She didn't want to run into Alex. Worse, she didn't want to run into Alex and another woman.

She might be a little less emotional, although the anger still burned like acid in her gut, but that didn't mean she was willing to test her limits. Avoiding his calls had been hard enough. Thankfully he hadn't bothered to stop by because she was positive she wouldn't have been able to ignore him then and she wasn't about to let him see what he'd reduced her to.

However, she'd known deep down that Alex wasn't up for grabs when it came to his heart, and this had proven that point. She just wished it didn't have to be quite so painful.

"What time?" Glancing at the clock on her computer, she wondered how much later they could push it. It was closing in on five o'clock.

"Let's meet at eight. Drinks. Dancing." Sam said. "We'll have fun."

"Is Sierra going?" Ashleigh wanted as many people as possible in the event she had to sneak out. She didn't want to leave her friend alone, just in case.

"Yes." She confirmed. "So are Logan, Luke and Cole."

Great. One big happy love fest. Just what Ashleigh needed to top off a not so impressive week.

"Alright." She found herself giving in. Staring at the walls was beginning to wear on her nerves and though she might run into Alex, at least she could get out of the house for a while.

"Perfect. See you there." Sam disconnected the call and Ashleigh clung to it like a lifeline.

She really should have said no.

~~*~~

When Logan called to invite Alex to Club Destiny, he'd been hesitant, but if there was a possibility that Ashleigh would be there, he was going. Come hell or high water. Or Jessie.

For two days, Jessie had been driving him crazy. She was crying all the time, giving him one sob story after another about this or that and Alex was growing increasingly more irritated with her.

He tried to be friendly, but she was refusing to go home and Alex needed her to get back on her feet. His white knight days were coming to an end. At least when it came to rescuing his ex-wife.

She was part of the reason Alex had only tried calling Ashleigh, not going to her house insisting she talk to him.

Now it would look like he was trying to save face and there would be no way to explain Jessie's presence at his house. Only a select few even knew about his long ago sham of a marriage, and Alex tried to keep it that way. Logan knew of course. He'd been around at the time. Dylan knew because Alex had shared that much of himself with his closest friend.

But neither of them knew why he had gotten married in the first place because Alex didn't want to share Jessie's hardships with everyone. Another way he tried to protect her. Again, at his own expense.

"Where are you going?" Jessie asked when Alex walked through the living room an hour later.

"Out." She didn't need to know more than that.

"Where to?" Her voice was closer as she followed behind him.

Turning on her, he stopped just outside of his kitchen. "Does it matter?"

A conditioned response, Jessie flinched and took a step back. Alex didn't concede to her timid reaction this time, he merely turned away from her.

"Did I do something wrong?" Jessie asked.

Yes. You overstayed your welcome. "No." Alex barked. "Shit. Jessie. Look." He turned to face her again. "Don't you think it's time you went home? Hell, I'm paying for the damn house. I'd rather someone live in it."

Fuck. He hadn't meant to go that far. Jessie knew as well as he did who paid for the house. And the utilities. And her car. Shit. There wasn't a damn thing the woman did pay for, except food maybe. As thin as she was, Alex even wondered about that.

"I'll get my stuff." She turned on her heel and headed across the living room.

"Wait, Jessie." Following behind her, Alex thrust his hands in his pockets. He hated this shit.

"What?" She turned on him this time, furious. "I get it. I'm in the way. Cramping your style. I'll go home."

Alex wished she was serious about that, but he knew better.

"Tomorrow." He told her. "I'll take you home in the morning, Jessie. Stay here tonight. I'll be out late, so just stay here." It wasn't what he wanted to tell her, but he couldn't bring himself to throw her out of his house, even if he wanted to.

A subtle nod was her response. She'd won again. She always won, but Alex was pretty sure she knew that.

An hour later, Alex pulled into the underground parking garage at Club Destiny. He needed a drink, and a couple of hours of mindless entertainment to help him get past the week he'd had. Having Jessie at his house for damn near five days was way more than he could handle. Not seeing or talking to Ashleigh for that amount of time had been even more frustrating.

Walking in the back doors, Alex nodded his head in greeting to a couple of people he recognized and then went in search of Logan and the others. He stopped suddenly when he saw them sitting at a table in the corner, all seven of them. Luke, Cole, and Sierra were sitting across from Logan and Sam, talking. Tag had just stood from the table, smiling that devilish grin that seemed to attract the ladies, but it was what he was doing that had Alex ready to knock that smile right off his face.

He was holding Ashleigh's hand, leading her to the dance floor.

With his hands balled into fists, Alex turned away, making a beeline for the bar. He needed a drink.

"Hey, Alex." Kane greeted him when he approached.

"What's up, man?" Alex tried for normal, but his words came out with a hint of the irritation building in his gut.

"Not much. I see the whole gangs here tonight. What's up? Someone else getting hitched?"

Alex laughed, not a hint of amusement in the gruff sound. "I'll take a shot of whiskey. Make it a double and I won't bother you for a little while."

"Sure thing." Kane disappeared for a moment before returning with a glass tumbler filled with liquid gold.

"Thanks." Alex took the glass and turned back to the floor, his eyes immediately zoning in on where Tag and Ashleigh were dancing much too close for Alex's peace of mind.

He wondered how Sam was taking it. For the last couple of months, Tag had signed on to be the third in Logan and Sam's relationship and from the bits of gossip Alex had received, the three of them were having more fun than ever. Apparently being a third lacked the jealousy associated with being in a relationship, or so it would seem.

Alex wouldn't know because he didn't share his women. Ever. His friends were all into the threesome thing, and that was all good and fine where he was concerned. To each his own and all that. But Alex couldn't do it.

He didn't share well. Which was another reason he and Jessie hadn't lasted more than a few months. There had been a brief time during the marriage that Alex wondered if he should actually try to make a go of it. They might've gotten married so Jessie could get out of her abusive father's house, but it had been a monumental step for Alex.

That brief thought had died a painful death when Alex learned Jessie was sleeping with a couple of Alex's buddies. Since she had been seventeen at the time, Alex had vowed not to touch her, regardless of whether they were married or not. His friends didn't seem to have a problem with it.

And now, leaning against the bar, watching Tag hold Ashleigh close, he knew he'd never be able to share her. Having another man's hands, lips, or any other body part on his woman didn't do it for him. Logan got off on it, big time, but Alex didn't want her anywhere near another man.

The red haze was damn near blinding him, but he had to remind himself that Ashleigh wasn't his. It didn't matter that they had sex. It didn't matter that he knew she had been a damn virgin that very first time, even if she hadn't told him as much.

The thought still made his dick hard. He was the only man she'd ever been with and up until a few nights ago, he'd planned to keep it that way. But Jessie had to go and interfere, answering his damn phone, and now he didn't even have a chance to explain because Ashleigh wasn't having any of it.

Not that he blamed her. He'd been on that side of the fence a time or two, and he hadn't listened to any explanations either. If you stepped out on the one you were with, you deserved to be left. But he hadn't. He never would either.

A cold blast of fury raced up Alex's spine when Tag leaned down and kissed Ashleigh on the lips, a laugh breaking loose from the man's chest as the two of them walked back to the table.

"What're you hanging out over here for?" Cole's deep voice broke into Alex's thoughts.

Alex turned to look at him, but didn't say a word. He wasn't sure he could speak at the moment. When Cole turned and looked back to see what Alex was looking at, he knew.

"It's nothing, man." Cole told him. "Nothing at all." Stepping in front of Alex, Cole crossed his arms over his chest.

"What?" Alex tried to play dumb, but Cole wasn't having any of it.

"He's trying to get her to smile. Something's obviously wrong, and she needed a little cheering up."

Alex knew something was wrong. She wasn't answering her damn phone, that's what was wrong. He needed a chance to tell her what was going on.

"Why don't you join us?" Cole asked, then turned to Kane. "I'll take a beer and get Alex another one of these."

Alex looked down and realized he'd downed his drink entirely. Too bad the whiskey wasn't numbing him the way it should.

"Come on." Cole said, handing Alex the drink before turning back the way he'd come.

Alex followed behind him, his stomach tightening in knots at the thought of what he'd just witnessed.

When they approached the table, everyone glanced up. Everyone except Ashleigh.

"Hey." Sam greeted, smiling as she leaned into Logan. "Where've you been?" She asked, glancing from Alex to Ashleigh and back again.

"At home." He told her, unable to take his eyes off of Ashleigh. Even pissed, she was the most beautiful woman he'd ever seen. Her long, glossy hair hung down to the middle of her back, board straight and begging him to run his fingers through it. Or better yet, to wrap it around his fist and pull her to him.

Alex shook off the thought. Thinking about the last time they'd been together, in his office, still made his dick throb in eager anticipation. Admittedly, Alex hadn't expected Ashleigh to give in to him, and when she did, she'd blown his mind. Since then he'd thought of very little else besides all of the things he wanted to do to her.

Not that it mattered at this point; she wouldn't even look at him. Side glances darted between everyone at the table. The tension was obvious, and Alex could damn near taste it.

He just didn't know what to do about it.

~~*~~

This was the very reason Ashleigh hadn't wanted to go out tonight. She knew with as many people as were getting together, Alex would show up. The only person missing at the moment was Dylan, and she suddenly wondered where her brother was.

"Has anyone heard from Dylan today?" She asked, glancing at Cole and then Logan. She wasn't about to ask Alex, although if anyone knew, it would be him.

"I saw him at the office earlier this morning, but I didn't have a chance to talk to him." Sam offered.

"He's supposed to be here." Alex contributed, but Ashleigh didn't look at him. She could feel his heated stare on the back of her neck, but she wouldn't turn to look at him because she was pretty sure she was too weak to resist him, no matter how pissed off she was.

"How's it going, Alex?" Logan asked, apparently oblivious to the tension at the table, or speaking up because of it, Ashleigh didn't know.

"It's going."

Ashleigh grabbed her glass, downing what was left and then stood from the table. She needed another drink. And a moment to breathe. "I'll be back." She said to no one in particular and then walked away, not making eye contact.

When she approached the bar, she sat her empty glass down and smiled at Kane. "Belvedere and Sprite, please."

"You gonna ignore me tonight?" The dark, seductive voice slid down her spine and made her hands tingle. Why did he have to follow her?

"No." She told him, then making the mistake of looking at him. Those brilliant green eyes saw more than she wanted him to ever see. "I was planning to ignore you *forever.*" With that, she turned back toward Kane, who was sitting her drink on the bar.

Grabbing a five dollar bill from her pocket, she dropped it in the tip jar and thanked him before she turned away.

She'd intended to go back to the table, at least there she could pretend not to notice Alex, and she could certainly ignore him better, but when he put his warm hand on her arm, she almost dropped her drink. Glancing down at the spot where he touched her, she trailed her eyes back up his exquisite body until she locked eyes with him once again.

"We need to talk."

"We don't have anything to say to one another, Alex." She told him, doing her best not to pull away. She needed to show him that she didn't care. If only it were that easy.

"I need to explain –" He began, but she quickly cut him off.

"There's nothing to explain. I get it. You're bedroom has a revolving door. Since I'm not interested in sharing, unlike my friends," Ashleigh tilted her head in the direction of the table Sam and Sierra were occupying, "I don't have anything more to say to you."

When she tried to walk away, he gripped her arm more firmly. "I don't know what you thought, but honey, you're wrong." His tone was laced with a hint of anger which only fired her up.

"Thought?" She said turning to face him fully. "I didn't have to think anything, Alex. Your girlfriend was courteous enough to tell me how busy you were. In detail."

Ok, so maybe that was a little lie, but the woman had told her Alex was in the shower. She'd also hinted that he was busy and that if he had time, he'd call her back.

"That woman is not my girlfriend. She's my ex-wife." He bit out, still holding her arm.

"Even better." Ashleigh's stomach plummeted to the floor in one fell swoop. That was the last thing she expected.

Chapter Eighteen
*** ~~ *** ~~ *** ~~ ***

Ok, so that definitely didn't come out the way he wanted it to. "I'm not seeing anyone, except you, Ashleigh." He told her, trying to recover the inadvertent derailment of the conversation.

"See, that's where you're wrong, Alex. You aren't seeing me. Not anymore." She stared down at his hand on her arm before shrugging him off and walking back to the table.

Before he could follow her, Dylan walked up.

Perfect fucking timing.

"Woman troubles?" He smirked before edging up to the bar and ordering a beer.

Alex wasn't about to go into it. Not even with Dylan.

"What's Jessie doing at your house?" Dylan asked, surprising Alex.

"What?" How the hell did he know that?

"I called the other night. She answered your phone. Please tell me you aren't seriously seeing her again."

"Fuck no." Jessie was the last woman Alex wanted to be with. If he'd been smart, he'd have cut ties with her all those years ago. Instead, he'd tried to do the right thing, and he was beginning to think she was taking advantage of him.

"You might want to let her know that."

"It's not like that. Her fucking boyfriend beat the shit out of her again, and she called me. I brought her home from the hospital, and now she's refusing to leave."

"Well, I suggest you don't leave your phone unattended." Dylan said, taking a deep pull on his beer. "You'll have hell to pay if Ashleigh gets wind of this."

Alex looked down at his glass and then away.

"Fuck." Dylan didn't need an explanation. "She knows?"

"She won't let me explain. Jessie answered the phone when she called too. I have no idea what she said to Ashleigh, but your sister's as hard headed as they come. She won't give me the time of day."

"That's Ashleigh. She's not big on second chances."

If that wasn't the damn truth.

Dylan sauntered off toward the table and Alex followed. Shit, he didn't have anything else to do. Might as well get the cold shoulder while he could. By the end of the night, she'd have to hear him out.

Two hours passed, and Alex wasn't making any headway with Ashleigh. She was still refusing to look at him, but he did notice she'd had more than her fair share of alcohol, and she was in no shape to drive. Alex had cut himself off after the drink Cole had gotten him earlier. He knew he needed a clear head if he expected to talk to her and have any chance that she would listen to him.

When Logan hauled Sam out on the dance floor, Alex decided to make his move. No way was he letting Tag get his hands on Ashleigh again. Not if he had anything to say about it.

Walking around the table, he came up beside her and took her hand when she wasn't paying any attention to him.

"Dance with me." He told her, pulling her until she slid from her chair. She was reluctant, but he could tell she was trying not to cause a scene.

A slow song came on, which was right up his alley. Alex didn't do that hard core, body grinding shit. But this he could do. Within seconds, he had her pulled flush against him, and his body was fighting a losing battle not to be affected by her nearness.

Tilting her head so she had to look him in the eye, Alex held her gaze. What he saw there was so unexpected, his chest constricted. She was close to tears, and the sight of her glassy eyes hit him like a punch in the solar plexus.

Leaning in, he kissed her gently on the lips. She didn't pull away, which was a surprise, but she didn't kiss him back either. Sliding one hand into her hair, he cupped the back of her head and kept her face turned toward him.

"I'm not with Jessie. Or anyone else, for that matter." He told her, hoping she wouldn't pull away.

"It doesn't matter, Alex. You can see whoever you want."

"I'm having a problem on that front." He told her, keeping her pressed against him. "The only one I want is you, and you've been ignoring me."

"It's obvious I can't handle a man like you." She said, but Alex barely heard the words. He didn't think she meant to say them out loud.

"What?"

"You were right. I'll never be enough for you."

What the hell was she talking about? When did he ever say anything like that? If anything, Ashleigh was more than he deserved. "Who said that?"

"You did." She told him, then turned her head away, but she didn't pull away.

"When did I say that?"

"It was a long time ago. It's no big deal." She said, trying to shrug him off.

Taking a step back, Alex had to pull her off the dance floor and out of the path of the other dancers before they were trampled. He took her hand and led her to the darkened hallway where at least it was a little bit quieter.

"What are you talking about?" Alex crowded her against the wall, blocking out the people walking in and out of the restrooms behind them.

When she looked up at him, she looked far away. "You came to the guest house that night, and you told me I would never be enough for you."

Alex didn't remember the night she was referring to and for the life of him, he didn't remember ever going to the guest house.

"I'm sorry." He said, knowing it wouldn't change a damn thing, but if he'd ever said anything of the sort, he couldn't blame her for trying to keep distance between them.

"You remember?" She asked, sounding both hurt and hopeful at the same time.

"No, baby. I don't."

"Of course you don't." Ashleigh sighed. "You kissed me that night."

Alex dug deep into the dark corners of his memory but didn't remember ever having kissed Ashleigh before recently. He was sure if he'd had those sweet lips on his, he'd have remembered it. But he didn't doubt what Ashleigh was telling him.

"But it doesn't matter, Alex. I think you're right. I'll never be able to handle you."

Alex thought back to the first time he'd had her or the many times after... she hadn't had any problem handling him then.

"Up until recently, you were treating me like I'd break. I don't want a man who's going to hold back from me."

Alex was pretty sure they'd gotten past that part because if the other day in his office, when he'd fucked her ass like a wild animal, was anything to go by, he wasn't holding anything back. And neither was she. Before he could tell her as much, she pulled away.

"I really need to go." She said, but then she swayed when she pushed away from the wall.

"I'll drive you." He insisted, knowing she was far too drunk to drive.

"No. I'll drive... whoa." Ashleigh put her hand on the wall to steady herself. "I'll have my brother take me home."

"I'll take you home, Ashleigh. No arguments." Alex was not going to let up on this. He was taking her home.

Her muddled brain told her this wasn't a good idea. She should argue; she should go back to the table and insist that Dylan take her home, but when Alex put his arm around her, it felt too good to resist. As much as she wanted to be angry, Ashleigh couldn't deny that her heart hurt and being near him soothed that ache, even if it was only temporary. Leaning into him, she allowed him to walk her back to the table as he said their goodbyes.

Ashleigh's eyes met Sam's and she saw the other woman's concern. She hadn't asked if something was wrong, but there was no way her body language would have fooled anyone. And now, she looked like a complete idiot, one who lacked a spine, allowing Alex to take her home.

When he pulled her along beside him, she put one foot in front of the other, although the room was beginning to spin. She definitely shouldn't have had that fifth drink. But by the third, she was beginning to feel no pain.

Alex helped her into his truck, even buckled her seatbelt while she sat back and closed her eyes. That was worse. Forcing her eyes open, she tried not to focus on any one thing for too long because her stomach began to churn.

Oh, God. She was going to be sick.

"Alex." She warned him, but then thankfully he pulled over to the side of the road immediately, and she pushed open the door and vomited right there in the grass. Her stomach heaved, the alcohol pulsing through her blood until she was puking again, then dry heaving when there was nothing left.

Alex, bless him, had come around to her side of the truck and managed to help her back in; got her resituated before once again climbing behind the wheel. "We'll be home in a few minutes, baby. It'll be ok."

With that, Ashleigh did close her eyes, and she willed sleep upon her. There was no way she would live this down.

The sun crept through the slats in the mini blinds, teasing the edges of Ashleigh's vision and making her want to cover her head with a pillow. Reaching out, she felt the bed beside her and thankfully she was alone.

That would be the last time she drank. Ever. Well, the last time she indulged in hard liquor anyway.

At least Alex wasn't there to watch her relive it. Her head was throbbing, but not as bad as it would have if she hadn't choked down the aspirin he insisted she take before she passed out in her bed.

And now, she had to go to the bathroom and that was going to be hell in and of itself. Pushing up from the bed, she walked lightly across the cold, wood floor to the bathroom before closing herself inside. Maybe a shower would help.

Fifteen minutes later, she felt like a different person. Before she had gotten in, she'd downed some ibuprofen, and that had taken some of the heat from her headache. The next item on her agenda was coffee.

When she walked into the living room, she stopped dead in her tracks.

There on her couch was Alex, sound asleep. His bare chest drew her eye, the sleek, tanned muscle teasing her. No matter how angry she was at him, he was still the sexiest man she'd ever seen. Taking advantage of him sleeping, she took a minute to look her fill.

"Keep looking at me like that and I can't promise you I'll keep my distance."

His smooth voice drifted from across the room, sending chills down her spine and jolting her into action. She turned abruptly and headed to the kitchen. She could not handle him this morning. Not even if her headache was subsiding.

A few minutes later, armed with her blessed morning coffee, Ashleigh took her laptop and went out onto the back porch. Hoping if she acted as though she needed space, Alex would take a hint and go home.

Not that she wanted him to, but she should have. After all he'd put her through and everything she didn't know about him, having him there was too much of a distraction.

"Morning." He whispered when he came up behind her, wrapping those strong, warm arms around her. She stiffened, his action reminding her of the last time he'd approached her on the back deck. Despite the hurt that still pulsed in her heart, she secretly enjoyed the seductive scent of him as it drifted through her senses.

"Ashleigh, we need to talk." He told her when he took a step back.

"No talking. I've got to work." She insisted, pretending to be doing something on her computer. Her fingers wouldn't work because from her peripheral vision, she could see he was still absent a shirt, and all of that gloriously tan skin was still there, still beckoning her to look.

She couldn't.

"Call me later." She told him, trying to brush him off.

It didn't work.

"Now. It can't wait until later. I have some things I want to tell you."

Alex was as relentless as they came; she knew that much about him. If she didn't give him a chance to talk, he'd never let up, and she'd never get him out of there.

"Talk." Ashleigh said, daring to look up at him.

Mistake.

Taking a seat in the chair across from her, Alex waited patiently until she closed the laptop and gave him her full attention. As if she had any other choice. Couldn't he have at least gotten dressed?

"I was married once." He began.

She knew that much. She'd known when she met him, which was one of the reasons she kept her distance. At such a young age, he'd already been divorced. "I know."

"But you don't know the circumstances."

She wondered what this had to do with anything. If he had been married, past tense, then why was his ex-wife at his house?

"I met Jessie when I was twenty-one years old. She had only been seventeen at the time, but she was working in a strip club because she lied about her age. It didn't take long to realize she'd come from a very abusive home, and for some reason, I couldn't sit back and watch her continue to suffer. After some coaxing, I managed to convince her father to let her marry me. That, or he was going to go to jail because I was going to turn him in."

Ashleigh was dumbfounded. She couldn't have said a word even if she had to.

"So, I married her. Only it didn't take long to realize that she had just wanted out of her father's house as much as I had wanted her out. She wasn't faithful, not that she and I were having sex, but she wasn't happy with me either. So, needless to say, we had the marriage annulled." Alex said, pausing before glancing out at the water. "It should've been done and over, except Jessie kept finding herself in these situations, and when she called, I came running because I didn't want to see her hurt."

"Why?" The word blurted out before Ashleigh could think better of it. "Why did you keep going back?"

"Hell if I know. I've always had a problem with a man who put his hands on a woman in anger. Jessie seemed to be a magnet for men like that. Instead of turning my back on her, letting her finally grow up and take some responsibility for her own actions, I kept coming to her rescue."

Another pause and Alex's gaze returned to hers. "That's what happened last week. She called. Said she needed me and I came running. Not because I have any feelings for her, but because I knew she couldn't take care of it on her own. When I showed up, her boyfriend was there and they'd gotten into it. I found her beaten and battered, her wrist broken, and the bastard was drunk and still in the house. So I called the police."

"So why is she at your house?" That was the part Ashleigh couldn't wrap her mind around. So maybe Alex was a decent guy, with a heart of gold, apparently. That didn't explain why this woman was at his house, answering his phone while he was in the shower.

"I brought her home from the hospital, and she said she was too scared to go back to her house. I fell for it, and I took her to mine."

Made sense even if Ashleigh didn't want it to. A little.

"I didn't realize what she was doing until I confronted her about answering my phone. She won't admit it, and she keeps playing up the scared card, but I think she's just playing me."

"So why don't you kick her out?"

"I told her she needed to leave this morning. I'm supposed to drive her back to her house."

Ashleigh wondered where her anger was. Where was the disbelief? The hatred for her man seeing another woman? But he wasn't, was he? Alex didn't belong to her, and from what he said, he wasn't seeing anyone else.

At least not according to the story he'd just given her. No, if that was the truth, and she feared it was, Alex was just too kind hearted for his own good. She didn't know Jessie at all, but she was inclined to agree with him. The woman had a hidden agenda. And her guess was the agenda was Alex himself.

Ashleigh went to take a sip of her coffee, but realized the cup was empty. More caffeine was needed to deal with this situation. Grabbing her empty mug, she got up from her chair and went inside, not saying another word. First of all, she was stunned. What was she supposed to say?

By the time she got to the kitchen, Alex was directly behind her. "Talk to me, Ash." He sounded... worried.

"What do you want me to say?" She asked as she poured another cup. "You're a saint, Alex. You're out to save the world, and I don't know how I fit in with those plans."

That was the honest truth.

But when he took her arm and turned her around to face him, effectively backing her up against the cabinet, Ashleigh's breath lodged in her chest.

"I don't care about the world. I care about you."

It sure didn't sound like it from where she was standing. He couldn't seem to let go of his past. What did that say about him?

"I need you." He whispered, not an inch between them and yes, having his body pressed against hers made her forget. About everything.

Her headache.

Her heartache.

Some jealous woman from Alex's past.

All of it. The only thing that mattered was his warm body pressed against hers, chasing away the cold loneliness that had infused her since the moment that other woman answered his cell phone.

"Let me feel you." He said, pressing his mouth against the sensitive skin of her neck. "I need to touch you, baby."

And damn it, she wanted him to touch her. Everywhere. For the first time that morning, Ashleigh put her hands on him, and the electrical current sizzled between them once again.

His smooth skin was warm, and he smelled so damn good. That sultry cologne he favored and the unique scent of Alex. Mixed together it was a heady combination, and she was defenseless against him.

When his lips landed on hers, she tasted his hunger, the urgency in his kiss. And then it all came flooding back. The ache she fought to bury, but lost every time. The need for him to take her – roughly and in spite of everything going on.

But when he started to pull her away, she planted her feet firmly on the tile and resisted going anywhere with him. "What are you doing?" She asked, still rubbing her hands through the spattering of hair on his chest.

"Taking you to the bedroom." He said, kissing her neck.

"No." She said, and the warmth he'd infused her with moments before was suddenly stolen from her when he stepped back.

The question in his eyes deserved an answer, and she fought to scrounge up the courage to tell him what she wanted.

"Not the bedroom." She said, staring into those brilliant emerald green eyes filled with a driving hunger she knew he battled with. "Right here. Right now."

His left eyebrow cocked as though he were trying to understand what she was telling him, and Ashleigh took the opportunity to get it out in the open. "I won't break. I think I've proven that." She whispered. "I don't want gentle and easy all the time, Alex. I see the hunger, and you forget, I know you. I know the real you. The dominant side. Don't treat me like I'm fine china."

He still didn't seem to understand what she was saying, or he was just letting her talk. Either way, she knew she was on a roll, so she kept going. "You've read my books; you know what I write about. Those are the things I dream about. I want hard. Fast. Dirty. Not gentle and loving all the time."

The growl he let loose said he understood.

"Right here." She repeated as she put her hands on the waistband of his jeans, feeling daring and bold, maybe more so than ever before.

Unhooking the button, she turned them until he was against the counter and she had more room to move. Easing to her knees, right there in the middle of her kitchen, Ashleigh made quick work of pushing his jeans and underwear down over his magnificent hips until they were around his ankles.

She slid her hands up his thighs, letting the course hair tease her fingertips, his cock standing proud and tall not far from her lips.

The first time she had done this, they'd been in his shower and she'd been nervous. Intimidated by the newness. Now, just like every time since, Ashleigh wanted to explore. Chancing a glance up at him, she was awash with the heat in his eyes.

"Right here." She told him again.

Chapter Nineteen
*** ~~ *** ~~ *** ~~ ***

Alex couldn't have moved if the house was on fire. With Ashleigh on her knees in front of him, undressing him like she couldn't wait another second, he couldn't control the burning need that welled up inside of him.

Gripping her head with one hand, his cock with the other, he pulled her closer until the head of his cock brushed the soft, fullness of her lips. "Open."

She'd tapped into the part of him that Alex fought to keep buried when she was around, although, in recent days, he'd been unable to hold himself back. Which was why he continued to worry that he'd push her too far, and he found himself hiding that part of him, reverting back to the first time he'd taken her and the realization that she had been a virgin.

She was right, he was a dominating man. One who sought his own pleasure and the pleasure of his lover. He'd been holding back with her, not wanting to scare her off. Apparently, he'd been mistaken about what it was she needed.

From the look in her amber, gold eyes, her hunger was stronger than he gave her credit for. Pushing his cock against her lips, he felt the tremble in his hands as he tried to tamp down some of what he'd continued to try and hold back.

"Don't hold back with me, Alex." She said before she sucked him entirely into the hot cavern of her mouth, the warmth of her tongue torturing him upon impact.

"Fuck." He grit out between clenched teeth. It was too good.

The softness of her lips, the warmth of her mouth, the determination in the way she sucked him. She was overwhelming his senses, making him want to fuck her mouth hard and fast, push as far as he could to see how much of him she could take.

And he didn't hold back. Guiding his cock into her mouth, he kept a firm grip on her hair, pulling her head back so he could control the movements. "Put your hands on my thighs."

He didn't want her using her hands. He needed this, there was no mistaking that. "Open wider." He demanded. "Close your lips around me, baby." God it was so damn good. "Suck me. That's it, Ash. Damn, baby."

Her fingernails dug into his thighs, but her mouth was firm and gentle, doing everything he told her to do. "Take more of me." He said as he pushed in deeper. "Relax."

Just like the first time he'd taken her, he wanted to go balls deep in her mouth, feel the head of his cock hit the back of her throat as she fought to take all of him. He began a rhythmic motion, pushing in, pulling out, her lips brushing down the length of him as her tongue slid over and around his spike hard shaft.

"That's it, baby. Let me fuck your mouth. Hard and fast." He growled as she tried to pull him closer, but he kept her head still, secured by the grip he had on her hair.

"You want me to come in your mouth?" He asked for the simple pleasure of saying the words. He knew what she wanted, and the vibrations that tingled straight up his spine from her moans confirmed it. "Harder, Ash. Suck my cock. That's it, baby. Fuck, it's so good."

He couldn't stop the words as they spewed from his mouth, his cock tunneling in and out of those sweet lips, the excitement in her eyes spurring him on and bringing his orgasm that much closer.

He was holding on for as long as he could because the sight of Ashleigh on her knees in front of him was something he'd only dreamed of for years. To have her there, it still didn't seem real, even if it was becoming more familiar. Forcing her to take him as far as she could, the furnace of her mouth heated him, making his balls tighten until he knew he couldn't hold on much longer.

Pulling her closer, he plunged into her mouth, holding her there and hoping he wouldn't make her gag, but he couldn't control himself. "Your mouth is so fucking hot." With each word, he noticed her eyes darken, smoldering with passion. "That's it. Suck harder."

He thrust over and over, harder and faster until the electrical current of release ignited at the base of his spine, his orgasm rushing forth as he stilled, holding her head and burying his cock deeper into the unbelievable warmth.

His release erupted, and he growled, the rough sound barreling through the empty house as he fought to hold on, fought not to fall to his knees from the sheer pleasure of having her mouth on him.

Ashleigh pulled every last drop from his spent cock, bathing him in sweet warmth until he had no choice, but to pull her to her feet. "Now it's my turn to play." He told her, part warning, part promise. Her eyes widened and a smile tilted the edges of her lips.

He turned her until she was once again backing up to the counter and he quickly removed every last stitch of her clothing, his eyes raking over every inch of exposed flesh. She was beautiful. All gentle curves and soft, pale skin.

Because he was unable to help it, he laved her nipples, cupping her full breasts in his hands and lifting her to his lips. When he nipped the puckered tips with his teeth, she moaned, throwing her head back and he took note of what she liked. How had he ever thought she'd only want sweet and gentle? Ashleigh Thomas was fueled by the same driving hunger he was, and she continued to prove it each time they came together.

Stepping back, he walked to the kitchen table and pulled a chair away before returning to where she stood, gripping the countertops, fully naked and trembling with desire.

Sexy as fucking hell.

"Put your foot on the chair." He told her as he crouched between her legs, separating the soft, pink folds and opening her to his hungry gaze.

Perfectly pink, her pussy begged to be touched, and his tongue longed to taste her. Every inch until she couldn't take any more.

For long minutes, he explored her with his tongue, spreading her swollen lips with the fingers of one hand while teasing her with one finger of his other. He raked over her clit, spurred on by her erratic breathing and desperate moans, and plunged one finger deep inside of her.

He continued to play, devouring her, lapping up her sweet juices as she tried to grind against his mouth, holding his head in her hands and pulling him closer. He gave into what she wanted, spearing her with two fingers, driving deep, retreating, then going back for more.

When he latched onto her clit with his lips, flicking his tongue over the sensitive nerves, she jolted, gripping his hair painfully hard and thrusting against his mouth.

"You're gonna make me come." She screamed. "Alex!"

He didn't relent, continuing to bury his fingers inside the hot depths of her pussy, using his tongue to torture her until he knew she couldn't take anymore. He began fucking her with his fingers with blazing speed, pushing deep and sucking harder on her engorged clit until she filled the kitchen with her sensual moans.

"I'm coming!"

Ashleigh's entire body tensed, her legs locked, her back straightened, and he felt her pussy spasm around his fingers, her clit throb against his tongue as her orgasm ripped through her. It was the sexiest fucking thing he'd ever seen, ever tasted, and Alex vowed that from here on out, there was no holding back with her.

If he wanted her to give him everything, and he did, he was going to have to give her everything in return.

~~*~~

Ashleigh had died and gone to heaven. That was the only explanation for what she was feeling. Her body was sated, a sense of euphoria washing over her even as she fought to remain upright. Thankfully she didn't have to use her legs much longer because Alex lifted her in his arms and carried her to the couch.

"Don't go to sleep, baby. I'm not done with you yet." Alex kissed her neck, her chest, took one nipple into his mouth.

"I – Oh! Don't stop." From sated to wanting in one second flat.

His mouth was doing wondrous things to her body, causing her womb to spasm. She needed to feel him inside of her and at this point, she didn't give a damn how he made that happen.

When he flipped them so that she was straddling his hips, she smiled down at him. Now this she could get used to. "I'm hoping you have a condom." She said sweetly, her gaze wandering over his sinful body until she reached his eyes.

"My jeans." He told her, apparently not planning to move from his position. Ashleigh made her way back to the kitchen, found the lone condom and returned seconds later.

"Put it on me." He ordered.

Ashleigh stared down at the foil packet, then back at him. She hadn't done this before. Apparently he picked up on her hesitation because he continued instructing.

"Open it." He said, gripping his cock and stroking slow and easy. "Now put it over the head of my cock and roll it down."

She could do this.

"Easy, baby. You could make me come just touching me."

She seriously doubted that, but she did slow her pace, not wanting to hurt him. She slid the latex over the solid length of him, and his groans lit a lingering ember inside of her. She could feel her pussy growing wet, eager to feel him buried inside of her again. When she had the condom in place, she looked up at him once again.

"Now sit on my cock, baby." Alex demanded, and Ashleigh shivered. "Ride my cock and show me what you like."

Her nerves rioted, right along with her hormones. Easing over him, she aligned herself with his long, hard length as he gripped the base and angled the head toward her opening. Long moments passed as she worked to fit him inside of her. His words of encouragement did wonders in making her relax so her body would accommodate the intrusion, and then he was seated fully inside of her, and she was moving over him.

He laced his fingers with hers and allowed her to use his upturned arms for leverage as she pushed up and lowered, going slow at first but then faster. Her movements weren't graceful by any means, and she feared she was doing it wrong.

"Come here." He whispered, and she leaned forward until her breasts were crushed against his chest. "You're pussy's so tight, baby. So fucking tight."

He sounded as though he were in pain, the words coming out gruff and choppy. Then he pulled her head down until their mouths touched, and his tongue thrust deep inside of her at the same time he tilted her hips and thrust up inside of her.

She moaned. It was exquisite.

He broke the kiss, but kept her face close to his. Controlling their movements, Alex gripped her hips with both hands, lifting her slightly as he began to pound inside of her.

"Alex!" It was so good. He filled her, grazing every exposed nerve ending, every inch of sensitive tissue, and her muscles clenched around him.

"Tell me." He demanded. "Tell me how it feels."

"So good." She said, barely able to speak.

When he slowed his movements, she tried to pull back, but he kept her close. "Tell me, Ash. I want to hear you say it. How would you write about it in your books? What does it feel like to have my cock buried in your pussy?"

His words ignited a mini explosion, and she tightened around the sensual intrusion. She was quickly learning with Alex that writing the words on paper was the easy part – speaking them aloud was an entirely different story.

"Deeper." She said, battling between nerves and need. Need won out. "Fuck me harder, Alex."

"Like this?" He asked as he thrust into her.

"Yes. Harder." She demanded. "I want you to fuck me, harder. Faster. I'm going to come, Alex." Just from the erotic conversation alone.

"I love the feel of your pussy on my dick. So wet. So tight. The way you squeeze me. Heaven, baby." Alex groaned. "Buried inside of you is the only place I ever want to be."

Ashleigh couldn't think when he began to move faster, holding her hips still as he pounded from beneath her. "Alex. It's too good."

"Never too good." He groaned. "Come for me, Ash. Come around my cock."

That was all she needed before her orgasm raced through her, exploding as she gripped his hair in her fingers, trying to keep herself grounded as she tumbled into oblivion yet again.

Chapter Twenty
*** ~ *** ~ *** ~ ***

Still riding a high that had been strong and steady since he'd fucked Ashleigh for the second time that morning, Alex had to force himself to go home. Not that he wanted to, but Ashleigh had a deadline that she had to meet – or so she said – and he had something he needed to take care of.

Namely Jessie.

When he pulled into his driveway, the house appeared just the way he'd left it the night before. He could only hope that the only thing different would be Jessie being gone. He wasn't going to hold his breath.

When he walked in the door that led from the garage to the kitchen, he cocked his head, trying to listen for any sounds coming from the back bedroom. She wasn't in the kitchen or the living room, but he knew instinctively that she was still there.

Having to leave Ashleigh had been one of the hardest things he'd done in quite some time. After finally breaking down those walls they'd both inadvertently built in recent weeks, he had only wanted to stay. Happy to have sat on her couch for the rest of the day and watched as she wrote those fascinating stories that had him captivated.

Instead, he'd decided to come back to his house and try to take care of the situation at hand. It wasn't going to be easy, which was why he wanted to put it off as long as possible.

Walking through the house, he didn't notice anything different, but he didn't hear a sound coming from the guest room. Maybe Jessie had left. Sticking his head in the room, he found it empty. His hopes ignited. How would she have gotten home?

Turning to his bedroom, he found the door shut, which immediately set his senses on high alert. He hadn't shut the door, never having reason to. When he pushed the door open, he found Jessie lying in his bed, sprawled out naked.

"Damn it, Jessie." Alex said, immediately turning back the way he'd come. "Fucking get dressed and get out of my damn bed."

"Alex, wait." She called out to him, and he froze in the doorway, his back to her.

"Jessie, get dressed. Then come talk to me."

"No, wait. I need you." She said, and Alex heard her attempt at seduction. He wasn't buying it.

"No, you need to get your shit together so I can take you home." Feeling like a total jackass that she'd played him yet again, he stepped into the hallway.

"I love you." She called out.

Was this her way of showing it? Did she think sex constituted love? "Get dressed."

He slammed his bedroom door and went to the kitchen.

That's where he found the something different.

His liquor cabinet was open. And there were two empty bottles of Jack Daniels sitting on his counter. That would have been his first sign that she'd fallen off the wagon. The fact that there were two glasses, both containing the last remnants of an apparent drunken bender made his hackles rise.

Who the fuck was in his house?

He rushed back to the bedroom, not giving a shit whether she was dressed or not. He threw the door open, sending the solid wood into the wall behind it, echoing in the open space.

"Where the fuck is he?" He asked, knowing exactly who she'd invited over.

"Who?" Jessie asked, trying to sound innocent and not making any attempt to cover her naked body.

"Jeff. He better not be in my fucking house, Jessie." Alex moved through the bedroom, a man on a mission. He threw open the bathroom door, but it was empty. Turning to the closet, he glanced at it and then back at Jessie. Her eyes widened as he moved to the closed door.

Opening it slowly, he found exactly what he was looking for. A naked, and very drunk, Jeff was sitting on the floor.

"Get the fuck out." Alex said, trying to keep his anger in check.

He'd been played again.

"You've got five seconds to get the fuck out of my house, so you better move quickly. I'm about to call the cops."

How could she? Alex took a step back, holding his fists at his sides to keep from punching the shit out of the asshole hiding in his fucking closet. He was half tempted to start counting, but the idiot was fumbling enough as it was.

When Jeff was finally out of the house, five minutes, not five seconds later, Alex turned his attention on Jessie.

"Get your stuff together. I'm taking you home."

"But..."

"I don't want to hear it, Jessie. For years, I've listened to your sob stories. Came to your fucking rescue more times than I can count and how do you thank me? You live in a house that I pay for. You drive a car that I pay for. And you keep putting yourself in the same situations over and over again. I'm done."

He left her sprawled naked and intoxicated in his bed. It was time to do what he should have done seventeen years ago. It was time to cut ties with his past and strengthen those of his future. As far as he was concerned, Ashleigh was his future.

Now he had to convince her of that.

~~*~~

"Will you read it?" Ashleigh asked, holding her breath in anticipation. She'd never asked anyone she knew personally to read her unfinished manuscript.

Sure, she had a couple of critique partners who would contribute, checking for errors, or making sure the flow was good, but never had she requested someone she knew to give it a glance.

"Of course." Sierra squealed into the phone. "Oh, my goodness. I'd be honored, Ashleigh."

"Just keep in mind, its rough." She told her friend over the phone.

That morning she'd managed to put the finishing touches on the rough draft, finally getting it where she wanted it. Now she needed to sit back and give it a little time before she polished it for the final draft.

"I'll stop by your house this afternoon and pick it up. I've got to run some errands anyway." Sierra said.

"Sounds like a plan. What do you think Sam will say when I ask her?" Although their friendships had evolved in recent months, she'd never been one to ask much of her friends, not wanting to seem overbearing.

"Holy crap. Are you kidding? She'll be at your house first thing to make sure she gets it first." Sierra laughed. "I'll be there in a couple of hours. Hold her off if possible."

"I'll try." Ashleigh said, then hung up. Turning back to her computer screen she reviewed the title page. Now if she could come up with something that encompassed the entire story.

Her thoughts drifted to Alex, and she wondered what he'd think. After all, he'd been her inspiration. Or rather, the phenomenal chemistry that seemed to brew like a hurricane when they came together. It was hot. Probably one of the hottest yet. And the ménage she'd incorporated had put it over the top, in her opinion.

Two and a half hours later, Ashleigh's house was full of people.

Not only had Sierra and Sam come over, but they'd invited their significant others. Luke, Logan, and Cole were sitting on the back deck talking while Sierra and Sam sat on the couch, curled up with their own copies of Ashleigh's book.

Logan and Sam had brought food – enough barbecue to feed an army – and they'd all been hanging out, laughing and talking. The only thing that would have made it better would have been if Alex was there. Ashleigh hadn't bothered to call him.

She was nervous enough that Luke and Cole now knew who she was thanks to their irritating need to know exactly what Sierra had been doing. They'd plied Sierra with questions, followed by some kisses that still had Ashleigh's mind whirling.

It was the first time she'd seen something so hot – with the exception of the night Sierra, Luke and Cole announced their permanent arrangement. That had been the first night she'd seen two men kiss and holy hell, it had been hot. The thought still sent chills down her spine.

Ashleigh stepped out on the back deck with the men while the women chattered and sent some heated looks at one another as they continued reading. It was one thing to hear their feedback, another to see how excited they were when they read the book. She didn't want to disappoint them.

"Where's Alex." Luke asked when she took a seat at the table, a glass of wine in hand.

"Don't know." She didn't either. She hadn't seen him since earlier in the week, insisting she needed to focus and he was a distraction unlike anything she'd ever known.

"I talked to him earlier this morning," Cole said. "I figured he'd be here this afternoon."

Ashleigh couldn't imagine why, she hadn't expected anyone to show up at her house, other than the girls.

"Why would he be here?" She asked, sounding entirely unsure of the conversation.

"Why wouldn't he?" Luke laughed.

So that didn't tell her much. Suddenly feeling her nerves take flight in her belly, she downed the rest of her wine and excused herself back inside. Once there, she came face to face with the reason for her nerves.

"Hey." She greeted Alex, stunned by his sudden appearance, and equally overwhelmed by how good he looked. And smelled. If she could bottle his incredibly scent, she'd make a fortune.

"Hey." He approached, pulling her into his arms and crushing his mouth to hers. Either he was oblivious to Sam and Sierra sitting just a few feet away in the living room, or he didn't care.

When he pulled away, she stared up at him. He was smiling. "What?"

"Nothing. I'm just surprised I wasn't invited to the party." He told her, keeping her body close, his hands wrapped around her waist.

"Well, it wasn't supposed to be a party." It wasn't.

"Well, I see food," he cocked his head in the direction of the kitchen, "I hear laughter," he tilted his head toward the living room, "and I see you've got security." This time he turned his eyes toward Logan, Luke and Cole sitting on the back patio.

Laughing, she pulled away. "When you put it that way..."

Alex followed her into the kitchen, a tiny measure of privacy that he immediately took advantage of. He pressed her against the refrigerator and pressed his lips to hers.

"If it weren't for all these people, I'd strip you naked right here and have you on your knees with my cock in your mouth again. I've missed that mouth." He traced her bottom lip with his finger and Ashleigh fought the urge to suck his finger into her mouth.

Leaning in closer to her ear, he whispered. "Or maybe I should do it anyway. They all like to watch."

Her belly fluttered, and her sex clinched. This was the side of Alex that she longed to get to know. The man who didn't hold back. Despite her nerves, she was tempted to do it just to show him how much she liked the promises he was making. Except she didn't have enough nerve.

"Do you want to be watched, Ashleigh?" He asked, licking her neck.

She didn't answer. She couldn't. The answer surprised even her. Yes, she wanted to be watched. Maybe not by her closest friends, but the idea intrigued her. But she figured it was only in the hypothetical sense.

"Damn, baby." He said when he pulled back. "It's a good thing my shirts not tucked in. Every one of them would know exactly what you do to me." Taking her hand, he placed her palm against the hard ridge behind his zipper and Ashleigh eagerly rubbed him, wanting him to keep going.

He growled.

"Now, that's hot as hell." Luke said as he approached.

Ashleigh jerked away from Alex, her face heating with embarrassment.

"What's up?" Alex asked, acting as though they hadn't been groping one another only seconds before in the middle of her kitchen.

"Just getting some beers. Come join us when you're done." He laughed as he pulled three long neck bottles from the fridge and turned back the way he'd come.

"I've never been into the idea of being watched, but with you... I could get into it. Really into it." Alex said as he pulled her close once again.

Ashleigh laughed, a rough sound that broke loose. She was in over her head right now, and she needed to catch her breath before she did something stupid.

Alex retrieved a beer from the fridge before turning back to her. "Don't go far." He grinned and then walked off.

Ashleigh leaned against the counter, trying to get her bearings. Holy shit. How did he do that? Turn her into some wanton woman who'd do anything to please him.

With a deep sigh, she steeled herself for what was to come.

Chapter Twenty One
*** ∼ *** ∼ *** ∼ ***

Alex hadn't expected anyone to be at Ashleigh's when he got there. And what made him come on to her the way he had was beyond him. It had hit him the moment he saw her, looking sexy as hell in those tight jeans she seemed to love, encasing her beautiful ass so perfectly.

When he told her that he'd never been into being watched, that had been partly true. He'd done it on occasion. Once at the club, and a couple of times when he was younger, when the moment presented itself and his curiosity won out. But never with someone that he cared about. And he cared about Ashleigh.

It wasn't the idea of being watched that excited him, it was the idea of *her* being watched that intrigued him. First of all, he got the impression she wanted to venture into unfamiliar territory. Granted, he'd spent the last two days reading her latest novel and holy hell, he'd had a hard on that just wouldn't quit.

And he'd been making mental notes of some of the kinkier things he planned to do to her. All in an attempt to see how far she was willing to go. Which was what happened when he'd had her in the kitchen. The memory of the last time they'd been in there, his dick buried in her sweet mouth had sent the blood flowing straight to his groin, leaving him aching and eager.

But he wasn't serious. Was he? No, at least not at the moment.

Joining the others in the back, Alex geared up to be ribbed.

Luke didn't disappoint.

"Man, you might want to be careful." He started in on Alex the second he sat down. "You know how we feel about the whole voyeuristic thing. Turns us on."

"Shut the hell up, McCoy." Alex muttered, taking a long pull on his beer. "That's for my eyes only, and you know it."

"Is that right?" Logan chimed in. "From what it sounds like, you've got a wildcat on your hands. She might just push those boundaries you've put in place."

He didn't have boundaries.

Ok, he had a few.

"You telling me you want to watch?" Alex pushed.

"Don't knock it till you've tried it." Cole said, grinning.

"What the hell are you talking about?" Alex asked. "You telling me you're into watching? Or being watched?"

How they hell they'd ended up on this subject, he had no idea, but he hoped it would change soon.

"Both." Logan confirmed. "And if you're girl is anything like ours, you're in for it, so you better be a little more open minded."

Open minded? Hell, Alex had probably done things these three had never dreamed about. Not that he would tell them that. And not that he would try those same things with Ashleigh. He was all for getting her worked up and making her come, but with as little experience as she had, he couldn't push her too quickly.

"What's everyone doing here?" Alex asked, hoping to change the subject.

"Sierra and Sam are reading Ashleigh's manuscript. We thought we'd come along. You know. Moral support." Logan smiled.

Apparently Ashleigh's secret was out.

"And what type of moral support are you providing?" Alex inquired, glancing from one man to another.

"Shit, Sierra's so damn excited when she reads one of those books, we wanted to make sure we were here for her. You know... if she needed us." Cole said, straight faced.

Luke and Logan laughed.

Good grief. What the hell did these people do? Alex suddenly felt left out of the loop.

"Are you going to the club on Tuesday night?" This time Luke asked the question, directing it at Logan and Alex had no idea what they were talking about.

"Sam is hoping to. Tag had to go out of town for a few days, but she's hoping he'll be back by then."

Alex must've had a questioning look on his face because Logan followed up with, "You know. The monthly get together at the club. Turns out Sam has a fascination with it."

Alex did a double take. Seriously? The club?

"Sierra's been begging for the last two days," Luke added. "I think she's still mad at us for not taking her last month."

"You were all there at the same time?" Alex was suddenly intrigued by the idea. He hadn't considered taking Ashleigh to the club yet. Since she wasn't a member, he'd have to work on that in the meantime, but until then, it was definitely something to consider. He had a room after all.

"Yes." Cole said. "Definitely nothing like I expected it to be."

"I hear Ashleigh's been hitting Sierra and Sam up for information on threesomes." Logan said, leaning back in his chair. How the man could appear so confident when they were talking about the women sitting only a few feet away inside the house, was beyond Alex.

"What?" That was news to him. And something he would have to set her straight on. He was not into sharing. Hell no.

He was too damn possessive for that. But there were other things they could engage in if her curiosity was that strong. He dared a glance back at the house to see Ashleigh sitting in the living room with Sam and Sierra.

"Does she know you're not into that?" Luke asked, sounding serious now.

"It's not like we've talked about it, no." Alex said, suddenly worried about Ashleigh's fantasies and how far she might try to push him.

"Well, you might want to set her straight, man. Before you find yourself doing something you swore you'd never do."

Alex was beginning to think Logan was right.

~~*~~

Ashleigh couldn't believe her ears.

"I'm serious." Sierra stated insistently. "Being with two men is unlike anything else. Two pairs of hands, two mouths, two... well, you get my drift."

Laughing, Sam turned to Ashleigh. "She's right you know. That doesn't mean it's for everyone. But, you did a fantastic job capturing the allure. I think your readers will be extremely happy."

Ashleigh was grateful for that because as far as she was concerned, that lifestyle wasn't for her. She was more than satisfied with having Alex and only Alex.

For the next half hour, Ashleigh listened intently to the feedback her friends gave her. Finally, when she worried they were getting entirely too worked up, they all ventured outside to join the men.

A short while later, the seven of them were still sitting outside, laughing and joking when Sam captured everyone's attention with her sudden outburst.

"Truth or dare." Sam exclaimed, sitting on Logan's lap.

No way. There was no way Ashleigh was up for a game like that with this group of people.

Especially not after they'd been sitting outside talking so intimately about anything and everything. As it seemed, they didn't have any secrets. At least from each other.

"Woman, you're entirely too open for your own good." Logan stated, kissing his wife's neck.

"I'm game." Sierra chimed in, sitting on Luke's lap across from his twin brother.

"Of course you are." Luke groaned.

Alex glanced at Ashleigh before that seductive grin tilted his lips. "And what about you?" He asked her, apparently leaving the choice up to her.

"I don't know." She muttered, glancing back and forth between Sierra and Sam. "I'm not sure I'm in the same league as you two."

And that was the truth. Sam and Sierra were far more open about their sexuality, something Ashleigh hadn't gotten comfortable with entirely. Hell, she was new to sex, even if she'd been writing about it for years.

"Oh, come on. It'll give you some good material for your book." Sierra coaxed. "We're all friends. Just don't choose a dare and you won't have to do anything you aren't comfortable with."

Right. Because choosing truth would be the simpler way to go. She knew better. Not with the devious way Sam's mind worked.

"We don't have to play." Alex contributed.

Oh, he wasn't going to put this on her. No way.

"I'm up for it. What about you?" She asked him, smiling.

This would likely push every boundary she could have ever dreamed up, but suffice it to say, she was actually intrigued by the idea. And Sierra was right; it would likely give her some hands on experience that she wouldn't have another chance at getting.

It was just the hands on was the part that intimidated her.

"Ok. I'll go first." Sam exclaimed. "I'll make it easy on you this go round."

Ashleigh didn't believe her for a second.

"Wait." Ashleigh said before the freight train known as Sam took off and would likely get entirely too out of control. "If we're going to do this, let's move it inside. I'm not sure my neighbors can handle the likes of you."

"Good idea." Logan said. "Baby, I think she knows you well."

Fifteen minutes and another round of drinks later, everyone was situated in the living room. Sam was once again seated on Logan's lap in the oversized chair, Sierra on Cole's lap with Luke close by on the couch, and Ashleigh and Alex were sitting on the floor. At Sam's insistence, they had moved the coffee table out of the way.

The only person who looked excited about this game was Sam. Ashleigh was beginning to wonder whether anything was off limits with that woman.

"Ok." Sam said getting everyone's attention. "Cole, you're first."

"Fuck." He groaned, but Sierra ruffled his hair and he smiled up at her.

"Truth or dare?" Sam asked.

"I'm screwed no matter what I do here, aren't I?" He asked. "I might as well enjoy it. Dare." He told Sam, wrapping his arms around Sierra.

"Hmm... Ok." Sam acted as though she were pondering what she would have him do. "I won't go overboard just yet. Show us how you kiss Sierra when Luke isn't watching."

Cole grinned and Ashleigh couldn't help but laugh. When Cole turned Sierra's head to face his, he wrapped his fist in her long, shiny, black hair, pulling her down to him before locking lips with her. They obviously didn't have any issues with having an audience because Sierra began to moan relentlessly as Cole plundered her mouth.

The sight of it was hot enough to make Ashleigh squirm. She glanced over and noticed Alex was watching her closely.

"Damn, baby." Cole released the words on a sigh when he pulled away from Sierra. "I'm thinking Luke needs to be away more often."

"Your turn." Sam said, obviously anxious to keep the game on track.

"Alright." Cole said, glancing over at Luke, then back at Alex. "I'll pick on Alex first. Truth or dare?"

Alex didn't hesitate. "Truth."

Ashleigh tensed. After the few things she'd learned about him recently, she wasn't sure she wanted to know all of Alex's secrets.

"Have you ever had sex in a public place? If yes, then where?" Leave it to Cole to break the ice quickly. Ashleigh turned her attention to Alex.

"Yes." He said, not looking at her. "I'm a member of the club, aren't I?"

Ashleigh thought maybe the answer would suffice, but Cole merely cocked an eyebrow and waited.

"I've had sex in more than one public place. The most taboo, since I know that's what you're angling for, was a department store."

Cole grinned, apparently content with the answer. Ashleigh held her breath, praying no one would call on her.

A good forty five minutes later, the game had ratcheted up a notch, and Ashleigh was wondering whether she should turn the air conditioner on.

She had a feeling they'd toned down the first few questions and dares, for her benefit. And thankfully, she'd only had to answer one simple question. But now, the dares were becoming a little more sexually graphic. Ashleigh knew she should've been ready to bolt from the room, but she found herself hanging on every word, watching every movement. Surprisingly, they'd only gotten one more drink each, so she couldn't even blame it on the alcohol.

"Alright. I'm through being easy on you people." Sam said. "If you aren't game to take this to the next level, I suggest you speak up now because all bets are off. There are no rules. No limitations. So, in other words, it's going to get hot and nasty in here now."

"Lord have mercy." Logan grumbled. "I've created a monster."

The room erupted in laughter, but a chill ran down Ashleigh's spine.

Sam directed her gaze at Luke, and Ashleigh knew they were about to be in for it.

"Luke, truth or dare?"

"Give it your best shot, baby." Luke pinned Sam with that cocky, no nonsense grin. "Dare."

Ashleigh knew that out of all of them, aside from Cole, Luke had the least limitations when it came to sex. He was obviously bi-sexual because he was in a permanent relationship with both Cole and Sierra, which meant they probably did some pretty interesting things if she'd have to guess.

"I want to watch..." Sam paused, obviously for effect, "while you give Cole a blow job."

Ashleigh's pussy clenched, the idea of what she was about to witness the hottest thing she could have imagined. She'd never taken her books down that path – at least not yet – so, seeing this first hand was completely out of her element.

"Stay right where you are, baby." Luke told Sierra when she would have moved. She was still sitting on Cole's lap, but Luke maneuvered her so she had a front row view of what was about to happen.

From where they were on the couch, everyone in the room would have an up close view to... *oh holy crap!*

Ashleigh could do nothing but stare as Luke eased Cole's impressive cock from his jeans, stroking him with his large hard before his tongue darted out to lave the engorged head. She couldn't even breathe.

Not until Alex moved closer to her, pulling her in front of him, his hands gripping her waist as he leaned in close to her ear. She could feel his erection pressed against her back.

"You like to watch?" He whispered against her ear. She hoped he didn't expect an answer because as well as being unable to turn away, she couldn't speak either.

Watching Luke ravish Cole's cock with his mouth, using his tongue and teeth to apply just enough sensual torture to have Cole's face contorting in both pleasure and what she assumed was pain, was the most erotic thing she'd ever witnessed. When Sierra gripped the base of Cole's shaft, holding him firmly, sliding his cock between Luke's lips, Ashleigh gasped, as did others in the room.

Involuntarily, Ashleigh moved back against Alex, suddenly wanting his hands on her, but knowing she was too engrossed in the erotic scene to so much as notice if he did.

What couldn't have been more than two or three minutes felt like hours, before Luke slowly released Cole's still erect cock from his mouth, licking the head one last time before returning to his seat beside him.

"Holy shit." Sam exhaled, "That was so fucking hot." She was just as breathless as Ashleigh.

"My turn." Luke said, staring right at his twin, a wicked gleam in his eye. "Truth or dare, little brother?"

Ashleigh held her breath, wondering whether Logan would take the easy way out because at this point, there couldn't be a single secret that would have been harder than what Luke likely had in store for his dare.

"Dare." Logan retorted, obviously pushing Luke.

"I dare you to convince your wife to strip naked so the rest of us can see her amazing body."

Ashleigh felt like a bystander, not an active participant in this little escapade. The way Sam was pushing Luke and Luke was pushing Logan, it was obvious they were trying to see who would go the farthest. To her surprise, Sam only smiled as she looked down at her husband.

"Stand up." Logan ordered, and his terse words sent a chill racing down Ashleigh's spine, although he was talking to his wife, not her. Just the dominant tone would have been enough to have Ashleigh jumping to attention, willing to do anything he instructed her to do. It was the same tone Alex had used on occasion, but not nearly enough.

Sam stood before Logan, her back to the room, obviously waiting for his next instruction.

"I want you naked. Completely." He ordered, and Sam grinned yet again. In a record amount of time, Sam was standing before them all, totally naked, and looking more confident than Ashleigh had ever felt, even when dressed.

"Now sit on my lap, baby." Logan said firmly.

With Sam once again on Logan's lap, his hands lingering on her breasts, teasing her while the rest of the room watched, Ashleigh waited to see who Logan would target next. She had a feeling she wasn't going to get by with sitting on the sidelines for much longer.

"Truth or dare?" Logan said, before pinning her with his gaze.

"Truth." Ashleigh said quickly, chickening out yet again.

"Have you ever done anything like this before? And if you say no, I want to know how far you are willing to go."

Ashleigh knew this was the opening for her consent for them to include her in this erotic interlude. They'd obviously been leaving her out, probably hoping she'd get her bearings. She had them, alright. "No." She said, not breaking eye contact with Logan. "I've never done anything like this before." Steeling herself by taking a deep breath, she answered the second part of his question, "And as for how far I'll go? Try me."

~~*~~

Alex knew his exhale could be heard throughout the room. He had held his breath, anticipating what she would say; unsure which way he wanted it to go. Evidently they'd be participating like the rest of them. He was both eager and hesitant.

"My turn." Ashleigh said, sounding more confident than he would have given her credit for. "Sierra, truth or dare?"

Sierra grinned, obviously hoping someone would call on her. "Dare."

Alex waited patiently for Ashleigh to come up with something, and when she didn't, he leaned in so only she could hear and offered his input.

Logan laughed while Luke groaned, Ashleigh merely smiled. Alex knew that once Ashleigh did this, it would likely come back on her, but he was tempted to see how far she would actually go. He would be the first to admit that this type of situation wasn't normally his forte, but seeing Ashleigh open up, watching as she got more and more turned on by what was going on around her, had him waiting patiently for his turn. It was erotic as hell, and yes, he was interested in seeing where it led them.

"I dare you to get as naked as Sam."

Surprisingly, Sierra looked hesitant for a moment, but then she stood from her seat on Cole's lap, removing every last stitch of clothing and revealing her stunningly beautiful body. Alex was just as consumed by the sight as everyone else in the room, the same way he had been when Sam undressed. Sam and Sierra were definitely attractive women, but neither held a candle to Ashleigh.

"My turn." Sierra smiled, looking back at Ashleigh. Or rather, just past Ashleigh as it would seem. "Alex, truth or dare?"

Since he'd picked truth the two other times he'd been called upon, he knew it was time to up the ante so to speak. "Dare."

"Since your girl's the only female left with any clothes on, I dare you to take them off of her." Sierra said, mirroring Luke's words from earlier.

Ashleigh was close enough that Alex could hear her slight gasp. That certainly wasn't a dare for Alex, but rather a sneaky way to get back at Ashleigh. He didn't hesitate before he instructed her to stand up. He also stood, both of them nearly in the center of the room.

Keeping his eyes locked with hers, he slowly slid her t-shirt up over her breasts, then over her head and tossed it to the floor behind them. With teasing fingers, he slid his hands down her chest, sliding them underneath the lace of her bra, and then circling each nipple once with the backs of his fingers.

When she shuddered beneath his touch, his cock throbbed in answer. He unhooked the front clasp of her bra and allowed the lace to fall to the floor as he glanced down at her beautifully puckered nipples.

Locking his gaze with hers once more, he stalled for a moment, waiting to see if she would back out, but she didn't.

Lowering himself to his knees in front of her, he made quick work of the button and zipper on her jeans, then lowering the denim, along with her panties, to the floor at her feet. She stepped out of them before standing before him in a move so provocative, he damn near came like a teenager who'd pilfered his first porno.

"You're beautiful." He whispered, not giving a shit who was in the room because truth be told, having their eyes on them was a turn on like he had never remembered.

Taking her hand, he pulled her down until she was in his lap before he turned his attention on the room. He wasn't sure who he would go after, but it was time for a little payback.

"Sam." He finally decided. "Truth or dare?"

The twinkle in her eye said she would only have one answer from there on out, and she confirmed it with a confident, "Dare."

"I dare you to sit on the edge of that chair, spread your legs, and let your husband lick your pussy... until you come." Alex said boldly.

At least the woman had the decency to appear a little nervous as she glanced around the room before turning her gaze on Logan.

Alex knew she'd become almost more than her husband could handle, based on the bits and pieces of conversation he'd picked up on, but until tonight, he hadn't realized how much.

Alex watched, along with the rest of the room as Logan's eyes smoldered with heat, when Sam situated herself on the chair, her pussy open and inviting her husband's eager tongue.

For a brief second, Alex glanced down at Ashleigh only to find she was riveted on the lascivious scene. To his surprise, she'd slipped her hand down between her legs and was gently caressing her mound. Unable to help himself, he slipped his hand between her legs, over hers, and guided her fingers to her clit.

"It's so fucking hot to watch a man eat a woman's pussy." Alex whispered in her ear, low enough that only she could hear. "But it's even hotter to watch you play with yourself."

Ashleigh moaned at the same time Sam did, as Logan's tongue thrust between her spread thighs. A quick glance showed Alex that Sierra was getting some extra attention from Luke as well when the man slipped his hand between her legs and began strumming her clit. The room erupted in sensual moans as all three women let loose while the men they were with gave in.

Only Logan was allowed to go all out though because this was Sam's dare and she was eagerly riding his mouth as he continued to eat her pussy in front of everyone. When Sam moaned, followed by her announcement that she was coming, Alex was surprised it had taken that long.

It took her a moment to catch her breath before she eased back into the chair, rubbing against Logan's obvious erection as she glanced around the room. "Ashleigh, truth or dare?"

Ashleigh was still breathing heavy, but her hand had stilled between her legs. She was gloriously naked, but she didn't seem to be bothered by it in the least. "Truth." She said, surprising the room. Alex thought she was worked up enough that she would have asked for a dare.

Sam's eyes narrowed on her. "Do you like watching and being watched?"

"Yes." Ashleigh stated firmly, her eyes never wavering from Sam's.

Ashleigh took her turn, throwing out a truth question when Cole selected. Then they bounced around the room randomly, everyone seeming to need a moment after the last dare until finally it was Sam's turn again. Alex wasn't surprised when she turned her attention on Ashleigh again.

Ashleigh opted for a dare, and Alex held his breath as he waited for what Sam would do. "I dare you to let Alex eat your pussy." Sam said crudely, but he could see the concern in her eyes. She might be pushing her friend, but she had her best interest in mind. If it came down to it, Alex knew Sam would call the game.

When Ashleigh turned back to look at Alex, Sam caught their attention again. "On the coffee table."

That didn't surprise Alex one bit. The point was to push the boundaries and having Ashleigh spread out like a centerpiece would likely end the game as they knew it and change everyone's actions.

Alex didn't figure they'd make it another round because in about five minutes, there would be a massive orgy going on right there in Ashleigh's living room.

Chapter Twenty Two
*** ~~ *** ~~ *** ~~ ***

Ashleigh's body was on fire. Every inch of her skin screamed for relief, by the only man capable of doing so. She needed his touch, his kiss, whatever it took to alleviate some of the intrinsic longing that had built up over the course of the last couple of hours.

With him easing her down on the coffee table which Luke had so kindly relocated back to the center of the room, Ashleigh was a jumble of nerves and hormones. At the moment, she didn't know which was fiercer, but with Alex touching her, even slightly, she knew which was going to win out.

The room seemed to disappear, along with everyone in it with the exception of Alex. When he made good on the dare, lowering himself to the floor so he could maneuver between her thighs, Ashleigh didn't care where they were at the moment. As long as he put his mouth on her.

When his tongue slid through the sensitive folds of her pussy, she fought back the urge to hurdle herself into the ether, snagging every ounce of bliss from the eager manipulation of his tongue. She was so hot, so bothered, even the slight movement of air from the ceiling fan was too much for her hypersensitive skin.

Spreading her legs farther apart, she willed him to go deeper, to bury his fingers inside of her and make her explode around them.

Only the subtle sound of harsh breathing around her brought her back from the edge. No longer was anyone paying them any mind, but rather they were doing their own thing. Which included Sam sitting astride Logan, who was now completely naked and buried deep inside of Sam as she rode him with wild abandon.

On the other side of the room, Sierra was sitting on Luke's lap while Cole was on his knees, nestled between their thighs, using his tongue to make them both moan in ecstasy.

It was too much – so much so, when Alex penetrated her with one finger, her orgasm detonated on impact, shattering what was left of her and leaving her in a million pieces, right there in the middle of the living room.

Sitting up when he pulled her, Ashleigh immediately dropped to her knees before him, going after his jeans like a crazed woman until his erection sprang free. Completely oblivious to everything else going on in her house, she focused on one thing. Pleasing this man.

Long minutes later, Alex was gripping her hair, holding her to him as he groaned out his release, filling her mouth with his salty taste. When she thought he would have mounted her right then and there, the way the others were doing, he surprised her by picking her up and carrying her to the bedroom.

The bedroom door clicked shut behind them as he deposited her on the bed, coming to lay beside her, halfway covering her with his body.

"Damn, baby." He whispered, sounding as stunned as she felt.

"I need to feel you, Alex. Inside me. Now." She urged, trying to pull him over her. Before he did, he reached into the drawer of the bedside table, retrieving a condom he'd placed there the last time he was at her house. Apparently he didn't want to be left without protection.

After what felt like days, but could have only been seconds, he was sheathed and buried to the hilt inside of her.

"Look at me, Ashleigh."

Her eyes opened to see the glittering green emeralds staring back at her, filled with so much more than just lust. Using his hands to hold himself above her, he ground his pelvis against hers, effectively driving his cock deeper and deeper, but never actually retreating.

She clung to him, never wanting to let him go, trying to pull him closer even though they were as close as two bodies could be. When he dipped his head down, claiming her mouth, she kissed him back with all of the pent up sexual energy that the erotic game had inspired and then some.

Before she knew it, her orgasm was taking over, igniting deep in her core before radiating outward, sparking flames in its wake. Screaming his name as she came, Ashleigh gave in to the darkness when it came over her.

Two hours later, Ashleigh and Alex emerged from her bedroom after a much needed nap. It was dark outside, but after sleeping like the dead, her body entirely sated, she was more than a little energetic. Thankfully the house had cleared out, and the only two left were Ashleigh and Alex. Just the way she wanted it.

"So, what's on the agenda tonight?" Alex asked, picking up a copy of her manuscript that she'd left on her kitchen table.

"Hmmm..." She could think of a few things, but she'd let him figure it out for himself.

Dropping the papers, he made his way over to her. "I was thinking we could go back to my place and pick up where we left off in the swimming pool."

She definitely wasn't opposed to the idea. Smiling up at him, she let him pull her into his arms. "I could –" she didn't complete the thought because it suddenly dawned on her that he had a house guest. One Ashleigh had no intention of meeting.

Pulling away, she busied herself cleaning up the kitchen.

"What's wrong?" He asked, catching on to her drastic mood swing.

"I don't think that's a good idea."

Alex walked up behind her, pulled her against him and then nuzzled her neck. "She's gone, Ash. I wouldn't put you through something like that."

Relaxing against him, she soaked up his warmth for a minute. Could she do this? It would be so easy to forget what had happened, to accept what Alex told her about his ex-wife, but Ashleigh was still anxious.

Letting him in had been hard enough, but if they continued to pursue what was happening between them, she was risking so much more than the hurt she'd endured already. If for some reason this didn't work out, Ashleigh's heart would be forever shattered, likely irreparably.

Being in his arms, feeling the warmth of him surrounding her felt so right, so real, Ashleigh feared what would happen if she didn't give in to this. If she held herself back from him, even a tiny piece, she'd be cheating herself out of something she'd waited years to discover. She had to trust him. She had to. There was no other option.

Inhaling deeply, she whispered, "Ok. Let's go."

When they walked into Alex's house, Ashleigh still felt the nervous tension, as though the woman who had been there would pop out of nowhere just to surprise him. Relief washed over her when no one came slinking out of any of the rooms. Instead, Alex went to the kitchen, grabbed two bottles of water and then took her hand before leading her out to the back.

It was dark outside, and he had flipped on one of the outdoor lights. It wasn't shining directly on the pool, rather leaving it in shadow, but illuminating a portion of the yard beyond.

"Take your clothes off, Ash." Alex ordered, his voice coming out stern and ridiculously seductive.

She turned to face him, about to ask him if he was serious. The look on his face said he was.

Her insides throbbed, both from nerves and from the longing to feel his hands on her. She'd never undressed for a man before. But then again, there were so many firsts she'd already experienced with Alex, why wouldn't this be another?

"Naked." He told her, sitting the water on the table and then moving closer. "For my eyes only this time." He whispered.

With fumbling fingers, Ashleigh found herself doing as he instructed. First her t-shirt, then her shoes, followed by her socks and jeans. She left her bra and panties on just to test him. Had she not already gotten naked in a room full of people, she might be a little hesitant about being completely naked outside, for the entire world to see.

"I think you forgot a couple of pieces." He told her as his eyes trailed over her skin.

She unhooked her bra, sliding the straps down her arms and letting the lace fall to the ground along with the rest of her clothes. Stepping out of her panties required a little more coaxing, but her fingers eventually caught on.

Standing back to her full height, feeling incredibly exposed and more than a little nervous, Ashleigh tried not to fidget.

"So damn beautiful." Alex said with a hint of awe in his tone that made Ashleigh blush. "I've dreamed about seeing you naked. Did you know that?" He asked, but Ashleigh couldn't answer. "For ten long years, I've wanted you."

Ashleigh could relate, but she wasn't about to tell him that. "I want to taste you. But, I think it's only fair if I were naked too." Alex said, staring back at her.

For a brief moment, she waited for him to undress, but then Ashleigh realized he wanted her to do the honors. She wasn't about to argue because seeing Alex naked had become one of her fantasies come to life. Sliding her hand under the untucked edge of his shirt, she raked her nails over his taut abs, lifting the shirt as she went. Within seconds, she had his shirt off, discarded to the concrete beneath her.

The evening air was cool, a welcome relief to her suddenly overheated skin. Before she moved on to his jeans, she took a moment to look her fill, gliding her hands over the muscular planes of his chest, scraping her fingernails over each of his nipples, watching as they hardened beneath her touch. She suddenly wanted to suck them to see what he would do. Feeling bold and brazen, she moved in closer, flicking her tongue against one small, brown disc, twirling around the hardened nub before using her teeth to nip him.

"Keep it up, baby. Just remember, paybacks are a bitch." He teased in that gruff tone she loved so much, slipping his hand in her hair and holding her head close to his chest.

Ashleigh moved to the other nipple, teasing it briefly before lowering her hands to release the buttons on his jeans. After lowering the zipper, she pushed the denim down his legs. Grateful that he managed to slip off his shoes, she helped undress him completely until he stood before her in all of his masculine glory, just as naked as she was.

Without another word, Alex led her to the pool, descending the steps while holding her hand. She followed along behind him, her gaze raking over his beautiful body. For a moment, she allowed her eyes to trace the bold, black outline on his back, the intricate pattern that formed the tiger's face on his back. She had the sudden urge to taste him, to trace the tattoo with her tongue.

Pulling away from him, she pressed up against his back, using her finger to trace the black outline before using her tongue to do the same. She'd noticed it before, just as intrigued then as she was now. With him naked, she wanted to graze each impressive line, taste the salty, warmth of his skin.

"Damn, baby." He groaned as he stood motionless in the water. She pressed her breasts against his back as she continued to explore him with her mouth, placing light kisses over his skin, licking the artwork that only accentuated how utterly male he was. The animal peering back at her was an ironic replica of what she thought of him. A jungle cat, always on the prowl. Strong and beautiful.

"My turn." Alex said, turning abruptly before turning her away from him. "Put your hands on the edge of the pool and don't move." He ordered her, and she immediately followed his instruction.

She loved that about Alex. His need to dominate, to be completely in control. It had taken him some time to finally open up to her, but once he did, Ashleigh hadn't been disappointed.

~~*~~

Alex placed his hands on the curve of Ashleigh's waist, gliding down her hips, her thighs, before bringing them back up.

The way she'd touched him, the way she'd run her tongue over his back had him gritting his teeth and squeezing his cock. He loved that about her, her need to explore him, but he was hanging by a frayed thread at the moment. He needed the control or he wouldn't last all of five seconds.

Placing his mouth on the back of her neck, leaning over her, he kissed her slowly, moving his tongue down her spine, similar to the way she had done to him only seconds before. Sliding his hands around her ribs, he cupped her breasts in both hands.

A sudden image of her flashed through his mind. She was on her knees, his cock buried deep in her mouth. They were at the club. In the playroom and there were others around. An overwhelming need flooded him, and he pushed it away. He'd spent too much time with the McCoy brothers. If he wasn't careful, he'd be thinking about threesomes next. His dick throbbed at the thought.

Squeezing her breasts, using his thumbs and index fingers, he pinched her nipples gently until she moaned. "You like when I play with your nipples." It wasn't a question because her reaction was evidence enough.

He trailed his mouth down the toned muscles of her back, her skin petal soft against his lips. Going lower, he released her breasts and gripped her hips, kissing the sweet dimples at the small of her back before continuing lower.

When she stilled, just at the point he was trailing his tongue over the beautiful curve of her butt, he paused. When she didn't pull away, he continued, kneading her hips with his fingers, he used his thumbs to gently separate the soft rounded globes of her ass, delving his tongue into the very edge of the crack that separated them.

He'd developed an obsession with her ass. After having teased her, then fucked her, the way Ashleigh had reacted made him want her all the more. Now that she'd allowed him to fuck her ass, he was convinced she was just as turned on by it as he was.

Slipping one hand between her thighs, he found her pussy slick from her juices, not from the water they were submerged in. Hoping they could stem off the chill by their body heat alone, Alex wanted to play for a few minutes. He only needed a minute or two to explore her the way he wanted.

"Don't move." He warned her as he pushed his middle finger into her tight channel, feeling her vaginal muscles tense around the intrusion. He wished it was his cock buried inside of her.

At damn near forty years old, Alex had no idea how he managed to keep up with her, but even after he'd come twice earlier in the day, he was raring to go again. That's what she did to him.

Thrusting his finger slowly, he continued to tease her ass cheeks with his tongue, delving between them from time to time as her moans increased. She was enjoying it, based on her reaction.

"Spread your legs." Removing his finger, he lifted her bottom, helping her to open wider, effectively putting her pussy on display for him. "Move closer to the edge."

When she was closer, he put his hand on her back, pushing her chest down onto the concrete until her ass lifted out of the water, and he had access to the soft pink folds between her thighs. Using only his tongue, he lapped at her pussy, gently thrusting inside once, twice, before gliding up over the puckered hole he'd exposed as he separated her butt cheeks.

Reaming her hole with his tongue, he felt her body shudder, her moans increasing as she enjoyed what he was doing to her. She'd been a virgin when he'd taken her for the first time, and he hadn't known it. When he'd fucked her ass, it was clear she'd never allowed another man there either. To know he was the only one, he fully intended to keep it that way.

"Alex!" She screamed as her thighs tensed.

He pulled back, easing his tongue back into her warm, wet pussy as she squirmed against his mouth. She tasted like honey and spice, and he could feast on her for hours, but he knew she wouldn't be able to take much more.

Helping her back down from the edge, he pulled her into deeper water, holding her against him, her breasts crushed against his chest.

"I want to bury my cock in your ass, Ashleigh." He told her, watching her eyes widen from his crude words. "Did you enjoy when I fucked you there?"

She didn't answer, but he hadn't expected her to. "Tell me, Ashleigh. Do you like when I take your ass?"

He eased his hand between them, guiding his cock into the warm depths of her pussy as she held onto him, her arms wrapped around his neck.

"Oh, God." She groaned when he pushed in deeper.

"Fuck." She was still so damn tight, her pussy milking him. "Tell me."

"Yes, Alex. Yes!" Ashleigh moaned as she began to ride his cock. "I loved when you fucked my ass."

Stopping her movements, he began to thrust his hips harder, slamming into her, because the sudden, overwhelming urge to come was too much. The thought of being buried in her ass had him riding a sharp edge of need, nothing there to hold him back as he quickly hurdled toward oblivion.

"Come for me, baby. Come on my cock."

"Yes!" Ashleigh moaned, her nails digging into his back as her pussy spasmed around his cock and he let go, a sharp tingling sensation erupting at the base of his spine and racing outward until he exploded, coming hard and fast inside of her.

And then it hit him with the force of a tsunami.

Pressing his forehead to hers, he didn't pull out of her, just held her close. "Ashleigh."

"What?" Sated and limp in his arms, he knew what he was about to tell her would likely change everything they'd built thus far.

"Baby, I –" God he couldn't get the words out. "We –"

Fuck.

How did he tell her that they didn't use a condom?

~~*~~

Ashleigh still couldn't get over the intense rush that rattled her to her very core. What Alex had done to her only moments before, something she'd thought about ever since the first time he'd done it still excited her beyond her wildest imagination.

When he'd used his tongue to tease her ass, the exquisite warmth rasping over highly sensitive nerve endings, she'd barely refrained from coming right then and there.

She could tell something was wrong, but she couldn't imagine what it could be. Didn't he realize she'd liked what he did to her? She wanted it more than she ever thought possible, and if he had wanted to fuck her ass right then, she'd have given in to him at that very moment. That's how hot she was for him.

Pulling back, she looked into his eyes, the brilliant green glow she was used to seemed dimmer somehow. "What's the matter?"

"Baby, we didn't use a condom."

Ashleigh processed his words.

No, no they hadn't used a condom. At least as far as pregnancy was concerned, they were safe. She hadn't made it that far in her life not knowing she was responsible for herself when it came to protection. After the first time they'd slept together, she had immediately made an appointment with her doctor to get on birth control. It was her responsibility as much as it was his.

Now as far as the other concerns, no, they hadn't been safe and they would have to deal with that fall out. Feeling a little deflated, she eased out of his arms, but didn't move far away. "I'm on birth control. I won't get pregnant." She told him. "And as far as disease —"

"Baby, you don't have to worry about that." Alex said quickly, pulling her close. "I've always been safe. I promise you that. I've always used a condom."

That was definitely good to know, but it didn't explain how he had forgotten with her.

"I've never been with anyone else." She said aloud, realizing she'd never admitted it to him until now.

"I know." The possessive tone in his voice sent shivers down her spine. "And if I have anything to say about it, you'll never be with anyone else."

She wanted to tell him the same, but that would constitute a relationship, and she wasn't sure Alex was ready for that. She had absolutely no intentions of straying – he was more than she could handle as it was – but she wasn't about to make him feel tied down.

When he pulled her back to him, lifting her until she wrapped her legs around his waist, letting the buoyancy of the water carry her, Ashleigh relaxed into his arms.

She didn't need sweet words or promises, just as long as she could hold on to him for a short period of time. At least until she had sated the craving she'd been harboring for the past decade.

The only problem... she was pretty sure she'd never get her fill.

Chapter Twenty Three
*** ~~ *** ~~ *** ~~ ***

Three months later...

Ashleigh was sitting at a table in the front of the children's section of a local bookstore, smiling and talking to the kids who had come to listen to her read her latest book. For the most part, that had gone well, only a couple of unruly kids who weren't too happy with having to sit still for longer than five minutes, but really, who could blame them?

As much as she enjoyed these public interactions, she was anxious to get back home. Her latest erotica book had released that day, and she was eager to see what her fans were saying about it. Since this one was for a much more mature audience than the one she had entertained for the last hour, she couldn't very well pull it up on her phone just to see.

Not that spending a Tuesday afternoon with a group of kids who loved to hear about barnyard animals, especially those that talked, wasn't a nice way to pass the time. It was. But, being that the last few months had been steady going with her writing, much of her inspiration thanks to Alex and his wild ways, she was anxious to get some feedback.

Speaking of Alex...

The man walked in the bookstore, looking way too handsome for his own good. For three months, they'd managed to spend a significant amount of time together, both exploring one another in the physical sense as well as each other's interests.

They'd checked off a few more items on her list, and a couple that weren't listed because they were for her eyes only.

Between riding four wheelers, taking a long weekend to go skiing before the weather warmed too much, and taking in her first major league baseball game, Ashleigh was having the time of her life.

As she watched him move closer, that devilishly sexy grin sending all sorts of erotic images through her mind, Ashleigh noticed a few other women glance his way.

That happened quite often. He was definitely a man that drew attention. Both from his sheer size and his extraordinary good looks, women seemed to flock to him.

"Hey." He said when he approached, leaning down and kissing her on the cheek. "Is it time to sneak out of here yet?" The last part was for her ears only, and she was grateful because there were still a couple of little ones wandering around.

"Five minutes."

"Perfect. I'll meet you up front when you're done." He said, grinning before he took off to another part of the store.

Ashleigh didn't know what he was up to, but, for the last few days, he'd been particularly restless. Namely when it came to sex. If she didn't know better, she was beginning to think their activities were becoming a little stale for his taste. Since she was inclined to agree, though she would never tell him that, it wasn't necessarily a bad thing.

It just seemed as though they had run out of ideas in recent weeks. Ever since that raunchy game of Truth or Dare, they'd been having some of the best sex ever. And a lot of it. Which explained the rut they had found themselves in.

Ashleigh could think of a number of new things they could try, but she wasn't sure she should be recommending them. After all, Alex had pretty much staked his claim and since the afternoon of libidinous games they had played with the McCoy clan, he was keeping things pretty tame. Much to her dismay.

Ten minutes later, Ashleigh was wandering through the store until she came upon Alex checking out at the front. She waited for him by the door as he paid for his purchases, the pretty, young sales clerk flirting relentlessly with him. When he turned to see her standing there, he grinned, and Ashleigh felt it all the way to her toes.

Being the center of his attention was definitely something she had never gotten used to, but something she hoped to never have to go without.

"Ready?" He asked when he approached, pulling her against him. She inhaled the now familiar scent of him, still getting a buzz from the sexy, intoxicating fragrance that was unique to Alex.

"Ready." She confirmed as he took her hand in his, linking their fingers as he normally did and led her to his truck. "Where are we going?" She asked as he was pulling out of the parking lot.

"I was thinking about taking you home and getting you naked." He said, throwing a glance at her before turning his gaze back to the road.

"What did you buy?" She asked, looking into the bag. Her heart stopped, then started with a jolt when she saw her latest release staring back at her.

"I figured I'd get an autograph from my favorite author." He grinned sheepishly.

"Awww. Are you sucking up?"

"Yep." He said, pulling onto one of the back roads that would take them to her house. Because of the location, her house was quite a ways out from the rest of civilization, and especially on a weekday afternoon, the roads were devoid of any other cars. "I was thinking about you today."

"Is that right?" Ashleigh asked, getting a sense that this was about to take a turn for the forbidden. She wasn't sure why, but she got the impression that Alex was up to his naughty best, and she was seriously liking where this was going.

"I was thinking about your lips." He told her, not looking at her. "Then I started thinking about how sweet they are around my cock."

Ashleigh felt her juices pool between her thighs, his words setting off a flash fire of heat down low. This was the Alex she'd been missing for a few weeks now. The one who had dirty thoughts and even dirtier words. She liked it. And she was pretty sure he knew she liked it.

When he pulled her hand, still linked with his, closer to him, Ashleigh knew where this was going, and her fingers suddenly itched to touch him. She leaned over the center console a little more, allowing him to place her hand on the hard ridge of his erection.

"Are you trying to tell me something?" Ashleigh asked, trying to sound innocent.

"God, yes." He groaned when she rubbed her hand over the rigid length of him. "Touch me, Ashleigh."

Ashleigh glanced out the window to ensure they were still alone on the isolated road before she leaned over farther, managing to release his cock from his jeans with quick, easy movements.

As he drove, she stroked the velvety soft shaft she'd uncovered, wanting nothing more than to put him in her mouth. Except he was driving and that was a distraction he could ill afford, so she settled for stroking him slow and easy, teasing him but never getting him close to where he wanted to be.

When he turned off, she recognized where they were going, and she smiled. This wasn't the road that led to her house; it was one that led to a secluded lake they'd discovered on one of their morning runs. Within a minute, he was parked near the water's edge, not another soul in sight.

"Baby." Alex groaned. "I need to feel your mouth on me."

Ashleigh unlatched her seat belt and leaned across the hard console, trying to get as comfortable as possible.

"I think it's about time I trade this bad boy in for one without a console." He chuckled as he gripped his cock, stroking a little harder than she had been. "Put your mouth on my cock." Alex insisted in that tone he knew she loved. "Fuck yes."

He wasn't sure what compelled him to take her for a drive, but he could feel her anxiety building. They'd been going through the paces for a couple of months, getting to know one another on more than just a sexual level. And although their relationship was going strong, Ashleigh was getting restless. Ever since that damn game of Truth or Dare.

Not that they were having issues when it came to sex, Alex just felt as though she wanted it to be a little more spontaneous.

Well, you couldn't get more spontaneous than this.

Gripping her hair, Alex held Ashleigh's head as she skillfully stroked him with her tongue. "That's it, baby. Fuck that's good. Suck me harder."

Alex had to grit his teeth when she began furiously ravishing his cock with her sweet mouth, using her hand to stroke him. It was so fucking good. Her mouth was like heaven, and he could have held off for hours, letting the warmth of her tongue slide over the swollen head, teasing the sensitive spot just beneath. Then she did that thing with her tongue and her teeth, pushing him closer to the edge.

"Baby." He warned, knowing he wasn't going to hold out. "I'm going to come in your mouth." He held her head in his lap, thrusting between her lips. "That's it. Fuck." Alex groaned.

Ashleigh gripped his shaft tighter, stroking slow and steady, matching the rhythm of her head as it moved up and down over his lap. He wanted to see her, but being that they were in the small confines of the truck, he had to settle with letting the urgency in her movements bring him closer to release.

"I love to feel your mouth on me." Alex groaned, hanging on by a very thin thread. "Fuck, baby." He was close. So fucking close.

Holding her head still, Alex's body tightened, trembled, then exploded as she continued to use her tongue to torment him as his semen flooded her mouth.

When she sat up and faced him, he cupped her face, pulling her to him so he could kiss her, tasting his own saltiness, mixed with her sweetness. It was a combination he'd never get tired of.

"I hate to spoil your fun," Ashleigh stated, smiling when she pulled back from him, "but if you don't mind, I'd like to go home. Today's the first day my book went on sale, and there are a couple of things I'd like to check."

Well. He could definitely accommodate that request, but he had only one stipulation. There was no way he'd make it easy on her. "Ok." He paused, mesmerized by the intense heat still lingering in her eyes. "Under one condition."

"What's that?" She asked, looking both intrigued and a little leery.

"As soon as we get inside, I want you naked."

"You're on."

Ten minutes later, they were walking into her house, but before Alex allowed Ashleigh to make it two steps past the door, he was pulling her backward until she fell into him. Her laugh filled the entry way and his heart with happiness. Alex loved when she laughed. It was one of the best parts of his day.

When she tried to pull away, still giggling, he lifted her feet from the floor and held her suspended in the air briefly before once again setting her back on the ground. Glancing down at her, he made sure she saw the demand in his eyes and the laughter ceased as did the smile, but in its place... blazing heat.

In the last few months, Alex noticed the way Ashleigh responded to his stern tone, so on occasion, he'd test her. He could pretty much predict she'd be wet and ready for him. Just the way he liked her.

"Naked, baby." He said, tilting her chin up to him. "Right now."

He took a step back, propping his back against the wall, crossing his arms over his chest and watching her as she fidgeted for a second before that steely determination he admired so much took hold.

With grace and sheer femininity, Ashleigh disrobed, even shedding her panties and bra without him asking. He sucked in a breath because she just did that to him. Anytime he caught her naked, she made him breathless. She was just *that* beautiful.

Before he could say another word, she shot him a sweet, seductive grin and turned away, heading right to her computer. His eyes were glued to the gentle sway of her hips and the luscious curve of her butt as she walked away.

Without an ounce of modesty, she took the laptop over to the couch and took a seat while he continued to stare at her from across the room.

He loved that about her. Well, it wasn't just her confidence and class because if he was completely honest with himself, he loved everything about her. *Everything.*

Taking a seat in the overstuffed chair facing the sofa, he crossed one ankle over the opposite knee and clasped his hands behind his head. In it for the long haul, he was.

"Put your feet on the coffee table and spread your legs. I want to see that pretty pussy."

She didn't falter. Instead, Ashleigh propped her laptop at a different angle, placing her feet exactly as he instructed. He was beginning to wonder how far she'd allow him to go, and he couldn't think of a better time to test the waters.

He allowed her to work for a few minutes while he admired her from a few feet away. She might've thought he didn't catch the way her eyes darted his way every so often, but he did.

Getting up, he didn't say a word as he disappeared into her bedroom. A week or so ago, he'd placed a couple of toys in the nightstand on the side of the bed he slept on when he stayed the night. They hadn't gotten around to using them. Yet.

He took the blue mini vibrator from the plastic package before inserting the batteries he'd brought and pocketed it before returning to his place in the chair.

Alex saw her confusion, but he also noticed the subtle way she squirmed in her seat. She was getting worked up, and he hadn't even touched her yet.

He was about to change that.

"Let me know when you can take a break." He said, trying not to smile.

"Did you need something?" She asked in that deceptively sweet tone. "I can take a break." Without further hesitation, Ashleigh set the laptop on the couch beside her, turning her attention to him.

Without the laptop obstructing his view, he was able to take in the mouthwatering sight of her stunning body. Ashleigh wasn't petite by any means, she was long and lean. Not to mention, sexy from her head to her toes.

There were so many parts of her body that had become his favorite, like the sleek column of her neck that he wanted to nuzzle with his lips, or the crook of her elbow, or her pretty pink tipped toes. Her long, shiny hair hung over her shoulders, resting just above her magnificent breasts and he wanted to run his fingers through it, to feel it's silkiness as she leaned over him, riding him until she came

Everything about the woman made his body come alive, but more importantly, she made his heart swell with emotion when he least expected it.

Leaning forward, he set the small blue toy on the table in front of her and watched her eyes widen, her mouth open in shock.

"Pick it up." He ordered, literally sitting on the edge of his seat. His dick had swelled and was throbbing with need, making it entirely too uncomfortable to be sitting down, but he forced himself to stay where he was.

Ashleigh leaned forward, reaching for the toy, and he noticed the slight tremble in her hand. He knew her well enough now that she wasn't trembling in fear, she was trembling with need.

Alex was the first to agree with Logan, the women they were with were slowly turning into sexual monsters, but Alex wasn't complaining. This woman had blown him away with her passion. Ashleigh didn't shy away from anything, at least not up to this point. He just prayed there wasn't a day that he couldn't hold her interest.

With the vibrator in hand, Ashleigh stared back at him, obviously waiting for what he would do or say next. "Lean back and spread your legs more. I want to see you play with your clit."

Her eyes widened even more, the golden brown shining with reserved anticipation, but she sat back, staring down at the blue toy in her hand like she'd never seen one before.

Admittedly, he was enjoying all of the firsts that the two of them were experiencing together. On the flip side, he wasn't all that fond of the patience he'd had to get a handle on in recent weeks. The woman was going to make his head explode.

~~*~~

Ashleigh stared down at the little toy in wonder. Not because she hadn't seen one before but because of what Alex expected her to do. She had learned in recent weeks that she'd had to pretend not to be intimidated by the sexual openness he lured out of her. It was becoming second nature to be naked around him, but to play with herself...

She wasn't so sure she could do it.

Not that she hadn't already done so many things she'd never expected to do with him, but each time she had to build up the nerve just to get through it. Like now.

Leaning back on the couch, she suddenly wished he'd join her. That would make it so much easier, but not Alex. He might be averse to having others watch, but he clearly enjoyed watching her.

"Turn it on, baby." Alex said, his voice coming out husky and eager. Ashleigh knew how he felt. She was pretty sure her voice wasn't working at the moment, so she didn't say anything.

Twisting the end, the little blue toy came to life. Just like every other time he pushed her to try something new, she wondered if she should just back out. That wasn't in her nature though, and secretly she liked how her actions seemed to please him.

He surprised her when he ripped his shirt up and over his head, tossing it to the floor beside the chair, his eyes never leaving hers. The sight of his naked chest and those magnificently formed abs had her body trembling as much as the vibrator in her hand.

"Put it on your clit." He said a little more firmly and she leaned back, spreading her legs, keeping her eyes trained on the plastic toy.

She was going to drop it, her hands were shaking so bad. Only the sound of his erratic breathing spurred her on, and she slipped the vibrator between her legs, easing it between her hypersensitive folds until she found the tiny bundle of nerves.

"Oh." She didn't hold back her moan because that was what Alex wanted, and quite frankly, the stimulation was more than she could stand. With the vibration on low, she wondered if she would come right there, touching herself while Alex watched.

"I wish that was my tongue," he said, standing.

She wished it was his tongue. The man could do wicked things to her with his tongue, and she had dreams about all the ways that he had explored her.

Pressing harder, Ashleigh's body tensed from the overstimulation, the sudden, acute tingle that radiated from between her legs had her clinching her teeth, trying to hold back.

She continued to play with herself while she watched him undress, uncovering all of those sleek, well defined muscles right there in front of her. The man was utter perfection with his smooth, tan skin, and lean, ripped muscle. The sight of him made her body ache for the feel of his weight pressed against her, looming over her as he thrust his powerful body into hers.

Another moan escaped, this one louder than the last, surprising her as much as it seemed to turn him on. When he was finally naked, he moved the coffee table before kneeling before her, his eyes intently focused on her hand moving between her legs.

"Touch me, Alex." She begged, pleading for his warmth, for his tenderness.

"So pretty." Alex said, then glanced up in to her eyes. "I will jack off to this memory for years to come."

Whether it was the way he said it, or the actual words, she didn't know, but Ashleigh nearly exploded. "Please." She needed more, and she was too worked up to do it herself.

Alex took the vibrator from her trembling fingers and expertly began stroking her clit as he used one of his fingers to delve inside her.

"More." She encouraged him, throwing herself into the cushions behind her as her body ignited. "I need more, Alex." She was begging, and it should have told her how far gone she was, but the way he touched her, knowing just the right amount of pressure to apply was making her body hum.

"That's it, baby." Alex whispered. "You're so wet. So tight."

If his husky voice was anything to go by, he was right there with her, wanting more, needing everything.

"I want to be inside you when you come." He told her, pulling the vibrator from her clit. "Stand up."

The insistence and hunger in his tone had her jumping, trying to do what he wanted because she knew it was the only way to assuage the ache that was building to astounding levels. He didn't disappoint because as soon as she stood, he sat down, the long, hard length of him ready and waiting.

"Sit on my cock, Ashleigh." He was no longer suggesting, he was demanding, and she was right there with him. When she started to straddle him, he stopped her with one hand on her though. "Turn around the other way."

Her mind attempted to understand what he was telling her, but she did as she was told, turning to face away from him. When his hands gripped her hips, pulling her down onto his lap, she realized what it was he wanted. Reverse cowgirl, she'd heard the position called.

Biting her bottom lip, Ashleigh cried out as he filled her completely, the feeling so wonderful, so familiar, she could barely stop herself from shattering the instant he was lodged deep inside. The angle was different and oh so perfect, his cock raking nerve endings she never knew she had, while he went deeper than she thought possible.

"Damn, baby." He groaned the words, digging his fingers into her hip as she eased onto him, slowly moving forward and back. "Take the vibrator. Put it on your clit."

Ashleigh's brain was fuzzy, but she managed to do as he instructed, taking the toy and pushing it against her clit as he lifted her hips with his hands, his biceps flexing and bunching as he held her weight before thrusting hard and fast into her.

"Oh, God!" She screamed, the vibrator slipping before she righted it and once again pressed against the bundle of nerves throbbing, moments away from an orgasm that would likely shake her to her very core.

"So fucking beautiful." He moaned. "Come for me, Ashleigh. Come around my cock, baby."

Ashleigh's thigh muscles screamed as she tried to lift and lower herself onto him, forcing him deeper, but she couldn't seem to move fast enough. Finally, he held her hips, forcing her to remain still as he pounded into her over and over until she couldn't hold back. The rush started between her thighs, a flame igniting in her womb before the spasms started and she was coming. "Oh, God! Yes! Alex!"

"That's it, baby. Ashleigh. Fuck!" Alex roared, and she felt him pulse and throb inside her as his orgasm took him, setting off another breathtaking explosion that left her weak and crumbling on top of him.

Good grief. She was pretty sure it didn't get better than that.

Chapter Twenty Four
*** ~ *** ~ *** ~ ***

"Congratulations!" Ashleigh squealed when Nate finally broke loose from the hordes of people demanding his attention.

Standing in Pops' living room, Ashleigh had been talking to Logan and Sam, everyone waiting anxiously for the graduate to arrive.

The ceremony had gone off without a hitch, and now her nephew was officially on his way to bigger and better things. To everyone's dismay, he hadn't revealed what his intentions were, but Ashleigh was just happy for him. Whatever his plans were, she didn't care, as long as he was doing what he wanted to do.

"Thanks, Aunt Ash." Nate said, putting his arms around her for a quick hug. "I'm just glad it's over. That was the most boring thing I've ever had to do."

That she doubted, but for an eighteen year old, she could only imagine.

"So, how does it feel to be finally finished with high school?" She asked, staring back at the handsome man she loved more than words could say.

"It's about damn time." He said gruffly, laughing. "I didn't think it would ever end, and to say that I'll miss it would be a lie."

"No, I wouldn't think you would." Ashleigh remembered her high school graduation and her need for independence, anxious to get on with the rest of her life. As an adult, she could look back on that time and wonder why she'd been so ready for it to be over, but at the time, it couldn't have gotten there fast enough.

"Have you seen Alex?" Nate asked, glancing around the room.

"He'll be here in a few minutes. He had to run an errand before he stopped by." Ashleigh told him, wanting to ask Nate why he was looking for him.

"Don't tell Dad, but I'm talking to Alex about a job." Nate whispered secretively.

"A job?" That was news to her, but he already knew that. He hadn't shared his intentions with anyone, no matter how many times they had all tried to get it out of him.

"Yeah." Nate looked down at her in all seriousness. "I met with Sam earlier in the week, and now I want to talk to Alex before I talk to Dad."

"You know I have to pry." Ashleigh smiled. "What are your plans?"

"I'm hoping to become a project manager like Sam." He told her, never breaking her gaze. "I've contemplated it for a long time, and she's been nice enough to talk to me a few times. Last week, I met with her again, and I'm convinced it's what I want to do."

"What about college?" Ashleigh asked, knowing Sam hadn't gotten where she was without it.

"Oh, I plan to go to college. I'm just hoping to work at the same time. Get some experience as I continue my education. Four years of school isn't all that exciting if you ask me, but if I have something to work toward, it might make it easier."

Holy crap. When had her nephew grown up so fast? She remembered the little rambunctious boy who ran around, pulling her hair, hiding behind chairs and making her laugh at every turn. Here before her was a grown man, his ambitions as clear as his brilliant golden eyes.

"Well, I think that's a good plan." She told him, touching his arm and squeezing gently. "I'm proud of you, Nate." Ashleigh felt the tears prick her eyes.

He didn't respond, just smiled back at her.

"Where's that young man I saw you talking to earlier?" Ashleigh asked, turning her attention to the others in the room to keep from sobbing like a baby. Her nephew didn't want her to get all emotional. It would likely cramp his style.

"Jake?" Nate asked with a hint of interest in his tone. "He had to go take care of something."

Ashleigh heard the disappointment, and she wondered for a brief moment what their relationship was. Not that she would ask because quite frankly it was none of her business. But hope sprung up like a spring flower. For the last few months, Nate had come into his own, and she was so proud of him. Both for graduating high school and becoming the man he is.

Having a nephew who was so strong, so true to himself was refreshing. Especially considering the hardships he would likely have to endure for the rest of his life. Ashleigh couldn't imagine that being openly gay was easy, but he was a confident, self-assured young man and her pride swelled up just looking at him.

"Well, if I see Alex, I'll let him know you're looking for him." Ashleigh told Nate. "Now, go talk to the others before they start hounding me about monopolizing your time." Reaching for him, Ashleigh gave him another hug before whispering in his ear. "I'm so proud of you, kiddo. So very proud."

When he pulled back, Ashleigh saw his own tears welling up, and she turned away quickly. He knew what she was referring to, the same as he knew she would always stand behind him. Whatever he chose to do, that boy was going to go far.

"Baby girl, come here." Pops called out to her when Ashleigh turned to go into the vast kitchen of her grandfather's massive home.

"Hey, Pops." She greeted, giving him a hug and a quick kiss on the cheek. "What's up?"

"Nothing, besides my favorite granddaughter doesn't seem to have enough time to come visit her old grandpa these days." Xavier said good-naturedly.

"What are you talking about?" Ashleigh laughed. "I stop by at least once a week."

"Like I said, not nearly enough." He grinned. "Where's Alex?"

Ashleigh tried to read her grandfather's expression, but couldn't tell what he might be up to. He was the second person who had asked her where Alex was and if she wasn't mistaken, her family had come to realize that the two of them had become nearly inseparable.

"He'll be here shortly." She told him. "Why? What's up? You aren't going to talk about work, are you?" She teased.

"Don't I always?" Xavier said with a smile.

"Of course you do. If you didn't, we'd think something was wrong."

Xavier chuckled, but then his eyes turned serious. "Have you seen your brother?"

Ashleigh hadn't seen Dylan since the graduation ceremony. She expected him to show up at any time, but they hadn't had a chance to talk, so she wasn't sure. "No, I haven't."

"Well, if you see him, tell him that I'm looking for him." Xavier glanced behind Ashleigh, smiled. "And don't run off without saying goodbye. I've got something I want to tell you."

Ashleigh glanced behind her to see Veronica Sellers, Xavier's exotically beautiful administrative assistant, as well as Sierra's mother, walking their way. If she wasn't mistaken, the woman was glowing.

"Hi." Veronica greeted Ashleigh when she came closer, keeping a couple of feet between herself and Xavier.

Ashleigh grinned. Those two were up to something. "Hi." she returned the greeting and turned back to Pops. "I've got to go talk to a couple of people, but I'll make sure to check in before I leave."

Ashleigh hugged her grandfather again before she left the kitchen. She heard hushed whispers behind her before Pops laughed again and she had the sneaking suspicion that they were about to get some really good news.

A half hour later, Ashleigh was wandering through the house until she caught a glimpse of her brother standing on the veranda. Before anyone could stop and talk to her, she snuck out the door and joined Dylan standing by the railing.

The skies were gray, lined with black clouds rolling in from afar, a few flares of lightening off in the distance. An early summer storm rolling in on the horizon.

"Hey." He greeted in that intense drawl he had.

"Hey, old man." Something was bothering him, she could tell, and she was pretty sure it wasn't the weather he was worried about. "How does it feel to have both kids now out of high school?"

Dylan turned to look at her and Ashleigh noticed the harsh lines bracketing his mouth and the dark circles beneath his eyes. Her heart cracked a little, knowing exactly what he was thinking about.

"She would have wanted to be here." Dylan said quietly.

Ashleigh touched her brother's arm, moved in a little closer and leaned against him. "I have a feeling she was."

"Yeah?" He didn't sound convinced, but he didn't say another word.

"Meghan's been with those kids every single day since the day she died, Dylan. She'll always be with them. And you."

"Maybe that's why it's so hard to let go." He stated, but there wasn't an ounce of humor in the words.

Ashleigh squeezed his arm. "You love her. Plain and simple." Turning to face him, she waited until he looked at her. "Dylan, it's alright for you to move on. Meghan would want you to be happy. You were the love of her life, and you gave her those two miracles. Just because she's gone, doesn't mean you have to merely exist in this life. It's not fair to you and it's not fair to her memory."

Dylan's mouth hardened even more, and Ashleigh knew he was going to argue with her. She put her hand up to stop him. "I would never tell you how to feel. I couldn't imagine what you've been through, and I won't pretend to. But I can tell you that you're missing out on so much by letting her memory haunt you like this. You'll never forget her, no one would ever want that, but you've got to see what you're doing to yourself and to your kids. Think about it, Dylan."

"That's the problem, Ash." Dylan said, his voice husky with emotion. "I think about it all the time. And I'm ready to move on which I think is part of the problem. I'm scared I'll forget her."

"You will never forget the love of your life. She was your soul mate. That will never change, even if you meet someone new, fall in love, Meghan will always be in your heart."

Dylan laughed, without mirth. "I can assure you, I'll never fall in love again."

Ashleigh wasn't about to argue with him. She begged to differ, but again, she'd never been in his shoes. She couldn't imagine life without Alex in it, and she was pretty sure if he was tragically taken away from her, she'd never fall in love again, so Dylan might be on to something.

The door behind them clicked as it opened and Ashleigh turned to see who it was. There behind them was a tiny, petite woman that rivaled Sierra in height. Her curly blond hair bobbed sweetly in the breeze, and Ashleigh didn't miss the way she eyed Dylan.

"Sara?" Dylan called out to her, his voice sounding different than only moments before, causing Ashleigh to turn and look at him.

So, maybe this woman was the reason for all of his internal turmoil. The way Dylan was looking at this waif of a woman was laced with heat and longing, something she feared she'd never see in his eyes again.

"This is my sister, Ashleigh." He introduced them. "Ashleigh, meet Sara Fulton."

Ashleigh held out her hand to shake the other woman's, noting the delicate hand that met hers. The warmth in Sara's navy blue eyes was unmistakable, making Ashleigh like her immediately.

"Nice to meet you." Sara said, her voice whisper soft. "I'm Jake's aunt."

Jake? Oh. Ashleigh could only assume she meant Jake, the man Nate was talking to earlier.

"Jake's one of the sales reps I recently hired." Dylan offered, and Ashleigh suddenly felt like an intruder. Turning to her brother once again, she smiled because the storm clouds in his chocolate brown eyes had dissipated. At least momentarily.

"Nice to meet you, too. I'd better get back inside," Ashleigh told them. "Oh, and Pops said to let you know he's looking for you."

Dylan nodded, but didn't say a word as his eyes seemed locked on Sara's. Without another word, Ashleigh snuck away, leaving the two of them alone.

Maybe the sun would come out after all.

~~*~~

Alex walked through the front doors of Xavier's grand estate, glancing quickly from person to person, looking for Ashleigh. He was late, he knew, and that was his fault.

Or rather Jessie's.

She had called him just after they walked out of Nate's graduation ceremony, and he'd ignorantly answered the call. As much as he wanted to ignore her, he hadn't been able to. During the short drive to her house, he'd wanted to kick himself in the ass for leaving Ashleigh, but by then it had been too late.

When he told her he needed to take care of something, he'd seen the concern in her eyes. And the worry. But she didn't ask any questions so he'd taken the easy way out.

Thankfully Jessie had just wanted to talk. Jeff wasn't at the house, and when he'd walked in, he'd been pleasantly surprised to find the house clean for a change.

When Jessie mentioned that she was going to start going back to her AA meetings, he'd been happy to see a turn for the better with her. For the first time in months, he actually thought he saw a glimpse of hope in her eyes, and he wanted to support her. Unfortunately, he'd done it at Ashleigh's expense, and that was bothering him more than he was willing to admit.

Why did he keep doing this to himself? He owed nothing to Jessie, yet he found himself going to check on her when she needed him. Not to mention, he continued to pay for everything she had, despite the fact that she didn't seem grateful in the least.

During their brief conversation, Alex had mentioned Ashleigh and alluded to the fact that what he felt for her was serious. Although Jessie seemed to take the news in stride, he wasn't so sure she was handling it as well as he'd given her credit for.

Only time would tell, though. And since he'd finally settled into the idea of being with Ashleigh, he wasn't as worried about what Jessie thought or even what she needed from him. He'd decided on the quick drive to Xavier's that it was time to let Ashleigh know his true feelings.

Now as he searched through the crowd, trying to find her, he felt his heart swell. That tended to happen just from the thought of seeing her, and being in her presence normally left him feeling elated. Something he wasn't used to feeling, because, in all honesty, he hadn't had a relationship thrive the way theirs was. He only hoped she felt the same because it was time they take things to the next level.

"Alex!" A deep, booming voice called out from across the room, and Alex turned to see Nate Thomas coming his way.

"Congratulations, man." He told Dylan's son when he approached, holding out his hand.

Nate clasped his hand with a firm grip before returning his hands to his pockets. "Thanks. Glad you could make it."

"Wouldn't have missed it." Alex admitted.

"Look," Nate began, looking a little intimidated but a strong sense of determination in his steely blue eyes.

That must've been a family trait because he'd seen the same look in both Dylan and Ashleigh's eyes from time to time.

"I'd like to come talk to you sometime this week if you don't mind."

"Sure, what's up?" Alex asked, trying to get a read on the kid.

"I'd like to talk to you about a job." Nate said quickly. "I'm not looking for a hand out, but I'd like to get your feel on what I might be able to contribute to CISS. I'm starting school in the fall, and I've talked to Sam a few times, and I've decided what I'd like to do."

Alex listened as Nate rushed through his spiel quickly, nervously. "I'd be happy to talk to you, Nate."

The idea of Nate Thomas working for CISS thrilled him. If the young man had half the determination and strong will as his father, Alex would definitely benefit from having him onboard. "Let's meet on Tuesday, at my office. That work for you?"

"It does." Nate's eyes lit up, and he thrust his hand out once again. "Thanks, Alex."

"Sure thing. Have you seen Ashleigh?" He asked when he realized Nate had nothing more to say.

"She was wandering around here earlier. I thought I saw her outside talking to my dad a few minutes ago."

Alex patted Nate on the back as he turned to walk away.

"Congrats again, Nate."

With a smile, Ashleigh's nephew turned and walked away.

"Hey." That sweet, familiar voice sounded from behind him, causing Alex to turn.

"Hey, beautiful." Ashleigh looked stunning in a frilly sundress, something he never imagined her wearing, but suddenly wished she'd do it more often.

"Everything ok?" She asked, that worried look haunting her eyes again.

"It will be." He told her, pulling her to him and kissing her softly on the mouth.

He was overcome with a sudden, intense need to take her to one of those empty guest bedrooms and have his wicked way with her. Leaning down until his lips brushed the soft curve of her ear, Alex whispered, "Can you sneak away for a few minutes?"

When she pulled back, he realized the worry was now replaced with a firestorm of intensity in the amber depths of her gaze.

"I think that can be arranged." She said, taking his hand and leading him toward the back staircase.

Once upstairs, Ashleigh pulled him down the hallway, toward one wing of the house that had been hers alone when she was growing up. When they reached the end of the hall, she opened the closed door before sneaking them both inside like she expected someone to find them at any moment. He wondered for a brief moment when this had turned into her idea.

When the door shut behind her, she flicked the lock, assuring them some privacy.

Her old bedroom looked just the way he'd remembered. Although he'd only seen it once or twice, and never when she was around, Alex had been fascinated with it. For such a tomboy, Ashleigh's bedroom was the complete contradiction of her outward appearance.

Pink, that's what it was. From the walls, to the rug covering the hardwood floor, to the comforter and endless supply of throw pillows. Everything in the room was pink and girly, and spoke volumes about the girly girl he'd come to know.

Remembering why he'd snuck away with her in the first place, Alex pulled her flush against him, pressing his now rock hard cock between her legs, letting her feel exactly what she did to him.

"Damn, I've missed you." He groaned as she began to grind her hips against his.

"Not as much as I've missed you." She said, her voice husky with need.

"I hope you aren't wearing anything beneath that dress." He groaned as he eased the silky fabric up her legs.

"I'm not." She smiled seductively. "Just for you."

"Ashleigh." He exhaled her name on a groan so intense, he worried others might hear them. "I need to be inside of you. Right now."

"What are you waiting for?" Her response was punctuated when she placed her lips on his neck, nipping lightly and licking away the stinging pleasure.

Turning her so that she was backed against the wall, away from the door, Alex lifted her dress to her waist, noticing that she hadn't been lying. She didn't have a stitch on underneath and the smooth skin at the apex of her thighs begged for his touch. Separating the soft, swollen lips, he found her wet and ready for him.

He had to let her go so he could undo the button and ease down the zipper of his slacks before freeing his throbbing cock. She had him so fucking hard, even the slightest graze from his own hand was nearly too much.

"Come here." He demanded, pulling her to him. "Hold your dress up."

With his slacks below his hips, he lifted her until she wrapped her sexy long legs around his waist, and threw her arms around his neck. There was no time for foreplay, nor did they need it. They were in tune to one another, and they both knew what the other needed, what the other desired, so they bypassed the small talk. Alex used the wall for stability, pressing her back against it before easing one hand between them so he could guide his cock into her velvety soft pussy.

Her body sheathed him like a glove, pulling him in deeper as her internal muscles clamped down on him. "Fuck. Do you even know what you do to me?" He asked, throwing out the first thing that came to his mind.

"Tell me." She whispered as she began to grip him tighter with her arms and her legs.

"I walk around with a hard on every time I think about you. Knowing your pussy is begging for my cock, makes me fucking crazy."

"Fuck me, Alex." Ashleigh bit out, her fingernails biting into his shoulders. "Fuck me hard."

Alex didn't deny her; he rammed his cock into her pussy, his hips thrusting him deeper until they were both panting with the sheer pleasure of his cock gliding through the silky warmth of her body.

"It feels so good." Ashleigh's words spurred him on, his hips pistoning at a frantic pace, the overwhelming need billowing around them, consuming his senses. He never wanted it to end, the feeling of being lodged inside of her, filling her luscious body while she ground her hips against his, trying to take him even deeper than was possible.

"Harder." She nearly screamed the command, her head pushing against the wall as she fought the same explosive urge to let go as he did.

Alex tilted her hips, pushing her into the wall as he slammed into her, slowing his movements as his cock tunneled in and out of the silken vice gripping him to the point of near pain.

"Come for me, Ashleigh. Let go and come on my cock, baby."

Ashleigh's body tightened around his cock as he continued to pummel her over and over, his legs straining as he fought to keep from coming. It was too intense, the feelings more than he could take as his body ignited, flames licking his balls as the sharp, tingling sensation started at the base of his spine.

"Fucking come for me." He groaned, using one hand to grip her hair because he knew she liked his rough side and she didn't disappoint, her pussy clamped down on his cock as she came with a muffled scream, her fingers scoring his skin through the shirt he still wore.

Alex let go, his orgasm ripping through him, his cock buried to the hilt in her body's sweet grasp as he came, filling her with his seed. For a brief moment, an image of Ashleigh round with his child flittered through his mind, and he couldn't hide the grin.

If he hadn't known it by then, he knew it now.

This woman owned him. All of him.

The rest of the evening was spent laughing, talking and ribbing the McCoy brothers who had shown up. By the time they were ready to call it a night, Alex wanted nothing more than to take Ashleigh home and hold her next to him for the better part of eight hours while they slept. He was exhausted.

"You about ready?" He asked when he located Ashleigh standing in the kitchen with Sam and Sierra.

"I am. I just need to find Pops before I go. He said he needed to tell me something."

As though Ashleigh's thought conjured the man up out of thin air, Pops walked into the kitchen with Dylan, Stacey, Nate and Veronica following behind him. Not far behind them were Luke, Logan and Cole. Everyone dispersed throughout the kitchen, turning their attention to Xavier.

"First, I want to thank each and every one of you for coming today. Today has been about my boy, Nate." Xavier said, turning toward his great grandson. "I'm proud of you, son. In more ways than you'll ever know."

Alex felt the emotions that flowed from Xavier's words, the man's pride obvious.

"And as for the rest of you, well, I've got some news to share." Xavier looked almost bashful for a moment, and Alex steeled himself for what was to come.

"I'm a very blessed man, to say the least. I've got my family," he said, glancing at Ashleigh and then Dylan, then to his great grandchildren, "I've got my company and no, it wouldn't be what it is today if it weren't for those of you who run it like it were your own." Xavier's gaze landed on Logan first, then Alex.

"And more importantly, I've had a second chance in life. Something I never expected." Xavier's gaze turned to the woman standing just inches from his side, and Alex didn't need to hear the man's heartfelt declaration to know what he was about to say. The love in his eyes was evident.

"I'm happy to say that Veronica has agreed to marry me and though I'm not sure I've ever done anything to deserve her, I'm selfish enough that I'm going to make her my wife."

Veronica blushed prettily when Xavier pulled her into his arms. Ashleigh, Sierra and Sam all three sighed, almost simultaneously. Alex glanced at Logan who shrugged, his admission that he had no idea. Alex had suspected as much, but neither Veronica nor Xavier ever gave the impression that they were more than business associates.

"Welcome to the family, Veronica." Dylan stated. "If you can put up with him, you're welcome to him."

The room erupted in laughter and then a round of congratulations before the conversations commenced. Alex just looked around, baffled at how much of a family they'd all become over the years.

Looking at Ashleigh, his heart swelled yet again.

He wouldn't do it now, but he promised himself that very soon, he'd show Ashleigh exactly what she meant to him and how he hoped to make her his family permanently.

Chapter Twenty Five
*** ~~ *** ~~ *** ~~ ***

Alex wasn't all that happy about having to drive to Austin yet again, but the opportunity was too great to pass up. This time he'd opted to go by himself, not wanting to subject Cole to yet another meeting that may result in nothing more than an agreement to think about it.

That's what Alex had been dealing with the last two times he'd visited the Walker ranch. He knew the time would come when Travis Walker would make the final decision to move forward with his plans, but as of yet, the man hadn't done it. Alex hoped that was all about to change.

Travis had called the night before, insisting he was ready to make a final decision and Alex figured it was worth at least one more shot. After all the work Cole had put into it, he couldn't just tell the man no. Not to mention, that was just bad for business.

Since Travis Walker was in the early stages of building a resort the likes of which hadn't been seen in the rural town he lived in just outside of Austin, Alex knew it was going to be well worth the investment. Not that CISS generally took part in startup companies, but after he'd met the Walker brothers and saw what they'd done with the company they already owned – Walker Demolition – Alex had been interested from the start.

Since Alex would be infusing CISS into the mix, it made it well worth his time in the long run.

Just north of Austin, Alex followed the 130 toll road on-ramp and dialed Travis' number, letting him know he was only about fifteen minutes out. They were meeting at the ranch so Travis could show him the plans for the resort.

This wasn't going to be just any resort either. The Walker brothers had a dream, and after having met all seven of the brothers in the last few months, Alex didn't doubt they could pull it off. That was if they could secure the land to do so.

Fifteen minutes later, Alex was driving down the dirt road of the Walker ranch, pulling up next to the large metal building that housed the offices of Walker Demolition.

Once outside of his truck, he was immediately greeted by Travis and two of his brothers – Kaleb and Sawyer.

"Thanks for coming." Travis Walker was a business man and based on what Alex had picked up, he did little else.

As for the other brothers, well, Alex knew they were a rowdy bunch, to say the least. But, considering they'd taken a small demolition company and turned it into a thriving business, Alex figured they knew what they were doing.

"Not a problem." Alex replied shaking the proffered hands before following the three men inside the building. "Is it safe to say you've acquired the land you were looking at buying?" Alex asked, hoping like hell they were going to say yes because if they didn't, this wasn't going to be a very long meeting after all.

"Not quite." Kaleb stated, taking a seat at one of the desks in the small office.

Shit.

"I don't have any doubts that we'll get the land." Travis injected, glaring at Kaleb who didn't seem the least bit worried about his brother's irritation.

"So why am I here?" Alex asked, suddenly confused.

"I wanted to show you the final plans for the resort." Travis stated, picking up a cylinder that had been lying on one of the empty desks. "I wanted your input."

Input? Alex wasn't quite sure what sort of input he could offer, but he kept his expression neutral.

"As you know, this isn't going to be the typical resort, and we're worried about security. That's where you come in." Sawyer added, and Alex suddenly realized what they were getting at. With a smile, he took a seat in one of the empty chairs, offering the brothers his full attention.

Two hours later, Alex was once again on the road. He'd already called Dylan and Cole, giving them a high level of the discussion he'd just had with the Walker's. Needless to say, they were both onboard, and Cole was going to talk to Luke and Logan.

After hearing the spiel, Alex knew this opportunity was right up their alley, and he wanted to see what their interest would be, if any. He got the feeling, the McCoy's would be right onboard with this type of venue, but he would have to wait until they called back.

Just outside of Waco, that call came in.

"What the hell goes on down there in Austin, anyway?" Logan asked when Alex answered the phone.

"Based on my morning, a little bit of everything." Alex laughed. "Right up your alley, man."

"Sounds like it." Logan agreed. "And they're looking for investors?"

"Yep. I think they could use a little help in the startup as well, which is where you and Luke come in. I won't lie, my mind is warped, but I think you and Luke take the cake on this one."

Alex spent the next twenty minutes filling Logan in on what the Walker's vision was and before he disconnected the call, Alex offered up Travis Walker's phone number. He'd let Logan and Luke deal with that side of things. He was only interested in the investment, and what they needed by way of security.

From his perspective, this might just be the business venture they were all looking for even if none of them had been looking in the first place. It would take some time, but Alex figured that the Walker's would have the place up and running in the next two years if their determination was anything to go by.

When Alex's phone rang again, he quickly answered, fully expecting either Luke or Cole to be calling him back. Instead, he was pleasantly surprised when Ashleigh's husky voice filled his truck's speakers.

"How'd your meeting go?" She asked sweetly after they greeted one another.

"Better than I expected." He responded. "Looks like we just might be getting close to a deal."

"Well, at least it wasn't a wasted trip."

No, it definitely wasn't wasted. At least Alex hoped not.

"What're you doing?" Alex had planned to head straight for Ashleigh's when he got back, hoping to make it in time to take her to dinner. There were a few things he wanted to discuss with her and now seemed like the appropriate time to do it.

"Sitting here, waiting for you."

Alex heard the smile in her voice.

"What are you wearing while you wait for me?"

"What if I told you I wasn't wearing anything?"

Ok, now this conversation was definitely going to be the highlight of his day. Could it be possible that his amazing girlfriend was interested in a little phone sex? That was one thing Alex had never done before.

"I'd say you need to take the phone into the bedroom with you."

"The bedroom?"

Alex laughed. He knew Ashleigh's aversion to having sex in the bed, but that was only because she insisted that's where he had insisted on being for the first few weeks of their relationship. Since that time, he'd like to think he'd proven himself to her.

"Yes." He confirmed. "Take the phone in the bedroom and I want you to lay on the bed. And Ashleigh?"

"Yes?" She sounded breathless.

"I want you to be naked."

"I am."

Regardless whether she was, he knew she would be in just a few seconds. There was some rustling on the phone and he waited patiently, keeping his eyes on the road and his hands on the steering wheel. Though his cock was begging for attention, Alex wasn't about to pull it out on the highway.

No, he'd settle for making Ashleigh come and then he'd hurry his ass back to her place so he could finish the job.

"What are you doing now?" He asked when she wasn't saying anything.

"I'm just getting on the bed."

"Wait." Alex had an idea. "Before you get on the bed, look in the nightstand on my side of the bed and pull out the black plastic bag that's in there. Don't open it."

He couldn't help but laugh when Ashleigh sighed in frustration. This was going to be fun.

Another minute passed by before Ashleigh finally spoke. "Ok, I'm on the bed, and I have the bag beside me. Now what?"

Ahhh... So that's how this was going to go. Alex could definitely be the director in this little play. Too bad he wasn't there to watch it in person.

"Are you lying down?"

"Yes."

"I want you to put the phone on speaker and so you can play with your tits." Damn, his cock was going to be as hard as fucking granite by the time this was over.

There was no sound on the other end, but Alex assumed she was doing as he told her.

"Tell me how it feels." He instructed.

"Not as good as when you do it." Ashleigh admitted, making him smile again.

"No? And how does it feel when I play with you?"

"So good." She said, but Alex picked up a little tremor in her tone.

"Are you touching your pussy?" He hadn't told her to, but the thought of her doing it was almost too much to bear.

"Maybe."

"Open the bag beside you and pull out the blue toy. And the lube."

Alex heard the plastic bag rattle near the phone, and he waited for her to say something.

"What is it with you and blue toys?" She laughed.

"Take some of the lube," Alex began, realizing it was getting hot as hell inside his truck, "and coat the toy.

"Lube?" She asked, but he knew she wasn't expecting an answer if she were looking in the bag.

"Damn I wish I was there with you." He told her.

"Where are you?"

"Just outside of Hillsboro." Actually, that was a lie. He'd made good time, and he was about fifteen minutes away from her house, but there was no reason to tell her that. If he timed it right, he'd be there just in time.

"You want me to stroke the toy?" She asked, again sounding breathless.

"Yes. Stroke it. Just like it were my dick. Do you like stroking me, baby?"

Holy shit. Alex wasn't sure who was going to get more pleasure out of this – him or her. Either way, he was about to find out.

~~*~~

Ashleigh couldn't believe she was doing this. Phone sex? Really?

Granted, she might have considered it when she called him, but she hadn't figured it would actually happen.

And no, when she told him she was naked, she hadn't been, but she certainly was now. It definitely hadn't taken long to rid herself of the shorts and t-shirt she'd put on before going outside that afternoon. And now she was stroking the silicone toy, her eyes closed, pretending it was Alex's beautiful cock.

"Do you, Ashleigh?" Alex's voice sounded from the phone lying on the pillow beside her. She'd put it on speaker so she would have the use of both of her hands.

Feeling a little bold, probably because he couldn't actually see her, Ashleigh opened her eyes and stared at the blue silicone cock. "Yes, I love to stroke your thick cock. Almost as much as I enjoy putting it in my mouth."

His groan had a shiver running over her skin, her nipples puckering.

"God, baby. I love when you suck my cock. Your mouth is perfection, and when you do that thing with your tongue... fuck!"

Ashleigh grinned, continuing to stroke the toy, waiting for his instruction.

"I want you to take the toy and put it in your pussy. Pretend it's my cock filling you."

Without hesitation, Ashleigh took the dildo and circled her opening, coating it with the slippery lube before sliding just the tip inside. "Ohhhh."

"Talk to me, Ashleigh. Tell me what you're doing, baby."

"I've got the toy in my pussy. It's so big." She moaned.

"Are you fucking yourself with it?"

"Yes." She hadn't intended to, but once she had inserted it into her vagina, she'd been overwhelmed by the intensity of what they were doing.

Phone sex.

Ashleigh still couldn't believe it.

"If I were there, I'd bury my cock in your ass and fuck your pussy with that toy."

Ashleigh heard the heat in Alex's tone, and she knew he was just as affected by it as she was and he couldn't see a thing.

"God, yes." She groaned, imagining what it would feel like to be filled completely by him and the toy at the same time. "I wish you were here."

"Take some of the lube and coat your fingers with it." Alex told her, and Ashleigh stilled her hand, reaching for the lube as he said.

She held the dildo inside of her by closing her legs, while she quickly squeezed some of the cool gel onto her fingers then waited with baited breath for him to tell her what to do next.

"I want you to ream your ass with your fingers while you fuck your pussy with the toy."

Ashleigh's breath lodged in her chest. Could she actually do that? It felt good when Alex played with her ass, teasing her with his tongue or his fingers and sometimes his cock, but she'd never imagined touching herself like that.

"Are you doing it?" He asked.

She wasn't, but before she answered, she eased her hand between her legs, reaching down to that forbidden hole, coating it with the lube. "Yes."

"Damn that's fucking hot." He groaned. "You make me want to pull out my cock and jack off right here in my truck."

Ashleigh could picture that in her mind as well. She remembered the one time he had jacked off for her when she asked. They'd been sitting in the living room, making out like teenagers, and the idea of watching him bring himself to orgasm had been overwhelming. When he had done it, Ashleigh had been so hot, she'd damn near come just from the sight alone.

"Are you fucking your pussy?" Alex asked.

"Yes." She had begun to work the dildo in and out of her pussy, trying to pretend it was him, but it wasn't the same.

"Turn over." Alex instructed and once again she stopped moving.

"On my stomach?" She thought that's what he wanted, but she had to make sure.

"Yes. On your stomach, but don't take the toy out of your pussy. I want you to move to the edge of the bed, on your hands and knees and continue to fuck your pussy. Then close your eyes and pretend I'm there, ramming my rock hard cock in your ass."

Ashleigh moaned. She might just come from his words alone. She took her time turning over, getting into the position he had told her, keeping the dildo buried in her pussy. "Alex."

"What, baby?"

Ashleigh must've made the phone move because his voice sounded different.

"I need more." She told him as she began to gently thrust the fake cock in deeper.

"How much more?" His voice startled her because he was no longer on the phone, he was right there with her. Had she not been so engrossed in what she was doing, she might've been startled, but having him there was exactly what she needed.

"Damn that's so fucking hot." His hands gripped her hips, and she felt the bed move as he put one knee on it behind her. He must've found the lube because his fingers were cool and slick as he teased her anus.

"Fuck me, Alex. Please fuck me now." Ashleigh was so far out of her mind with lust, all from having him talk dirty to her on the phone, she just needed to come.

He didn't say another word, but Alex did exactly as she suggested. Without using brute force, he eased his cock inside her ass, making her grit her teeth. Although they'd done it on multiple occasions, there was still that initial bite of pain. With the dildo still lodged in her pussy, Ashleigh felt the pressure when he moved in deeper.

"Fuck yourself, Ashleigh. Let me feel what it's like to have a cock in your pussy while I'm fucking your ass."

She could hear the restraint in his voice, and she knew this wasn't going to last long. With her chest down on the bed, her hands between her legs, she managed to move the toy in and out, trying for a steady rhythm, but her brain wasn't keeping up. She just wanted to feel.

When Alex retrieved the toy from her hands, she felt a measure of relief. And then there was the glorious friction from both Alex lodged deep in her ass and the toy buried to the hilt in her cunt. Instead of waiting for him to move, Ashleigh began thrusting back into him as he groaned in response.

"That's it, baby. Fuck me." He groaned, pushing in deep when she reared back, thrusting the dildo inside of her when he retreated. Before long they had developed a rhythm, and although awkward, it was incredibly stimulating and her body was reacting to the feel of two cocks buried inside of her.

"Yes!" She screamed when he began ramming her harder, the dildo pushing deeper. "Harder, Alex. Fuck me harder!"

Grabbing the dildo from him, she began fucking herself, rapidly thrusting the toy inside her pussy as Alex gripped her hips, fucking her until they were both groaning.

"Oh, God, baby. Fuck." Alex cried out. "I'm going to come."

With that, Ashleigh's orgasm ruptured, exploding as she tried to hold onto the toy. Then Alex stilled behind her, and she felt the heat of his release as he filled her.

Just before she drifted off from complete and total exhaustion, Ashleigh wondered why in the hell she had ever worried that their sex life might become stale.

Chapter Twenty Six
*** ~~ *** ~~ *** ~~ ***

"Alex." The trembling voice on the other end of the phone stopped him in his tracks. Alex hadn't wanted to answer, knew what he was walking into the second he did.

"Jessie?" He didn't need to ask, he knew exactly who it was because she had called him twice that morning when he'd been driving down to Austin and he'd ignored the calls. Maybe it was the fact that the last conversation he had with Jessie had gone fairly well, but this time he had a hunch it was not going to go as well.

Sitting at the table, staring across at the empty chair, waiting for Ashleigh to return from the restroom, Alex knew he should have ignored this one too. "What's wrong?"

"He's going to kill me." She whispered, as though she were trying to hide from someone.

Instinct told him she wasn't playing him. At least not at the moment. "Where are you?"

"At home." He barely heard her. "Please help me."

Alex caught sight of Ashleigh from across the room, and their eyes met. She must've seen the concern in his gaze because she hurried her movements until she was standing beside the table.

"What's wrong?" She asked, not bothering to sit down.

"I'll be there in a minute, Jessie. Stay right where you are." He ordered before disconnecting the call. The look in Ashleigh's eyes made him cringe.

"Where is she?" Surprising him with her question, he stood from his seat, tossing a fifty on the table to cover the bill before taking her hand and walking through the restaurant.

"Talk to me, Alex. What's wrong with her?" Ashleigh demanded, pulling on his arm.

"She said he's going to kill her." He bit his lip, both frustrated at the situation and pissed off at himself for feeling as though he needed to go see for himself.

"Let's go check on her." Ashleigh said the words and Alex stopped short.

Looking down at her in utter disbelief, he waited for her to continue.

"You heard me. We can't just stand here."

She wanted to go with him? Had she lost her mind? This time she was the one on the move, and he fought to process the situation as he followed her out into the bright Texas sunshine.

"Ashleigh, wait." He said, unsure of what he would say next.

"No. Let's go. Once and for all, we're going to get this woman some help." Ashleigh sounded entirely too confident and just a little pissed off.

He opened the truck door for her, waiting until she climbed in before shutting it. Still stunned, he walked around the truck and climbed in the other side.

"What did she say?" Ashleigh asked as she buckled her seatbelt, staring at him. "Start the truck, Alex."

Her instruction startled him into motion, reminding him where he was and what he was doing. For the next few minutes, they drove in silence, but he knew she was waiting for an answer.

"Ashleigh," he said, glancing at her before turning back to the road, "I don't know what I'm going to walk into. With Jessie, I never know."

She didn't say a word, but he could feel her gaze on him.

"Jessie needs help," he finally said.

"I know." Ashleigh sighed but continued. "I talked to Dylan."

Great. Now his best friend was sharing his secrets. He couldn't imagine what Ashleigh said when Dylan told her that Jessie had pulled Alex's strings for the last ten years, calling on him constantly, sometimes truly needing him, others just wanting to get his attention. He didn't know what she was pulling now, but he knew he couldn't just turn a blind eye to her situation.

For the last two weeks, Jessie had been calling, trying to talk to him, but Alex hadn't been interested in hearing from her. Even after she told him she was going to get on the straight and narrow, he knew she had been drinking again, and he knew that Jeff was coming around.

As much as he wanted to push her out of his life for good, he couldn't sit by while his ex-wife continued to throw her life away.

"What did he tell you?"

Ashleigh flinched, but she turned toward him. "I know she has problems, Alex. I know she calls you at all hours."

That she did. Alex had never tried to hide the calls from Ashleigh when he was with her, but he had wanted to. The thought of losing Ashleigh because Jessie was continuing to use him for whatever reason tore at him.

But, this was who he was. He couldn't change the fact that he didn't want to see Jessie hurt. Until recently, he hadn't realized he wasn't able to help her the way she needed. That had been a hard thing to swallow, but as the days passed, he knew he had to do something or things with Jessie would never change.

"Alex." Her warm hand came down over his, and he briefly glanced down at it. "Let's go see what she needs. We have to get her help. Real help."

He knew what she was saying, but he couldn't get past the "we". His heart swelled, aching with the need to tell her everything he felt for her. The woman was so giving, never asking for anything in return and here he was, dragging her across town to check on his ex-wife, not knowing what they would actually find when they got there.

"Let's just check on her." Ashleigh said, sounding entirely too reasonable. "Then you can decide what the best thing to do for her is."

"Why?" He couldn't hold back his questions anymore. He felt like he were being set up and he was suddenly scared of what might happen. He couldn't lose Ashleigh, but he couldn't turn his back on Jessie. He had to live with the consequences. Either way.

"Why what?" She asked, pulling her hand from his.

"Why do you want to go?"

"Trust me, I don't want to go." She retorted, then took a deep breath, sighed again. "Dylan told me about your relationship with Jessie. Between what he said and what you've told me yourself, I think the woman needs help."

She paused, then looked at him.

"Don't get me wrong, Alex, I'm not willing to be her friend, and I'm not exactly thrilled about sharing you with her, but it's clear you are concerned about her."

He was. But not the way Ashleigh thought. Maybe now was the time to tell Ashleigh the full story.

"My dad died when I was twelve." He said, keeping his hands firmly on the steering wheel. "For two years my mother sat around, depressed and lonely, until one day she met a man. Rick. She started dating him for a little while, and before I knew what happened, Rick was coming to the house. He'd stay the night once in a while, and I didn't ask questions. My mother seemed so happy, and that was the most important thing to me."

Ashleigh reached over, touching his arm and her touch seemed to calm him. Releasing one hand from the steering wheel, he laced his fingers with hers.

"As it turned out, Rick wasn't all that nice. They would argue from time to time, but I tried to stay out of it, unsure what to do or say. Time passed and they kept seeing each other, but their relationship kept getting more and more unstable." That was an understatement. "I was fifteen when he hit her for the first time."

Ashleigh's fingers squeezed his, but she didn't say anything.

"I was bigger by then, not like I am now, but I wasn't the scrawny little boy I had been when he started coming around. Long story short, Rick's anger only continued to escalate and so did mine. I was so pissed at my mother for just sitting back and letting that bastard beat on her." He paused to take a breath. The anger from those memories surged to the forefront.

"I came home from school one day to find him hitting her while she cowered on the floor. The rage set in, and the only thing I remember is pulling him off of her, so fucking pissed that she'd let him do that to her.

"Then he turned his anger on me, but I'd obviously been preparing for that day. Needless to say, by the time the cops showed up, they had to pull me off of him." That was the easy part. "My relationship with my mother was never the same again. She didn't forgive me for that, or for the fact that Rick didn't come back around." Alex hated that part, hated how his mother had put that man before her own son. "I can't stand a man that hits a woman, and maybe I should just back off, leave Jessie to her own devices, but I can't seem to do it."

"You shouldn't." Ashleigh said after a few moments of silence. "I don't fault you for caring, Alex. I just..." She didn't continue, and Alex didn't push her. They were pulling onto Jessie's street, and he just wanted to get through the next few minutes because once they were done here, he had some more things he wanted to tell Ashleigh.

~~*~~

Ashleigh followed Alex up the driveway to the tiny little house. Her own curiosity had her glancing around, taking in the outside appearance. The neighborhood wasn't fancy, but it was well kept, all of the small houses neatly maintained.

With the exception of Jessie's.

The yard was... well, there was no yard, just brown, crispy grass, long since dead.

She returned her gaze forward, following Alex up the two small steps to the porch before he opened the front door and walked right in. He didn't bother knocking.

Ashleigh was still reeling from Alex's story, feeling as though she had been given a glance into his soul. She may not like the way he ran to Jessie's rescue, but she couldn't fault him for it. He was just that type of man, one any woman should be proud to be with. They just didn't make them like Alex anymore.

"Jessie?" Alex called out as they stopped in the living room.

The house was a wreck. Empty bottles everywhere, food containers laying on every flat surface and it reeked to high heaven.

When Alex moved, Ashleigh followed. Jessie hadn't answered when Alex called out to her, and a sudden nervous tension coursed through her. She may not like the woman, though she had never met her, but she hoped nothing was wrong. Well, other than the obvious. The woman had a problem.

Alex pushed open a door at the end of the hall, and Ashleigh stood at his side, unable to see into the room.

"Fuck!" Alex huffed. "Put your goddamn clothes on, Jessie."

Turning away, he grabbed Ashleigh's hand and pulled her alongside him.

"Wait! Alex, please." Jessie called. "I need you. Please!"

Ashleigh pulled away, going back to the door and pushing it open with a rush. Before her was a very naked Jessie, sprawled out on her bed. Well! Apparently the woman needed Alex, but it had nothing to do with life or death.

"Who are you?" Jessie asked, sitting up in the bed, but not trying to cover herself.

Ashleigh stared at the emaciated woman. Jessie had to be in her mid-thirties, based on the math Ashleigh had done in her head, but she looked closer to fifty. Time definitely hadn't been good to the woman. Or maybe it was the drugs and alcohol.

"Get dressed." Ashleigh couldn't believe the anger that had grown to the size of a beach ball in her chest. "Now."

Slamming the door behind her, she walked back to the living room where Alex was standing.

"We should go." He told her when she walked into the room.

They should, she agreed. But that wasn't going to fix this little problem. "Not until you talk to her."

"I don't want to fucking talk to her, Ashleigh. You saw what this is about. I don't have time for this shit."

No one did, Ashleigh knew. "She needs your help."

"I can't fix *that*." Alex said, his green eyes sparkling with fury.

Before Ashleigh could say another word, Jessie joined them, at least moderately decent with an oversized t-shirt and shorts on.

"Sit the fuck down." Alex barked at Jessie.

Looking both pissed and a little remorseful, Jessie did as Alex told her.

"What the hell is wrong with you, Jessie?" His anger was a living, breathing thing and Ashleigh knew he needed to calm down before this situation escalated.

"Nothing." Jessie cooed. "I just wanted to see you."

Ashleigh watched in wide eyed wonder as the woman stared at Alex like he was a lollipop and she was craving sugar. It was almost as though she had no idea Ashleigh was standing right there, although they'd been inadvertently introduced not one minute before.

"Jessie," Alex said, thrusting his hand through his hair, "I can't keep doing this."

He sounded defeated, and Ashleigh felt sorry for him in that moment. Maybe there was more to this situation than she had originally given him credit for. He didn't look any happier about being there than Ashleigh was. But, since they were there, it was time they get some things straight.

"You don't have time for me anymore." Jessie whispered. "I just miss you."

Alex groaned, turning his back on her like he couldn't stand to look at her another second. Ashleigh didn't know what to say, but she was getting more and more uncomfortable with every passing second.

"Does anyone need a drink?" Jessie asked, sounding bubbly and cheerful, the complete opposite of just a few seconds ago. Ashleigh was going to have a headache just trying to keep up with the woman's personality changes.

"Don't you fucking move." Alex stated adamantly, turning back to face Jessie, but then looking over at Ashleigh. "We should go."

Ashleigh couldn't have come up with a better plan, but she knew they had to get this settled, or he would never be at peace. For the last few months, they'd been tiptoeing around the phone calls that went unanswered and now that they were presented with the opportunity to do something to fix it, she wanted to jump on it. If they didn't, she feared this woman, and her destructive need, was going to come between them. Something Ashleigh wasn't willing to let happen.

"Jessie," Ashleigh turned to the woman, suddenly more determined than ever, "what do you need from Alex?"

That surprised Alex as much as it did the woman sitting on the couch.

"What do you mean?" She sounded sincerely confused.

"Why do you keep calling him?" Ashleigh asked, realizing she was totally ill equipped to handle a situation like this.

"Because he loves me." She said, making direct eye contact with Ashleigh.

"He's your friend." Ashleigh confirmed. "But you can't keep doing this to him." *Or yourself.* She kept that last part to herself.

"Doing what?"

"Jessie," Alex interrupted, his patience obviously worn thin. "I don't know how to fix this."

"There's nothing to fix." Jessie said with a huff. "I just want to see you. I want..."

Ashleigh hung on the woman's every word, waiting to hear what it was she wanted. Or rather what she thought she wanted.

"I want you to take me back." Jessie finally said, looking down at her feet. "I need you."

Alex shot her a look, and Ashleigh saw the apology in his eyes.

"Have you been drinking again?" He asked, not moving.

"Yes, I've been drinking." Jessie yelled, standing up immediately. "It's the only thing that makes me feel better."

Ashleigh wasn't sure how this made her feel better. The stench of alcohol and old food filled the air, singeing her nostrils and making her want to vomit. How Jessie could live like this, day in and day out was shocking.

"Do you want to push Alex away?" Ashleigh asked, deciding they were getting nowhere and she felt entirely too awkward being there. She should have never asked to come along because it was obvious there was nothing that she could contribute.

"Are you deaf?" Jessie blurted, turning to face Ashleigh.

"No, I'm not." Ashleigh held her ground. "But I know what you're doing to him. Your frequent phone calls. Have you not noticed he doesn't answer the phone?"

"That's just because you're there. If he was alone, he'd answer my calls. He always does."

Ashleigh wasn't so sure anymore.

"You need to go back to rehab." Alex stated, coming to stand beside Ashleigh, putting his arm around her. The warmth of his body, his apparent need to hold her close was comforting.

"Fuck you." Jessie screamed, turning vicious. "She's turning you against me. The fucking bitch –"

"Don't." Alex's stern tone had Jessie flinching.

Ashleigh put a hand on Alex's arm and took a step closer to Jessie. "He's your friend, you know that, right? He cares about you. Even I know that." She did. "But you're tearing him apart, Jessie. Do you really want to do that to your friend?"

"He's my husband." She argued.

"No." Ashleigh said defensively. "He's not your husband. He was at one time, but not anymore." Taking another step closer, Ashleigh continued. "If you want him to be your friend, you've got to get some help. Like today."

"I don't want him to be my friend. I want him to be my husband." Jessie clenched her hands into fists. "That means you need to leave."

"It's not going to happen." Alex said, inserting himself between the two women. "I love her, Jessie."

Ashleigh's heart seized. *He what?*

"I've always loved her." Alex continued. "I don't want to choose between being your friend, and being with her because I will choose her, Jessie. Do you hear what I'm telling you? There is nothing that you can say or do that will get me to love you that way. I care about you. I'll always care about you, but I can't keep doing this."

Jessie sobbed, the sudden look of sheer disbelief contorting her sickly features. The woman was too thin and based on the state of their surroundings she probably wasn't getting much nourishment. Unless of course the various types of liquor she consumed had enough calories to sustain life.

Alex took a step closer to Jessie, tilting her chin up so she had to look at him. "Go to rehab. For me." He paused. "Please."

Ashleigh watched as Jessie seemed to crumble at his feet, but she never actually moved. Whatever she felt for Alex, whether it was based on true love, or just a deep need to be loved, Jessie was giving in to his plea.

~~*~~

"I'm sorry you had to be here." Alex said as they walked out to his truck. For the last two hours, they'd seen multiple sides of Jessie, ranging from hurt to rage and varying degrees in between.

At least she was going to get the help she needed. The help he never could give her. No matter how many times she'd said she would stop drinking, he knew she needed the professional help he couldn't provide. This would be her second stint in rehab, and thanks to his brief conversation with one of the counselors, he now knew how to help his friend.

"I'm not." Ashleigh told him, leaning into him. "I'm sorry she's sick."

And that's what the counselor had told them. Alcoholism was a disease; one Jessie had no fighting chance of overcoming on her own.

"Do you want me to take you home?" He asked, realizing their day had been thrown so far off course, Alex wasn't sure it would get back on track at that point.

"Sure." She answered, sounding unsure.

And that's what Alex did. He drove Ashleigh home, dropping her off and feeling at a total loss without her with him. Instead of coming in, he stayed in his truck. His emotions were all over the place, and it didn't get past him that he had admitted how he felt about Ashleigh, and she'd never said a word about it.

Chapter Twenty Seven
*** ~~ *** ~~ *** ~~ ***

One week later, Ashleigh found herself going stir crazy. Since the day of Jessie's incident, she hadn't heard from Alex. He'd dropped her off at the house, and because they'd been riddled with emotional churn for the better part of the day, she'd decided to leave him alone for a little while. Now she was beginning to question her decision.

Maybe he hadn't meant what he said after all. And yes, she remembered every last word.

I've always loved her. I don't want to choose between being your friend, and being with her because I will choose her, Jessie.

She couldn't get the conversation out of her head. Why hadn't he said anything? Alex had never given her the impression that what they had between them was anything more than some intense sex and a budding friendship. They had become close over the last few months, and the sex was phenomenal.

After the day he'd picked her up at the bookstore, Ashleigh had had high hopes that he was opening up to her once again. He had even asked her about becoming a member of the club, and she had acquiesced. Grinning on the inside, of course.

And now, as it would appear, he'd withdrawn from her both emotionally and physically. At least that was the impression she got from him.

Granted, she could call him just as easily as he could call her. And she hadn't.

No, she'd been reeling from his admission, wondering how in the hell she hadn't seen it. Or how she hadn't been able to tell him exactly how she felt about him. How she had always felt about him.

Her phone rang, startling her from her thoughts and she launched at it, praying it was Alex.

It wasn't.

"Hey." Ashleigh greeted her brother when she answered the phone.

"How are you?" He asked, sounding a little more cheerful than he had the last time she talked to him.

"Good. You sound happy. What's up?"

Dylan chuckled. "Let's just say this move has been good for me."

That was so good to hear, Ashleigh couldn't help but smile. She wondered exactly what he meant, but she didn't have a chance to ask before he started talking again.

"What did you do to Alex?"

"Ummm... excuse me?" *What she had done?*

"He's moping around this place. I told him if he doesn't stop, I was going to punch him. I guess I now know what it's been like to be around me."

Ashleigh didn't say a word.

"Ash? Is everything alright between you and Alex?"

"I don't know." She answered honestly, surprised by her admission.

"You know how I feel about people interfering, but..." Dylan let the sentence linger as though he were waiting for her to say something.

Ashleigh didn't know what to say. Knowing that Alex wasn't off gallivanting around, ignoring her on purpose gave her hope. Not that she wanted him to be upset, but at least she knew what she needed to do now.

"I need to go." Ashleigh told her brother. "I've got something I need to do. And, hey, thanks."

Dylan laughed, "Not sure what it was I did, but you're welcome."

With that, the line disconnected. Ashleigh didn't hesitate; she dialed Alex's number and waited for him to answer.

"Can you come over?" She blurted out before he had a chance to say anything more than hello.

"Is everything alright?"

Dylan was right, Alex didn't sound like himself.

"We need to talk." She said, trying to sound serious.

"Alright. I've got a meeting this morning, but I'll stop by after lunch. Does that work?"

"Sure." She threw in a little uncertainty, smiling into the phone. "See you then."

Now she just needed to get ready.

~~*~~

Alex suffered through his only meeting of the morning, but had it not been Xavier he was meeting with, he would have cancelled and rushed over to Ashleigh's.

Hope sparked in his chest when she had called; quickly doused when she told him they needed to talk. He wasn't sure what she wanted to talk about, but he had an idea.

It'd been a week since he saw her and the last time was when they had checked Jessie into rehab. After that little ordeal, he figured Ashleigh didn't want to have anything to do with him. And he almost couldn't blame her.

He might not be married to Jessie, he might not have any binding ties to the woman, but he cared about her wellbeing. He didn't figure Ashleigh wanted to deal with that kind of baggage, so he'd left her alone, hoping she'd call him.

He was walking out of XTX when he ran into Logan who was walking in.

"Hey." Logan called out to him. "You too good to say hi these days?"

"Sorry." He mumbled. He was too preoccupied at the moment.

"You're girl called me this morning." Logan grinned, and that got Alex's attention.

"She did?"

"Yeah. She wanted Luke's cell phone number."

What the hell for? He didn't voice the question, but he couldn't stop wondering.

"I gave it to her. She sounded a little out of breath. I figured you were with her."

"Funny." Alex retorted. "I'm heading over there now."

"Guess I'll see you around." Logan said, turning toward the entrance to the building, but suddenly turning back. "Hey, I wanted to ask you something."

"What's up?" Alex wanted nothing more than to run to his truck and haul ass to Ashleigh's to see what she was up to, but he stood firmly in place, staring back at Logan.

"The club's monthly get together is Tuesday. You coming?"

"Doubtful. Why?" He asked.

"Just wondering. Sam's been pushing me to ask. Apparently she thinks it would be good for Ashleigh." Logan laughed. "I've tried to tell her that not all women are as out of control as she is. She doesn't believe me."

Alex did laugh. Logan was right. Sam was out of control. Ashleigh wasn't nearly as reserved as he'd expected her to be, but he wasn't so sure she'd be willing to do some of the more carnal things that Sam was willing to do. Not that he minded in the least. Ashleigh was more than he could handle as she was.

"I'll talk to you later." Alex said and turned toward his truck.

A half hour later, Alex was rapping his knuckles on Ashleigh's front door, his heart beating ninety miles a minute. Having not seen her in a week, he was more than ready to, but he was worried about what she wanted to talk about.

When she answered the door, she smiled at him, and the noose around his heart loosened a little. Damn the woman was beautiful.

"Come in." She told him, turning away and leaving him to close the door behind him. As though it were a conditioned response, he immediately glanced down at her ass, admiring her as she walked away.

"What's going on?" He asked when he walked into the living room.

"I was just thinking we could play a game."

"And what game would that be?" He asked, noticing how the coffee table was pushed out of the way, and the chair was moved closer to the couch. He was tempted to pinch himself to see if he was dreaming because this was the last thing he expected, coming to her house.

"Truth or dare." She grinned before taking a seat on the couch.

He grumbled good-naturedly. Who was he to argue with her if she wanted to play truth or dare? After the last time they'd played, he was open to damn near any game she wanted to play.

"There are some rules." She mentioned, once again grinning from ear to ear.

God he loved when she smiled at him like that. For the last week, he had feared it wouldn't happen ever again. And standing before her now, he felt like he was in an episode of the Twilight Zone, not knowing what was going to happen.

"And those would be?" He asked, taking a seat in the chair across from her, fully expecting her to lay into him for not having called for a week.

"We each get two truths and three dares." She began. "And like always, you have to be honest. It doesn't matter what order you take them in either."

He had expected to be inundated with questions and for the two of them to hash out their differences. Never would he have expected to be trying to come up with the two most important questions that he wanted her to answer for him.

Nodding his head in agreement, he waited for her to start.

"Truth or dare?" Ashleigh asked him, leaning back as though she didn't have a care in the world.

"Dare." He figured that was the easiest at the moment, although the gleam in her eye said he should've picked truth.

"I dare you to take your shirt off."

Well, that was easier than he thought. He untucked his polo shirt, lifting it over his head by gripping the collar behind his neck and gently sitting it on the edge of the chair beside him.

"Your turn." Ashleigh said, her gaze caressing every inch of his chest, making his dick twitch.

"Truth or dare?"

"Dare." She answered easily, albeit much faster than he expected.

"I dare you to take your shirt off." He said, mirroring her dare.

Alex watched as she unlatched the small buttons on her shirt before sliding the cotton down her arms, leaving it to drop behind her. Clad in a sexy as hell red satin bra, his dick was no longer twitching, it was throbbing.

"Truth or dare?" She asked.

"Truth." He held his breath, unsure of where this would lead them.

"Did you mean what you said to Jessie the other day?"

Alex didn't have to dig hard to remember what she was talking about. When he had said the words out loud, he'd shocked himself with the admission. "Yes." He answered firmly, not taking his eyes off of hers.

"Truth or dare?"

"Truth." She answered, and for the first time, Alex noted a little unease in her amber eyes.

"Did it scare you? What I told Jessie?"

Ashleigh's gaze didn't waiver, but her bottom lip trembled just slightly. "No."

Ok, they were two truths and two dares down. Alex's body was hard as steel, aching to get close enough to touch her, but he remained where he was, hoping to make it through the next round of questions.

"Truth or dare?" She asked.

"Dare." Figuring they had to let the roundabout declarations simmer for a moment, Alex opted for the harder of the two.

He was stunned when Ashleigh's eyes turned glassy, unshed tears welling up. For a moment, his heart stopped beating in his chest.

"I dare you to tell me you love me." She whispered.

Alex launched across the small space between them, pulling her into his arms and pressing his mouth to hers, eager to feel her skin beneath his fingers, to feel her heartbeat against his chest. He didn't take her fiercely, but rather licked her tongue while he cradled her head in his hands.

Pulling away from her, he glanced down, drowning in her whiskey brown eyes. "I love you. I love you with everything that I am, everything that I ever will be."

A tear slipped down her cheek, and he brushed it away with his thumb. "Truth or dare?"

"Truth." She whispered, her hands cupping his neck.

"How do you feel about me? About us?"

"I love you, Alex. I loved you the moment you stepped foot in my grandfather's house. I've loved you every single second in between. You are my heart, my soul, my everything. You make me stronger than I thought possible and wilder than I could have dreamed." The last was said with a small grin.

Her admission had tears welling up in his own eyes. To think he'd kept himself away from her for so many years, because of this. This emotion she filled him with, the foreign feeling of wanting to protect someone, to love them unconditionally today and forever. He was overwhelmed with it.

"Truth or dare?" He asked, although it was technically her turn.

"Dare." She said, her eyes resting on his lips.

"Marry me." He whispered.

To his surprise, Ashleigh didn't answer; instead she pounced on him, making him laugh. Her mouth crushed to his, straddling him as he fell back on the couch. Sliding his hands through her hair, he gently pulled her head back so he could see her eyes.

"Answer me." He insisted, smiling.

"Yes!" She squealed. "I will marry you, Alex McDermott!"

Alex rolled until she was crushed into the back cushions of the couch, but he was now on top of her. Sliding his lips down the sweet smelling curve of her neck, he kissed and licked as she tried to wrap herself around him.

"Patience, baby." He said, lowering his lips over the swell of her breast. He snuck his tongue beneath the red satin, licking her nipple as she groaned. He didn't even get a chance to assist before she had unclasped her bra, using some behind the back move that had him shocked.

"What?"

Alex laughed. "Nothing, baby. Nothing at all."

Exploring lower, he kissed every inch of skin he saw and continued to do the same with the skin he uncovered as he removed her clothes. She was having none of his going slow business, and she told him as much when she pushed him off of her, all but ripping his remaining clothes from his body before she straddled him right there in the middle of her living room.

"Ashleigh." He groaned her name as she lowered onto his cock while brutal waves of pleasure crashed over him. "Baby."

"I love you, Alex." She repeated her sentiment from earlier and Alex rolled her onto her back, pressing into her from above.

"Forever." He said. "Tell me you'll love me forever." Pumping his hips, pushing deeper, Alex maintained a steady rhythm, trying to hold back but losing the battle.

"Forever. I'll love you forever and always." Ashleigh whispered, pulling his face down until their lips met.

Alex put everything he felt into the kiss, into the way he filled her body, taking everything she was giving him at the same time.

"Alex!" Ashleigh screamed his name, breaking the kiss, bowing her back as he thrust harder, faster until he could no longer contain the need to fill her with his seed.

"Come for me, Ashleigh." He grit out, holding back, until her body gripped him, milking his cock and forcing him over the precipice to free fall into complete and total euphoria.

Epilogue
*** ~~ *** ~~ *** ~~ ***

This was all Sam's fault. The woman had relentlessly pushed until Ashleigh had agreed to go to the monthly get together with Alex, though she was seriously rethinking the idea. Of all the things she'd done for the last few months, all of the ways she'd discovered herself, Ashleigh had never been compelled to delve into that dark underworld that Sam embraced with open arms.

"Are you sure about this?" Ashleigh asked for the hundredth time.

She hadn't stepped foot behind Club Destiny's double doors that held the taboo, not to be disclosed, section for members only. Until now.

When the doors closed behind her, she wanted to ask Alex the same question again. Louder maybe, because he didn't seem to be hearing her.

As they stepped down the impressive hallway, turning a corner, Alex took her by surprise, pressing her into the wall. "I'm always sure; don't you know that by now?"

"But..."

"Trust me." Alex looked so sincere; Ashleigh found it difficult not to trust him.

He took her hand and continued down the hall and from the short distance Ashleigh could see the playroom that Sam and Sierra had gone on and on about. Her nerves were rioting, and she was honestly scared to death, but the man beside her was her strength and she trusted him to take care of her in every way.

She was just about to take another deep breath, hoping to fortify her nerves when Alex stopped abruptly, pressing her against one of the doors that lined the hall. Expecting him to kiss away her nerves, she looked up into the brilliant green of his eyes and saw the love she'd always seen, but had never known what it was.

A sudden click behind her had her turning to see what he was doing, only to find herself being pushed backward into a separate room.

"What...? I thought –" Ashleigh was dumbfounded, unable to figure out what he was doing.

"Baby, haven't you learned by now? I don't share." Alex smiled, continuing to hold her close and walk her backward. "A game of naked truth or dare, a little public foreplay when friends are around is one thing. I'm game whenever you are, but I am not willing to share you with anyone else. Not even if it's only so they can watch."

Ashleigh loved so many things about the man, but his possessiveness when it came to her still blew her away. To know that she belonged to him and only him was so much more erotic than any threesome her friends could ever tell her about.

"So what are we going to do now?" She asked, glancing around the nicely furnished room. It resembled any normal apartment, except it was in the middle of a swingers club.

"First, you're going to get naked." He informed her, that erotically sexy demand filling his tone.

"Naked?" Teasing him, Ashleigh looked around. "And where would you like me?"

"Hmmm... good question." Alex sounded serious, but Ashleigh could see the grin threatening to break free. "I'm thinking the bed would be perfect."

"What did I tell you about that?" Ashleigh asked, reminding him of the long conversation they'd had about his need to constantly be in the bedroom.

"Are you saying I can't satisfy you in a bed?"

Ashleigh had to take two steps back when he began stalking her toward an open door that she assumed led to the bedroom.

"Of course not." It didn't matter where they were; Alex managed to satisfy every craving, every desire, in every possible way.

"Then get naked and get on the bed. Sit right in the middle and don't move."

Ashleigh's belly fluttered. Sit? This might get interesting. When he swatted her butt, she jumped. The heat in his eyes couldn't have been hotter if they had been standing on the sun.

Stripping as slowly as her eager hands would allow, Ashleigh managed to disrobe, leaving her clothes on the floor where they landed. Rubbing her hand over the velvety soft comforter before she climbed onto the massive bed, Ashleigh held back the smile when Alex growled. He was still working on his patience.

Crawling onto the bed, she tried for seductive, but probably landed more on ridiculous. She smiled anyway.

"Spread your legs for me." Alex instructed when she was finally in the middle of the bed. "You know, one of these days I might just have to spank that pretty ass of yours."

"Why?" A chill ran through her. The good kind.

"Just because I can."

Ashleigh sat in the middle of the bed, spreading her legs out in front of her while Alex discarded his clothes, somewhere on the floor beside hers.

"Now lay back."

So missionary was how they were going to play? At this point, she didn't care how she had him, just as long as she did. Lying back, she put her head on the pillow and watched him.

"So pretty."

Alex's heated words matched the warm graze of his hands over her ankle, and she shivered.

"I've waited so long." Alex groaned, lifting her leg and placing a kiss to the inside of her foot.

Watching intently, she damn near choked when he pulled a silk scarf that had obviously been tucked beneath the mattress at the end of the bed.

"What are you doing?" She asked, hesitant but intrigued at the same time.

"I'm going to tie you to the bed and have my wicked way with you of course."

And that's exactly what he proceeded to do, kissing her ankles before he tied them with the scarves and then did the same thing to her wrists when he bound them to the headboard. Her breathing had become erratic, anticipation making her writhe on the bed.

That's when he pulled out another scarf, but since she didn't any more limbs to tie down, she could only figure he was going to blindfold her.

He grinned and then he did just that.

"Excited, baby?" Alex's smooth voice trailed over her nerve endings, similar to the slow glide of his tongue as he began licking her. Everywhere.

Oh, God! If he wasn't careful, she was going to come right here and now... and all of his plans would be pointless.

With a gentle thrust of his tongue, Ashleigh's body ignited when he teased her clit, licking gently before sucking the bundle of nerves into his mouth. The caress sent sparks shooting through her nerve endings, her pussy throbbing, selfishly wanting his wicked tongue.

When he finally stopped torturing her, she was left waiting, completely in the dark with her eyes covered by the blindfold. She didn't know what to expect, and the not knowing was intensely sensual.

He remained between her legs because she could feel his shoulders as he situated himself there, followed by the heat of his mouth as he hovered just over her mound. Then his tongue was thrusting, teasing her until she was moaning his name, begging him to let her come.

With no idea what he was planning to do, Ashleigh had to give herself over to the sensations of his mouth on her.

"Oh, God!" She screamed when something cool and hard slid into her ass, not even a warning and the sensation was warring with the way he was thrusting his tongue into her pussy, over and over again.

She was just getting used to invasion when whatever it was he'd inserted into her began vibrating, sending shards of electrified pleasure coursing through her veins. She was not going to last.

"That's it, baby." Alex crooned. "Relax for me."

She was trying to relax, trying not to focus on the vibration in her ass and wondering at the same time what he was going to do next. Then the vibration intensified, only this time, it wasn't in her ass, it was on her clit. Oh, hell. He had two vibrators, and he was going to kill her with overstimulation.

"Alex!"

Oh, God. It was so fucking good. Her clit was pulsing as he pressed the vibrator more firmly against the throbbing bundle of nerves, and she moved her hips to get it in just the right spot.

She was so close, her muscles locking up as her orgasm ignited, the tingling in her womb intensifying, but when the bed dipped, more movement, her brain took over, and she tried to figure out what he was going to do next.

~*~~

Alex pushed up on his knees, holding the vibrator on her clit as he aligned his iron hard cock with her tight pussy, pressing into her slowly at first before ramming himself home.

Ashleigh screamed, her muscles locking onto his cock, making him grit his teeth. She was so fucking tight.

Grabbing the small remote, he turned up the vibration of the small plug in her ass until she began squirming beneath him. He then did the same with the small pocket vibrator he held against her clit, pressing more firmly, feeling the vibrations against his cock as he retreated before slamming into her again.

Leaning over her, he held himself up with one hand on the mattress, holding the vibrator against her clit as he began thrusting his hips, burying his cock deep inside her pussy. It took everything in him not to speak because he wanted her focused on the vibration and the friction of his cock inside of her.

He increased the pace, the intensity of the vibrator against his shaft was damn near too much to bear, as was the way her vaginal muscles clenched tighter and tighter around his dick.

Her soft moans turned into violent cries of pleasure, and he wasn't able to hold on any longer, the words tumbling out of his mouth as he began thrusting harder.

"You're mine, Ashleigh." He groaned, slamming into her over and over. "Mine." He wanted her to come; he wanted her to scream his name. "Your body is mine to pleasure." He punctuated the words with forceful thrusts inside her tight channel. "Your heart is mine to love." Harder, faster, the pleasure building to a crescendo that would likely send them both reeling into the oblivion. "Your soul is mine. Only mine."

"Yes!" She screamed. "Alex! Oh, God! I'm coming!"

The sound of his name on her lips sent him careening into the abyss, his orgasm detonating like a nuclear bomb, leveling him, shattering his senses and life as he knew it altered in that moment.

Everything came down to this woman. The one who owned him mind, body and soul. She was seduction in its simplest, purest form, and he wasn't sure how he'd survived the last ten years without her, but he vowed he'd never spend another minute, another second, without her.

And tomorrow, well, tomorrow was the first day of the rest of their lives... because tomorrow was the day she would take his name and make him the happiest man on the planet.

Visit Nicole at http://nicedwardsauthor.com/

Made in the USA
Lexington, KY
23 July 2013